© 2007 by Michael Gallacher

About the Author

Neil McMahon was a Stegner Fellow at Stanford.
The author of six novels, he is also a carpenter in
Missoula, where his wife coordinates the Montana
Festival of the Book.

Also by Neil McMahon

Praise for
NEIL McMAHON'S
DEAD SILVER

"**R**eading *Dead Silver* is like discovering that the great Raymond Chandler wrote a mystery about Montana. Neil McMahon is definitely up to the task of writing ground-breaking mysteries. Maybe that's why *Dead Silver* kept me entertained for the weekend."

—James Patterson

"**I**magine the Lone Ranger and Tonto as a pair of witty, profane, shot-and-beer construction workers—but still fighting for justice, in their fashion—and you have some idea of how much fun *Dead Silver* is. It's a terrific read—worldy-wise, scary, and as fast moving as a runaway truck on a steep mountain grade. Neil McMahon is such a skillful storyteller, it's easy to overlook how good he really is."

—Larry Watson, author of *Montana 1948*

DEAD SILVER

NEIL McMAHON

HARPER

NEW YORK • LONDON • TORONTO • SYDNEY

HARPER

A hardcover edition of this book was published in 2008 by HarperCollins Publishers.

HarperCollins books may be purchased for educational, business, or sales promotional use. For information please write: Special Markets Department, HarperCollins Publishers, 10 East 53rd Street, New York, NY 10022.

FIRST HARPER PAPERBACK PUBLISHED 2009.

Designed by William Ruoto

Library of Congress Cataloging-in-Publication Data is available upon request.

ISBN 978-0-06-134077-2 (pbk.)

09 10 11 12 13   OV/RRD   10 9 8 7 6 5 4 3 2 1

AGAIN, TO KUSKAY SAKAYE, WHO GAVE THE
GIFT OF HIMSELF TO MANY, AND THE GIFT OF
MADBIRD TO ME.

1933–2007

Many a time I've heard the tale from the men in the shipyards about the rat that could speak. I never laid no confidence in that before; but tonight, if I'd demeaned myself to lay my ear to the door of the further bin, I could pretty much have heard what they was saying.

—M. R. JAMES

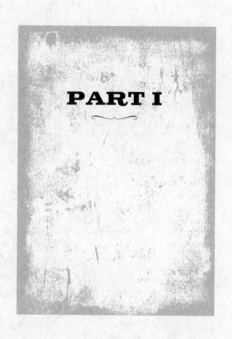

PART I

CHAPTER 1

FRIDAY AFTER WORK, MADBIRD AND I were drinking shots and beers at the Split Rock Lodge when his niece, Darcy, came prancing through the door. The raucous conversations of the dozen barroom regulars stopped like somebody had dropped a girder on a squawking radio. Darcy knew how to steal a scene.

She was Blackfeet, same as Madbird, and she was some smoke—just turned twenty-one, full-bodied and vibrant, with hair that fell almost to her waist and gleamed like a raven's wing in sunlight. She'd grown up on the tribal reservation in northern Montana, then spent her late teens moving from place to place, looking for the things you looked for at that age. Now she was trying her luck in our state capital city of Helena.

She was as wild as she was pretty, and Madbird did his best to keep tabs on her—he'd gotten her a job waiting tables here at Split Rock because he and I were working nearby these days, remodeling some motel units—but Darcy walked her own walk.

She waitressed the lunch shift on Fridays, then stayed through the afternoon to help clean and set up for dinner. She was a good worker, we'd heard—cheerful, energetic, and possessing that all-important quality of doing what needed to be done without waiting to be told.

Now she was finished for the day and dressed to party, wearing tight jeans, spike-heeled boots, a turquoise-colored low-cut sweater, and a black leather biker jacket studded with silver.

"Hi, Hugh," she said to me.

"Darcy, you're scorching my eyeballs."

She gave me a big smile and pulled up a barstool next to Madbird.

"Buy me a drink," she commanded him teasingly.

His mouth twitched in amusement, but the rest of his face remained unmoving. It looked like it had been carved out of a cliffside by a lightning storm, and his rumbling voice sounded like a diesel engine with a handful of gravel thrown in.

"Well, I guess, since you ask so nice," he said. "But I ain't sure they got Shirley Temples here."

"I'll kick your Shirley Temple ass," Darcy said scornfully. "Gin and tonic."

"Gin?" He frowned. "You got a note from your mother?"

She snapped a quick punch to his forearm, smacking his Marine Corps skull-and-crossbones tattoo.

"Whoa! Okay, goddammit." He backed away, rubbing the spot dramatically.

"See? He's not so tough," she whispered to me.

"You ain't got to say it so loud," Madbird muttered. He signaled the bartender and pushed forward a five from the pile of bills in front of him.

He wasn't much for vocalizing his feelings, but I knew that he had a special affection for Darcy. Even as an infant, she'd been uncowed by his fierce appearance, and she'd soon grasped his quirky brand of humor and learned to throw it back at him. This had developed into ritual sparring that both of them loved.

Over the years, he'd worried about her a lot, with reason.

Now he was concerned in a different way, and it showed in his next words.

"I suppose regular bar gin ain't going to be good enough for you, seeing as how you been hanging around with the rich and famous," he said.

Darcy's eyes narrowed just slightly, just for an instant. But she bounced back in a heartbeat with her mischievous smile.

"You got that right," she said, and called to the bartender, "Bombay Sapphire, please."

Madbird whistled softly. "Bombay fucking Sapphire," he repeated, to nobody in particular. He pushed forward another five-dollar bill.

"It's a pretty blue bottle. Almost this color." She plucked at her sweater.

"That what your boyfriend drinks?"

"Sometimes."

"He coming by here to pick you up?" Madbird said.

"Sure, why not?"

"I didn't say nothing about why not. I just wonder why he don't ever come inside."

"What, to meet you? You kidding?"

He slumped dolefully against the bar. "Well, ain't that the way it goes. Ashamed of your poor old uncle."

"I'm not ashamed of you! I'm sitting right here beside you."

"Yeah, long as I buy you fancy liquor."

"Hah. Play me a game of eight-ball." She grabbed his hand and tugged him away from the bar.

"I ain't played pool in a hundred years," he objected, but he didn't resist.

"Come on, Hugh," she said to me. "My poor old uncle needs help. You two against me."

I wasn't going to provide much help; I couldn't remember the last time I'd touched a cue myself. But I gathered our drinks and followed the two of them to the barroom's pool table, a sturdy old veteran scarred by countless cigarettes, stained by blood from fights and, according to rumor, occasional dousings of amatory body fluids as well. The conversation level in the bar had risen back up to normal, with the jukebox shifting from Bob Wills to Hank Snow doing "A Six-Pack to Go." Darcy punched quarters into the table and expertly arranged the rack, alternating stripes and solids and giving the centered eight ball a spin, then pressing the triangle inward with her fingers to clamp it tight.

Her newest boyfriend—the source of Madbird's concern—was a Montana state representative named Seth Fraker, from the resort area of Flathead Lake. The legislature had been in session in Helena for the last couple of months; Fraker and Darcy had met one evening when she was waitressing here and he'd come in with some colleagues to have dinner. He came from a well-established business family and he had all the trappings that went along with that—money, connections, and sophistication. Except for the inconvenient fact that he was married with kids, he seemed a big improvement over the aimless, troubled guys and sometimes outright criminals she'd run around with in the past.

But that was as far as the Cinderella story went. There was no glass slipper, just a variation on an old theme—an upper-crust white guy having a fling with a hot young Native girl. The deeper problem was, there were hints that Darcy was taking it more seriously. She'd suddenly decided to move to an apartment more expensive than she could afford, with money from a mysterious source. She gave off a new sense of excitement, like she had an important secret. She had let it slip that he described his marriage as being "in name only," without her seeming to realize what a stale ploy that was. While she was far from naïve in many ways, this situation was outside her experience, and maybe she was subconsciously blinding herself besides.

That happened to just about everybody, in some way, at some point, but it was hard to watch it happen to Darcy.

For sure, Fraker had no intentions of leaving his family and marrying her. At best, he was setting her up as a mistress; he'd have plenty of pretexts to come to Helena. If that was the case and she could accept it, it might be a cynical but advantageous arrangement for her until something better came along. But far more likely, when the legislative session ended a couple of months from now, Fraker would head back to his glossy home life and realize that maintaining the affair was too costly in a number of ways.

Madbird feared that, besides the hurt, it might knock Darcy into a tailspin just when she thought her life was turning the corner. And the situation reeked with the sense of a powerful white man figuring that since he was dealing with Indians, he was untouchable.

Very few things in the world pissed Madbird off like that did.

I knew that he was torn about whether to intervene. He hadn't, yet.

"Okay, it's ready," Darcy said, stepping back from the pool table. "One of you guys break."

"Friday's ladies' night out here," Madbird said.

"It is? When did that start?"

"New rule. Go ahead."

She lined up on the cue ball and broke with a crack I could feel in my teeth. The balls seethed around and careened off the rails; when they settled, the six had dropped into a corner pocket and three other solids were easy picks. She tapped in two of those and left the third blocking another corner, with the cue ball buried in a cluster.

Madbird and I managed to sink a couple of stripes, but mostly we duffed around while she continued to clear the table. At the end of the workweek, concentrated effort was very low on our priority list, and this spacious old lodge with its huge stone fireplace and vintage country jukebox was a good place to kick back. Split Rock was the kind of setup that had once been fairly common in the West—a main building that housed a restaurant-bar, and several smaller cabins that served as motel units. Like a lot of the others, it had been hand-built of logs soon after World War II, when tourism by automobile was becoming an industry. It stood facing the landmark for which it was named—a chunk of granite the size of a two-story house, cleft from the top almost to the bottom by a vertical V that looked hewn by a giant ax. Big plate glass windows gave expansive views of the still-pristine surrounding country, the foothills of the Elkhorn Range several miles south of Helena. Often, you could see elk foraging on the mountainsides.

A sudden sound, like a spray of elevator music on acid, made my head jerk. It was the ring of Darcy's cell phone. She dropped her pool cue on the table and flew to dig the phone out of her purse, then pressed it to her ear and walked a few steps away from Madbird and me, talking in a tone too low for us to hear, while her other hand smoothed her hair.

This was the situation that Madbird had tweaked her about. Seth Fraker would drive here to pick her up, but instead of coming inside, he'd call as he was arriving and have her go out to meet him—the modern equivalent of honking the horn. Sure enough, headlights were turning from the highway into the Split Rock parking lot. There was enough daylight left for me to see the vehicle when it got close—Fraker's huge new pickup truck with all the bells and whistles, including smoked windows.

Darcy closed her phone, slipped it back into her purse, and turned to face us. The next couple of seconds were a strange, tense freeze where nothing happened, but it seemed like a lot of things could.

Madbird and Darcy moved in the same instant. He started

walking around the table toward the parking lot. She scooped up a chunk of blue cue tip chalk and intercepted him. Her hand moved quick as a snake to smear a touch of it on his forehead. While I stared, she spun around and did the same to me. Just as abruptly, she broke into a brisk skipping dance, circling the pool table and both of us, chanting or singing under her breath.

Then she was gone out the door, leaving him and me standing there, looking like refugees from Ash Wednesday.

"What was that?" I said.

Madbird gazed stonily after her as she hurried across the parking lot and disappeared behind the darkened windows of Seth Fraker's big pickup.

"She threw something at us," he said. "Kind of a witchy trick, to get us off her case."

CHAPTER 2

THE NEXT AFTERNOON, SATURDAY, I spent banging around my cabin doing the chores that I let slide during the week. I was forever losing ground; it was like fighting a Hydra that grew back two heads for every one I lopped off. Besides the routine business of cleaning and laundry and such, new problems were endless—plumbing leaks, vehicle repairs, a garage roof caving under one too many snowstorms. Most often, I'd discover further wrinkles once I started trying to fix the original one; I'd end up driving to town for materials two or three times; and so on. By the time I got the situation under control, I'd have lost a couple more weekends, and the list kept on growing.

But that was far outweighed by the payoff. I could never have imagined a greater gift than this property, left to me by my father: twenty acres of conifers in the Big Belt Mountains, an area that was steep, rugged, and thickly wooded, with only a few gravel roads that were dicey at the best of times. Humans were rare.

If I hadn't had this place to come back to during a bad time in my life—the collapse of my marriage and career in California, more or less simultaneously—I wasn't sure I'd have gotten through. Keeping it cobbled together was sort of like living with somebody who drove you nuts, but who you loved and couldn't stand to be without. You did whatever it took to make things work.

I'd been thinking about the incident with Madbird and Darcy yesterday at Split Rock. He hadn't been headed outside to brace Seth Fraker—just to get a look at him, invite him in for a drink, size him up. But I understood Darcy's concern, too. Madbird already didn't like what he knew about Fraker; in all probability, he'd like him even less if they met, and that would be clear. Darcy was well aware of it, and in her view, she had nothing to gain and a lot to lose if it happened.

As for the "something" she'd thrown at us, paying any attention to it was silly. But I had come to suspect that there were cracks in the rational fabric of the universe, and such a "something" might just slip through once in a while and rattle cages. In other words, I'd gotten more superstitious instead of more levelheaded. There were a lot of factors involved, including that my nature and lifestyle tended toward the solitary. Then, too, the more I knew about the fairer sex, the more mysterious they became. That wasn't to say I'd bought into Darcy's gesture in any serious way. It just made me a trifle uneasy.

The supply of stove wood that I kept in the cabin was low, so I walked outside through the wet spring snow to stock up. When I got to the woodshed, my half-feral black tomcat—I'd never named him; I just thought of him as the other guy, which was probably how he thought of me—was crouched on a stack of split fir, staring intently toward the tree line, twenty-five or thirty yards away. I glimpsed the shape of an animal just inside there. It was good-sized, with the deep brown color of a mule deer. I hadn't seen any of them for a while, and I was vaguely interested that they were coming back.

But instantly, the real situation clicked into focus. This thing was sitting upright, which deer didn't do. It was built like a Rottweiler, with powerful shoulders, a heavy round head, and bone-crushing jaws.

This wasn't any muley. This was a big cat—the reason the deer hadn't been around lately.

I wasn't entirely surprised. I'd been seeing its tracks for the past couple of weeks, and assumed it was a cougar; this part of Montana had always been their turf. At a guess, he was a young male who'd been driven off by his elders and hadn't yet staked out his own claim. But there were some factors that didn't fit. Cougars usually kept moving around a large area, and they usually stayed well away from humans. I'd only ever glimpsed them in the backcountry, where I'd roamed a lot as a kid. In the past several years, since I'd been living in the cabin fulltime, I'd hardly seen a trace.

But this guy had been hanging around for a while, and he'd been coming within the boundaries of my property. Right now I was looking into his eyes, staring straight back at me. He must have heard me coming out of the cabin, and he hadn't budged an inch. No doubt he was hungry, too. Deer were the main staple of a cougar's diet. He must have been eking out a meager living on small critters.

Shy though cougars traditionally were, attacks on people were becoming more common. Probably they were getting used to us and losing their fear. They'd taken down several joggers around the West, and here in Montana not long ago, a pair of them had stalked a group of schoolchildren on an outing. Courageous teachers had gotten the kids to safety, but the cats hadn't even made any attempt at stealth.

I wasn't *too* worried, but I admit I suddenly found myself thinking about what I'd do if he came my way. The woodshed was just an open-fronted lean-to; the closest place that offered protection was the cabin, and I wasn't at all sure I could make it there ahead of him. My pulse rate started edging upward. But while I was trying to decide whether to stand my ground, or slowly work my way toward safety, or just flat-out run for it, he tipped forward from his haunches onto all fours and paced unhurriedly away.

That was when I saw his short black-striped tail, and realized he wasn't a mountain lion—he was a bobcat. The scenario started making more sense. They tended to find a home
territory and stay there, and they seemed to have learned fast
that we humans had our uses, such as providing livestock and
pets for meals.

"You better watch it," I told the black tom. "You'd be an
appetizer to him."

He kept staring with his wide green eyes, claws dug into a
chunk of fir and tail switching in agitation as his mega-cousin
leisurely moved out of sight, pausing every several yards to
sniff the air and look around.

When the bobcat was gone, I completed my mission
of carrying a few armloads of wood to the cabin. The tom
jumped off his perch and followed me back and forth, butting
against my ankles—wanting a drink of beer. I was ready for
one myself. I dug into the forty-year-old Kelvinator and found
a bottle of Moretti left over from a six-pack I'd splurged on
a couple of weekends ago. I poured a splash into a saucer for
the cat and worked on the rest myself, thinking about how to
handle this.

On the one hand, I was relieved. I'd never heard of a
bobcat attacking anyone. On the other hand, he was a really
big bobcat. While I knew that wild animals and fish always
grew with the telling, I also knew what I'd seen. I even wondered if a cross with a mountain lion was genetically possible.
Besides his size, his coloration, brown and mostly solid, was
more cougarlike; bobcats tended to be tawnier, with leopard-
like black spots. And yet, there was no mistaking that tail.

I didn't want to shoot him—on the contrary, I was glad
that creatures like him were out there, and I wanted to keep him
there. I was just nervous that he'd eat my pet—the tom was extremely canny, but everybody made mistakes—and maybe even
me. When the snow melted and the ground dried, he might head

into the backcountry in search of more satisfying game, but that wouldn't happen for several weeks. And then again, he might not. I considered contacting the Fish and Wildlife Department, but that was a can of worms—strangers stomping around my place, and me losing any say in the matter.

I started leaning toward the notion that the best thing for everybody concerned would be to give him a good scare—let him know that he'd better stay away from human beings. But that was easier thought than done.

I'd start carrying a pistol when I went outside, I decided— one that threw big slugs and made a lot of noise. If I met the bobcat with a burst of explosions and chunks showering out of the trees around him, that might get the message across. The weapon would also be a comfort when I came home after dark and walked from my truck to the cabin, just in case he was bold and hungry enough to take on something bigger than a bunny.

I finished the beer and went back to puttering, while the tom curled up on the bed to sleep off his adrenaline and beer. I stacked the firewood beside the stove and started scrubbing out the blue enamel roasting pan I'd had soaking in the sink— waiting until a decent hour before I headed downtown for a Saturday evening tour of the bars, and maybe hooking up with a lady friend who wasn't interested in anything long-term, at least with me, but occasionally enjoyed the kind of company that was gone in the morning.

When the phone rang, it brought me a routine touch of angst. I wasn't crazy about telephones—another of my regressive traits. I used mine mainly for work and other necessities, rarely for chatting, and it seemed to me that unexpected calls usually meant either hassles or outright bad news. But the news would come anyway, and answering was the only way to get rid of asshole solicitors who'd otherwise keep tormenting you forever, so I picked up and grumbled hello.

At first I was sure I'd guessed right—it was some kind of a pitch. The caller was a woman whose voice I didn't recognize, asking for Hugh Davoren. But she sounded pleasant, slightly uncertain, and she even pronounced my last name right, to just about rhyme with "tavern." I tried to sound a little less brusque.

"Speaking," I said.

"This is Renee Callister. Do you remember me?"

That caught me by surprise. I hadn't seen Renee or heard anything about her since I was a teenager. Ordinarily, I'd have stumbled over a name from that long ago. But I'd been thinking about her family because her father, Professor John Callister, had passed away earlier this week.

After all this time, it seemed unlikely that she was just calling me out of the blue. I guessed that her reason had something to do with her father's death, which added a poignant element.

Professor Callister had once been a prominent figure in Montana, a highly respected wildlife biologist and defender of wilderness. But his life was ruined when his young second wife was murdered, along with the lover she was in bed with at the time. Uglier still, Callister was the chief suspect. He was never formally charged, but the murder went unsolved and he was never cleared, either. He'd spent his last several years in a nursing home, after a series of strokes left him incapacitated and, eventually, comatose.

That was the legacy his daughter, Renee, had inherited.

CHAPTER 3

"GOOD GOD, RENEE," I SAID, regretting my grumpy hello. "Seems like light-years."

"A lot of ordinary years, for sure. I think the last time I saw you, you were about to leave for college, and your family had a backyard barbecue party."

My recollection wasn't that clear, but I trusted hers. She was several years younger than me, so she must have been about ten then. She'd be in her early thirties now.

I hadn't really grown up with Renee. Besides the age difference, our only point of contact was that our parents were acquainted, and that had ended when her folks got divorced and she'd moved to Seattle with her mother. My recollections of her were sketchy, mostly just images of a skinny, dark-haired girl. But she was sweet, solemn, and gentle in a way that wasn't just childish shyness—it was her nature.

"I'm here in Helena, for Daddy's funeral," she said.

"I saw the notice. I'm sorry." The sentiment was trite, but I meant it.

"It's a mercy, really. I don't think he'd been aware toward the end, except maybe of pain." She sounded a little shaky, which was understandable. Mercy or not, losing a parent was losing a parent.

"Is there something I can do?" I said.

She made a slight sighing sound, like she was frustrated.

"I hate to admit it, Hugh, but that's why I called. I feel guilty, barging in on you and asking for help right off. But there's so much going on, I'm overwhelmed."

"I know that feeling. And believe me, you're not barging in on anything."

"I was hoping you'd still be a nice guy," she murmured.

Still? I thought. I couldn't recall ever being anything of the kind to her, but it was good to hear her say it.

"Daddy never sold our old house, and I couldn't bring myself to do it while he was alive," she said. "But I want to now, and it needs some work. I heard that's what you're doing these days."

I grimaced; I was probably going to have to let her down.

"I am, Renee, but I'm committed to another job for the next couple months," I said. "Are you talking something major?"

"It's hard to describe. But no, I don't think it would take long."

Homeowners rarely thought otherwise.

"Well, how about if I swing by and look it over?" I said. "I could give you an idea of what you might need done."

"Really? You're sure it wouldn't be too much trouble?" I could hear the relief in her voice.

"I was heading that direction anyway," I said, which wasn't strictly true. But I was glad for an excuse to abandon my chores, and my curiosity had awakened about her, her father, and the situation. "Call it an hour or so?"

"Perfect."

I was just starting to move the phone from my ear to its cradle when I heard her say, "Hugh?" in that same anxious tone as before.

"Yeah?"

There came a pause that seemed longer than it was.

"Thanks. See you soon," she exhaled, and ended the connection.

I had a feeling that wasn't what she'd started out to say.

I hadn't forgotten my encounter with Mr. Bobcat. Before I left the cabin, I got out the loudest, most powerful pistol I owned: a .45-caliber government-issue Colt 1911 that my father had brought back from the Korean War. It had seen a lot of use; the bluing was worn and the action was limber, well broken in. I knew he'd been in a fair amount of combat, but he'd said very little about all that; I didn't know if he'd ever killed anyone with it, or if it had even been his. Still, I had a feeling that the usage hadn't all been on the firing range. I didn't shoot it often—a couple of times a year, for the hell of it—and I'd cleaned it not long ago. I checked to make sure the clip was loaded, the chamber was empty, and the safety was on, and carried it out to my pickup truck, a '68 GMC that was yet another of the valuable gifts that my old man had passed on to me.

The afternoon was waning as I started down the narrow dirt road of Stumpleg Gulch toward Helena. It was late March, the time of year when spring was encroaching but winter still clung to a hold, and the two conspired together to turn the outdoors into a tedious, unwinnable mud-wrestling battle. The roads were covered with a layer of self-perpetuating muck, snow that had melted and refrozen dozens of times and all the dirt that got trapped in the process. If you bothered to wash your vehicle, it would only highlight the greasy black splotches that reappeared as soon as your wheels started turning, like shooed flies flitting back to a picnic lunch.

The snowfields that blanketed the higher mountains were taking on a worn look, and the buds on the trees lower down were thickening. Patches of ice clung to the shoreline of Canyon

Ferry Lake, but most of its solid freeze-over had broken up, and its miles-long expanse reflected the slaty gray sky in the afternoon light. Soon there'd come a couple of days when the sky cleared for hours at a time, the temperature climbed enough to make you break a light sweat, and you could almost feel the grass and foliage greening around you. Leaves would start competing with pine needles for sunlight, and insects would start tormenting mammals and delighting fish.

Then, just about when you figured that winter was done for, you'd wake up early one morning to six inches of fresh snow driven by a howling, subzero wind doing its best to tear your roof off.

That was a quality of this country that I respected to the point of reverence. If you took anything for granted, you were likely to end up regretting it.

CHAPTER 4

HELENA HAD A FAIR NUMBER of stately Victorian houses, most of them dating back a century or more to when the area had been awash with mining money. The Callister home was one of them, up in the foothills toward the city's southeast edge. It was set comfortably apart from its neighbors, with a backyard giving way to forest that thickened as the terrain climbed.

The quietly elegant old neighborhood looked directly over the state capitol grounds, which were dominated by the grand, high-domed, gray stone main building. Before it stood a statue of ex–territorial governor Meagher, on horseback with sword raised like he was charging back into action in the Civil War. His fate remained one of Montana's fondest mysteries—he'd vanished off a ferryboat on the Missouri River at Fort Benton one night, and was never seen again.

North of the city, the land flattened out into the plains of the Helena Valley, bounded on the west by the foothills of the Rockies and on the east by the dark springtime glimmer of the Missouri. There was a lot of newer development that wasn't so attractive, but that was the price of living in a place that was becoming known.

Out of long habit, I started assessing the condition of Renee's house while I was still driving up to it. It had suffered neglect during the years that the Professor had been in the nursing home. The eggshell white paint was dingy and peeling, the bottom courses of clapboard siding and the front steps needed replacing, and there were other similar concerns common to such places. But by and large, the exterior seemed in pretty good shape. The roofing looked fairly new, and while the foundation was rock and mortar like most its age, there was no visible sagging or other structural damage. The inside might be a different story.

I parked on the street out front—leaving the driveway clear for the homeowners was another longtime habit—got out of my truck, and walked up the pave-stoned footpath to the house. As I got close, I glimpsed Renee's shape through a window, hurrying to the door. She must have been watching for me.

Then, when she stepped out onto the porch, I had an odd instant—a sudden wash of familarity, almost like a déjà vu. Maybe it was only because I'd known her long ago. But more than suggesting the past, this had an intriguing sense of here and now. It was a pleasant little shock, gone too soon.

She was trim, verging on slight, with dark brown hair cut above her shoulders and eyes about the same color. She still gave off the solemn gentleness I remembered from childhood. I wasn't sure whether she was thinking of me as an old friend or a carpenter there to look at a job, so I only offered a handshake. But she clasped my hand in both of hers, fine-boned and warm, then drew me into a light embrace.

We segued into small talk for a couple of minutes, catching up on our families and a little of our current lives. She was here alone; her mother was ailing and didn't travel well, and her brother was teaching in Japan and hadn't cared to make the long journey. Career-wise, she was doing well; she'd gone into science like her father, and was doing pharmaceutical research.

She was also wearing an engagement ring that looked like it would add up to a pile of my paychecks.

The strain she was under showed in her face, and she seemed nervous, like she'd sounded on the phone. I reminded myself that besides her worries, she was probably used to men whose clothes weren't stained with construction glue and who didn't drive the kind of vehicle you usually only saw in old Clint Eastwood movies. I changed the subject to the house, trying to put her more at ease.

"What I've seen so far doesn't look too troublesome," I said. "Paint and a little carpenter work. I'd say go for it. Jack your curb appeal way up."

"Thanks, that's good to know." She hesitated. "But there's another reason I called. Come on, it'll be easier to explain if I show you."

She led me back down off the porch and around the side of the house, across a tree-dotted lawn that I remembered as lush and well kept but now was just a grass-stubbled mud patch, past flower beds gone to ruin.

At the rear of the property stood a smaller building that the Callisters called a carriage house, but which probably had been quarters for the domestic help. Her father had converted it into his study.

When Renee opened the door, I faced the most dismal sight I'd ever seen.

The place had been infested by pack rats. Books, carpeting, upholstery, insulation—anything they could get their teeth into—they'd chewed to shreds and used to build their warrens or just strewn around. Worse, almost every surface was layered with their foul pelletlike dung.

While I stared, she told me how this had happened. During the past years that her father had been in the nursing home, the main house had been occupied by a lowlife shirttail relative. He'd run it into the ground, using it as a crash pad for cronies and girlfriends, and when the pack rats invaded this outbuilding, he'd never lifted a finger to stop them.

Renee had made a game start toward swamping out the mess, clearing pathways here and there and trying to rake it up. But it was unpleasant work, and heavy—a hell of a lot to take on for a woman to cope with by herself, while mourning her father to boot.

I had to admit, realizing that this why she was courting my assistance was something of a comedown.

Ordinarily, I wouldn't have touched it. I was no prima donna, and I'd done my fair share of grunt work through the years. But by now I was well qualified in a range of skills that were much in demand, from heavy highway and commercial concrete work through any kind of framing—my specialty—to high-end remodels. About all this called for was a flat shovel and a strong stomach.

Then again, I didn't know anybody else who'd touch it, either; she'd be stuck with it herself. I decided that a day or two of slogging through rat shit wouldn't kill me. In a metaphorical sense, I did it often.

"I could start tomorrow, if you don't mind me banging around on Sunday," I said. It would probably take longer, but I could miss Monday out at Split Rock and make that up next weekend.

Renee didn't answer. She looked straight at me with her solemn gaze, like she was trying to make up her mind about something. I could just see her front teeth touching her lower lip. And it seemed to me that her eyes showed more than her earlier anxiety—pain, and maybe even fear.

Then she threw me a curve that eclipsed everything else.

CHAPTER 5

"THERE'S A LOT MORE TO this, Hugh," Renee said. "I found something really creepy. I don't know what to do. I need somebody I can trust. But I know it's not fair of me to ask you. So if you want to leave, go ahead. Just please don't say anything to anybody."

That was a lot to take in during those few quick, breathy sentences.

I was gun-shy about a lot of things these days and I'd started looking at people more warily, for good reason. But my sense of Renee's sincerity hadn't faltered.

I decided to go ahead, but to step very carefully.

"I'll listen, Renee, and I've gotten pretty good at keeping my mouth shut," I said. "I can't promise more than that."

She gave me an anxious smile. "That's a lot."

I walked with her back to the main house, this time noticing the many rock outcroppings on the mountainside that boundaried the property's rear—the primary homes of pack rats. There must have been a thriving community in there, aggressively expanding its turf.

Renee had gotten the bigger house pretty well cleaned up from the tenant's trashing. It was a splendid old place—nine-foot ceilings, oak floors, and the kind of finely wrought trim that had become as extinct as gaslight streetlamps.

She left me in the kitchen and went to another room. A minute later she came back with a manila envelope and shook out its contents on the table—a dozen bits of ragged-edged paper, ranging in size from a postage stamp to a playing card.

"I found these when I was trying to clean, mixed up in the rat gunk," she said, arranging the scraps and flipping some over.

I was puzzled, and more so when I realized what they were: fragments of photographs. The images were unclear—the colors had faded with time, and the rats had both chewed them up and stained them—but when I started to make them out, the strangeness factor of this day took another jump.

They appeared to be nude shots of a young woman. In a couple of them, she was wearing a costume—cowboy boots, a fringed leather vest opened to bare her breasts, and, in the only one that showed a complete face, large dangly earrings and a cowboy hat tipped rakishly low above her mischievous smile. It was hard to judge their quality; about all I could guess was that they weren't from a magazine or straight computer download—they were printed on photographic paper. There were no markings on the back, no clue as to who the photographer might have been.

I'd started to understand why this would upset Renee. Her father had always seemed a dignified, somewhat austere man, and no doubt that was how she wanted to remember him. Finding his study despoiled by vermin had to be yet another blow that she had suffered since coming here—a cruel trick of fate that mocked and underscored his ruined life. Learning that he'd kept a stash of cheesy porn would cheapen his memory further. But the way she was treating this like a nuclear secret seemed a bit overblown.

Just as I was thinking that, Renee touched the fragment that showed the model's full face, with the earrings and hat.

"This is Astrid," she said.

Her words took a few seconds to register, but when they did, they hit hard.

Astrid was Professor Callister's second wife, the one who had been murdered.

CHAPTER 6

RENEE AND I TALKED THE situation over for the best part of another hour. After she assured me that she was doing fine and had everything she needed, I headed home. My notion of going downtown had vanished, although I still wanted a stiff drink.

The afternoon was deepening toward evening as I drove back toward Canyon Ferry Lake. Houses became sparser and traffic disappeared. My truck had been over those roads so many times it practically handled itself, like an old horse heading for the barn. I let it do the work; I had plenty to think about.

Not surprisingly, Renee clung to the belief that her father was innocent of Astrid's murder. The job she had in mind for me was tied to that, and was far more intriguing than just cleaning up the rodent superfund.

It centered on the photos of Astrid. Renee had made the realization that originally, there must have been a lot more of them. Only a few of the fragments that she'd found fit together; when she laid them out on the table, they were like a jigsaw puzzle with most of the pieces missing. She'd gone back and looked through desks and bookshelves and everyplace else accessible, and even raked carefully through the rat debris—that was why she'd cleared the pathways I'd seen—but still came up far short of the total.

She suspected that the rest of them might be stashed someplace she hadn't been able to get to—maybe inside a wall or floor cavity. The rats had found them, chewed them up like everything else, and dropped scraps around haphazardly. She wanted to find the missing fragments in the hope that they might contain some detail, like handwriting or other marks, that would lead to information about Astrid's murderer—and that this, in turn, would help to vindicate Professor Callister.

So Renee had asked me to tear into the carriage house structure, in search of the missing photos.

Several questions hung unanswered. There was no hint as to who the photographer was, but Renee was convinced that it couldn't have been her father. He'd had no interest in that sort of thing—never had so much as a *Playboy* magazine lying around. He'd have found salacious photos of his wife offensive, especially after her death.

Then what were they doing in his study? One far-fetched possibility was that they comprised evidence relating to the real murderer's identity, and for some reason he'd held off revealing it—then had been incapacitated by his strokes.

Another scenario that occurred to me was even less likely but more disturbing. I didn't mention it to Renee. Sex killers often kept souvenirs, usually objects with some intimate connection to the victim. They would handle these or otherwise use them to heighten their pleasure in reliving the crimes. During my years as a newspaper reporter in California, I'd become well aware of such instances, and difficult though it was to imagine Professor Callister like that, they'd included outwardly normal, pleasant men who harbored hidden evil sides.

When I added it all up, my take was that even if I could find more photos, the odds of that helping Professor Callister's cause seemed slim—if anything, the opposite was more likely. Renee was realistic enough to recognize that; while she hadn't exactly said so, it was why she wanted to keep this secret.

Still, I'd agreed to start the job tomorrow morning. I was uneasy about it, for fear that her hopes would get crushed for good. But she was willing to take that risk, and the decision was hers to make.

I turned off the highway at Stumpleg Gulch and drove the final two miles up the gravel road to my place. The forest closed in thicker as the elevation rose, with the road narrowing to a track that petered out in the mountains just beyond there. Grainy snow crunched under my boots as I walked to my cabin, keeping a wary eye out for the bobcat, with the pistol in my hand. I felt a little silly, but I was glad to have it.

The fire in my stove had died, leaving the cabin with the peculiar kind of chill that could make a building seem colder than outside. I rekindled it, poured a splash of Old Taylor, and opened a beer chaser.

I'd been living in California when Astrid was killed, but I had followed the story as well as I could. Not many specifics were released; the era was arriving when everybody was so gun-shy about potential lawsuits and mistrials that authorities stayed tight-lipped.

I recalled that she and her lover had been trysting in a cabin she owned up in Phosphor County, roughly sixty miles northward of here. They'd both been shot at close range.

There'd been a backdrop of bitter political controversy, involving an outfit called the Dodd Mining Company starting operations in the area. Most of the local residents were thrilled at this infusion of lifeblood to their stagnant economy.

But opposition had also been fierce—and Astrid, a fervent environmentalist, had spearheaded it.

Of course, there was suspicion that she'd been murdered out of hatred over that, or to get her out of the way, but nothing along those lines was ever established. Ironically, though, the company abandoned the project soon afterward, and the

Dodd Silver Mine became known as the Dead Silver Mine, or just Dead Silver.

I was feeling restless, like my place was uncomfortably small. Maybe it was because of my somber line of thought. I got the pistol and walked outside into the last of the twilight. Except for the always restless treetops and the barking of a distant neighbor's dog anxious for dinner, this was about as quiet as a place could get. The air was damp, sharp, and laced with the fine piney smell of smoke from my stove. I could just see the lights of Helena, a bright cluster that thinned out to pinpoints over the surrounding miles of ranch land and forest.

As a journalist in California, I'd gotten almost inured to brutal crime. But here on my own turf, it felt much closer.

I'd known Astrid from a distance when we were growing up. She was a year older than me, and I was a relatively invisible kid; my contact with her hadn't ever gone beyond an awkward smile and "hi." But I'd been far more aware of her than that, and so had pretty much everybody else.

For openers, she was a very attractive blond—not a Barbie type, but athletic, vibrant, and a track star and straight-A student besides. She loved attention and she brimmed with self-confidence. There didn't seem to be any question in her mind that if she wanted something, she should get it, and if she decided something, she was right. Besides her looks and talents, she came from a prominent ranching family, the Seiberts. Modern Montana and feudal Europe might have been separated by hundreds of years, thousands of miles, and a vast gulf of technology, but they had one thing in common—big landowners tended to be aristocrats, and vice versa.

According to the teenage grapevine, Astrid had brought the same attitude to romance. If she liked a boy, she didn't hesitate to let him know it in the most time-honored and convincing way. But she'd be equally quick to dump him and move on to the next one who caught her fancy. By the end of high school, she had already junked a string of young hearts and left them abandoned along the road.

Clearly, getting married hadn't ended her amorous penchant. She'd been trysting with a lover at the time of her death—a powerful motive for murder, at the hands of a jealous husband. Physically, Professor Callister was capable of the crime; he'd been a hardy woodsman and hunter.

Back inside, I poured another drink, then picked up the phone and called Madbird. I'd told Renee I wanted to bring him in on this, if he was willing—that his experience and way of thinking would bring insights I'd never see on my own, and that I trusted him more than I did myself—and she was fine with it.

When he answered, his gravelly voice had an edge that startled me. He was always a little gruff, but not like this.

"I was going to run something by you, but maybe this isn't a good time," I said.

"It ain't you—I'm just pissed off. Me and Hannah"—his longtime live-in girlfriend—"got some stuff to give Darcy for her new apartment, and she was supposed to come by and decide what she wants. We drug it all out and cleaned it up, and she never fucking showed or called."

"Ouch."

"I should of known better. She's pulled shit like this before."

It sounded like the cumulative strain of worry and annoyance was getting to Madbird, and that didn't happen easily.

"So I'm glad for a excuse to quit thinking about it," he said. "What's going on?"

I gave him a quick description of the chaos in Renee's carriage house.

"Pack rats, hey?" he said, with his tone back toward normal. "I had a old Ford Bronco a while back. One night, three o'clock in the morning, my dogs start going apeshit. I look out the window, the rig's on fire. Turns out one of them fucking rats chewed up the wiring harness. Melted the dashboard out."

"I wish they'd done the same thing to that carriage house," I said. "This job's going to be ugly, and I'm not asking you to work on it—I'd just appreciate you thinking about what I told you. Let me know if you have any notions."

"Right off, the way it sounds, I wouldn't bet you're going to do any good," he said.

"I hear you."

"I remember them murders. Ten, twelve years ago?"

"Right around then."

"I suppose you ain't doing it for the money."

I'd been thinking about my reasons, enumerating them. I was drawn to Renee and wanted to help her through this trouble. I'd respected her father, and I'd even admired Astrid for her brash allure. The damage they'd all suffered made my heart ache. And I was pissed that someone might have gotten away with the crime. I knew it was naïve to imagine I could make a difference, but as long as I admitted that, I felt free to try.

"It comes with a story," I said, and gave him another quick rundown—this time about the photos.

Roughly ten seconds passed in silence.

"Well, Sunday morning, I can't show up too early," Madbird finally warned. "I got to go be a altar boy."

"Huh. I thought you'd moved on to hearing confessions."

"Only from women. I got a special clientele. That's in the afternoon, so I'm gonna have to take off early, too."

"A lot of people would be surprised to find out you're so devoted to caring for lost souls."

"Hey, call me Mother Mag-dah-kee." That was his real, Indian name. It meant "bird of prey."

I smiled. "I'll see you when I see you."

CHAPTER 7

I WAS LEFT WITH A Saturday evening to kill. Earlier today, I'd figured I'd grab some dinner downtown, but after I left Renee's it had slipped my mind. I foraged through the refrigerator and found the chunk that was left of the weekly pot roast. I usually cooked one every Sunday and lived on it for lunch sandwiches, chili, stew, and other spinoffs. This one came from an elk Madbird had shot last fall, and was about as good as meat could get. I decided to make my own style of Stroganoff. I stirred a splash of red wine, a lot of garlic, and dashes of this and that into the oniony drippings, and put the pan on the stove to warm. With sour cream added at the last, poured over sourdough toast, it would be redneck gourmet.

Then I turned on the computer I'd bought myself last Christmas—my major concession, to date, to the twenty-first century. I'd learned basic skills during my journalism stint, but I'd phased out of that a decade ago, and I had a lot of catching up to do. It was a no-frills Compaq desktop, but at first I'd felt like a Neanderthal piloting an F-16, and I still spent a fair amount of time trying to extricate myself from blunders I didn't have a clue how I'd made. But by now I could get around reasonably well on the Internet, which was my main interest. It wasn't much of a substitute for a warm and breathing companion, but an agreeable time-passer for a solitary night, and it spurred me to dig into matters I was curious about but otherwise wouldn't take the time to pursue.

I spent the next couple of hours, with a break to savor my elk concoction, trying to refresh my memory about Astrid Callister's murder. I didn't really learn anything new. The online archives of Montana newspapers didn't go back that far, and I wasn't able to find much on the national archiving services I tried. There were a few breaking stories on the crime itself, but nothing about the follow-up investigation. I decided I'd stop by the *Independent Record* when I got a chance; probably they'd have their older records on microfiche.

I'd fallen into that near-trance state of being like a lab animal trained to press a bar for a pellet of food or a jolt of pleasure to the brain. I kept clicking my finger, dancing the arrow across the screen, hoping for my own little reward in the form of a morsel of intriguing information.

Then, on a whim I hadn't even realized was in my head, I typed the name Seth Fraker into the search window.

About four hundred entries turned up, fewer than I'd expected. Most involved minutes of the current legislative session or other business where his name was attached in some perfunctory way. He was also mentioned in political websites, occasional news articles, and a few blogs, although he didn't seem to generate much interest with those. There were a couple of photos and snippets of personal information. His looks defined the term "clean-cut." He enjoyed wholesome sports like skiing and boating, and had played on the golf team at Arizona State. He believed piously in God, his country, and, of course, family values.

The single factor that at first seemed to stand out was his claim to be a moderate in a Republican party that generally leaned far to the right. But even that started looking like just a way to play it safe. I didn't see any record of him taking a strong stand on any controversial issue, or even speaking out. In a couple of instances when he was pinned down by questions from the press, he'd hedged, saying that he was still giving the matter serious thought. But his voting record was straight party line.

None of that was surprising or interesting, and my brain and vision were dulling toward slumber. But my robotic finger kept clicking the mouse, and after a few more pages, I caught an entry that opened my eyes again.

It was in French, apparently from a newspaper on St. Martin, in the Caribbean. The heading read only *Le St. Martin Courrier*, and was dated way back in February 1997.

> *Tragique noyade accidentelle au Lagon Blanc. . . . La victime se baignait toute seule le soir et a disparu . . . malgré l'insistence de son ami M. Seth Fraker qu'il a fait tout effort pour la sauver. . . .*

I'd studied French through high school and some in college; my grasp of it had never been anything to brag on, and like most of my other formal education, had suffered with the passage of time. But I got the gist.

A woman had drowned in a tragic accident, while swimming alone at night in White Lagoon. A man named Seth Fraker had tried to save her.

My first hit was that this was unrelated to the Seth Fraker I was checking out—that it referred to another guy who happened to have the same name.

Still, I opened the file.

The *Courrier* was a small weekly that billed itself as "The Voice of French St. Martin." It had a semi-tabloid presentation, with graphics that tended toward garish and catchy headlines, the lowdown that you wouldn't find in the mainstream press. In fact, most of it consisted of ads; the news was limited to a roundup of a dozen items from the previous week, none much over a hundred words. The drowning story was one of those, and, at least via my clumsy translation, as tame as hand crème.

Guests had been staying at a seaside villa. Late in the evening, they'd noticed that a young woman, one Lydia Korzina, had slipped away. They found her clothes on the beach. Seth Fraker had swum into the night-bound lagoon and searched for her until police arrived. Her body was recovered next morning. She wasn't a St. Martin resident—it was thought that she was originally from somewhere in Eastern Europe. Authorities were trying to locate her family.

That was all.

I clicked on the link to the newspaper's website to see if there was a follow-up story, but got a "can't be displayed" message. The same thing happened when I tried a general search. At a guess, *Le St. Martin Courrier* was defunct. I took a stab at penetrating the archives of the island's major paper, the English language *Daily Herald*, but the names Seth Fraker and Lydia Korzina turned up nothing. I drew another blank going through the remaining entries on Fraker. Maybe there was information in there, but I wasn't the guy to find it.

But why would there be? If it even was the same Seth Fraker, he had simply happened to be present when a sad accident occurred, long ago and far away. There was no hint of scandal; his political opponents surely would have brought that to light.

Although one bit of nuanced phrasing, in such a brief account, struck me as a little odd—Fraker "insisting" that he'd made every effort to save her.

As if maybe there'd been a suggestion otherwise.

CHAPTER 8

MADBIRD PUSHED MY OLD WORM-DRIVE Skilsaw horizontally across a plaster wall in the Callisters' carriage house, with a sound like a freight train braking hard along a mile of rusty track. Sparks flew out in sprays when the blade hit lath nails, and clouds of stifling white dust billowed forth, hanging in the air like they had a half-life. I followed along behind him, digging my hammer claw into the plaster and ripping out chunks.

By now, it was early Sunday afternoon. We'd already checked the obvious places where the photos might be hidden, then sifted through the toxic Zonolite insulation in the attic. Next came the walls. Since it was impossible to guess where somebody might have eased a piece of siding loose and slipped something inside, we'd decided to open them up—carve channels that later could be filled with drywall, taped, and textured to match the plaster. There was an additional benefit: The ancient knob-and-tube wiring was a fire hazard, and this would clear pathways for rewiring.

Besides the main room that the Professor had converted into his study, there was also a small bathroom and an unimproved back area. The rats hadn't left a square inch of it untouched. Cleaning up the mess just so we could walk around, every bit the ugly job I'd warned Madbird about, took us half the morning. We'd managed to tear up the sodden carpet and drag it into the yard, then mucked out the rest with shovels. A couple of armchairs and a small couch were far beyond saving, so they'd gone, too. The resulting heap of trash would damn near have filled a Dumpster.

I'd never dealt much with pack rats before. Between my tomcat and predators like a resident badger family, my premises stayed pretty clear of varmints. But I knew other people besides Madbird who'd had run-ins with them, and as often as not come out second best.

They tended toward the large end of the North American rodent family, almost the size of cats. They could chew like chain-saws. A construction pal had told me about a ceiling that collapsed under the weight of dog food they'd hoarded up there. Another friend from northern California reported that they loved marijuana plants and were a bane to the region's growers—an army of feral four-legged narcs, stealthily searching and destroying by night. Like most critters, they avoided humans, but while others would run if you surprised them, pack rats tended to stand their ground and stare right back at you, even if you were pointing a gun. Whether this was because they were bold or stupid, nobody seemed sure.

They were probably best known for their penchant for pilfering small objects and leaving others in their place. The consensus was that they didn't deliberately swap objects on a quid pro quo basis, but if a rat was carrying something and saw something else it liked better, it would drop what it had and pick up the new item. They were particularly attracted to shiny stuff. Eerily, they tended to trade up in value, as if they had an aesthetic sense. They'd abandon a scrap of cloth for a scrap of tinfoil, the tinfoil for a beer tab, and the beer tab for a coin. If you left any jewelry where they could get at it, you could kiss it good-bye.

Their peculiarities also included a fondness for flowers. They'd strip gardens of them, not to eat, but to decorate their turf—touching, considering that otherwise, they were about as destructive and filthy as creatures could get.

They'd sure proved that here.

The Skilsaw's shriek died off as Madbird finished his cut and released the trigger. When the blade stopped spinning, he jerked the saw out of its kerf and laid it on the floor. Blessed quiet settled over the room, and the swirling dust clouds settled over us.

"Hope there ain't any hantavirus in here," he muttered. "Be just right—die from mucking out the shit of the rat that killed you."

"Hugh? Can I come in?" Renee called from the doorway. She'd probably been waiting for the commotion to stop.

"Stay there, we'll come out," I said. We groped our way outside into the cool damp day. Spring was still taunting but not yet delivering.

When Renee saw us, she actually started to laugh before she caught herself. I didn't mind. It was the first time I'd seen worry leave her face. And we had it coming. Madbird looked like an extra in a *Road Warrior* movie—his body was white with dust except for dark goggle rings around his eyes, and his thick black hair was tangled with a nest of plaster chunks that suggested he'd gone through a wall headfirst. I was sure I was no improvement.

"My God," she said. "I'm sorry, I had no idea it would be so—chaotic."

"That's why we get paid the big bucks, darlin'," Madbird said. His gravelly voice was reduced to a parched croak.

"I baked fresh cookies," she said timidly. "And there's coffee."

"That sounds real tasty," Madbird said. "But you know, there's nothing works up my appetite for cookies like a couple cold beers."

I nodded agreement. We didn't usually drink while we were working, but this wasn't usually.

"Oh, *no*," she said. "I should have thought of that. I'll run get some."

"Half-rack of Pabst." He fished a twenty out of his wallet and handed it toward her, trailing dust. "Try Louie's; they keep it almost froze."

She pushed his hand away gently. "I'll buy it, don't be silly. Let me grab my keys."

While Renee walked to the house, Madbird and I stayed outside to suck down a few more fresh breaths. The sky was blue-gray with a threatening storm that sent occasional flurries of spitting snow and the breeze had a sharp edge, but it felt damned good.

"You know that couch for Darcy?" Madbird said. The question seemed abrupt, but his mind worked in mysterious ways.

"Yeah?"

"We could probably use another hand getting it up them stairs."

"Like, her boyfriend?" I said.

"You got it."

He'd mentioned earlier that Darcy had finally showed up at his and Hannah's house last night and picked out some of the furniture they'd offered her. Her new apartment was on the second story; the two of us were going to move the heavier stuff tomorrow, including a couch.

I'd told him about the drowning incident involving Seth Fraker on St. Martin island—not because it was important, but just because. That must have gotten him thinking about Darcy's situation; he'd decided he'd had enough of Fraker dodging him, and had seen a way to force his hand, by inviting him to join in a manly effort to help his girlfriend. If he refused, that would be a serious loss of face. Darcy would try to head it off, but Madbird could handle her. It was going to be interesting.

"Let me know what time," I said.

As Renee stepped out the door with her purse, a rumbling sound in the distance was getting louder and more jarring, fast. A few seconds later, its source rolled into sight—one of those yacht-sized sedans that Detroit had made in the '70s, with a body faded to bilious green and a vinyl top that was peeling like a bad case of eczema. Besides the shot muffler and disintegrating engine that the noise advertised, the car belched smoke and was cancerous with corrosion. A great old line from Raymond Chandler flashed through my mind—in this pretty, peaceful place, the big rust bucket stood out like a tarantula on a slice of angel food cake.

I recognized both car and driver the instant I first glimpsed them.

His name was Ward Ackerman. He was the tenant who'd lived in the Callisters' house for the past several years and had let it go to hell. The blame for the unchecked invasion of the pack rats and all the damage they'd done lay squarely at his sorry-ass door.

While I tried not to stereotype people, I couldn't help myself with Ward. I seemed to be noticing more and more guys like him these days—neither tall nor short, fat nor thin, with longish greasy hair usually covered by a baseball cap, smudgy goatees, and lots of tattoos. It was often hard to tell whether they were closer to twenty or fifty in age.

He came from an extended clan of similar relatives, who occupied a settlement of trailers and run-down cabins outside of town. They tended to be well represented in the newspaper's weekly DUI and crime reports; I knew that Ward had done jail time for petty stuff like dope and theft.

But the Ackermans were distantly related to the Callisters through some convoluted genealogy; when the house needed a caretaker, that and Ward's claims to be a skilled builder had persuaded the family to give him free rent and utilities in return for upgrading the place. Renee had visited her father often in the years since then, overseeing his medical needs and managing his finances, and she'd realized early on that Ward wasn't even pretending. But she lived several hundred miles away, with a demanding job. Trying to lever him out and make other arrangements was too much of a hassle, so she'd followed the path of least resistance until the Professor's death.

The only direct contact I'd ever had with Ward was a couple of construction jobs where he'd hired on as a laborer, and never lasted more than a few days. I'd never had any personal reason to dislike him. But now I had a couple of good ones—the mess he'd left Renee, and an uglier problem that he was causing her.

Ward didn't have a shred of legal claim to the house and wasn't even mentioned in her father's will. The property was clearly and indisputably left to Renee and her mother and brother. But when she informed Ward that he had to move out, he'd argued that he should inherit it, coming up with a bullshit rationale involving the work he'd supposedly done, his blood ties to the Callisters, and squatter's rights. She'd had to threaten eviction before he would finally leave.

Of course, he was furious, and he'd started a campaign of stopping by a couple of times a day on some pretext, such as that he'd left something that he had to look for. Then he'd bully her, telling her he was going to take this to court, he'd sue her if she tried to sell, and so on. He hadn't been overtly threatening, at least not yet, but she was constantly nervous that he'd show up, and a little scared when he did. She was right to be. Ward was a pissant, but there was no telling what kind of psycho state he might work himself up to, especially dealing with a woman alone.

Ward's car charged up the driveway and stopped just inches behind Renee's, blocking her so she couldn't move. He threw open his door and started to climb out.

Then he saw Madbird and me. He casually withdrew the foot he'd put on the ground and stayed where he was, draping his arm over the seatback like that had been his intention all along.

So we walked on over to him.

"Glad you came by, Ward," I said. "Renee's been bringing me up to date about all the improvements you made around here, and now I get to tell you personally how much I admire them."

He looked at me with studied insolence, fingers drumming on the seatback.

"I know you?" he said.

I almost smiled. That was another thing I was noticing more and more—people who seemed to learn their lines from TV.

"Aw, come on, Ward," I said. "Don't you remember punking studs for me a couple years back, framing that Ramada Inn out on the strip? You were there at least two days—maybe even three."

He made a little sound of derision. Then he turned to Renee and whistled, like he was summoning a dog.

"Hey," he called to her harshly. "What's going on? I didn't tell you you could change anything."

I ached to jerk him out of his seat. When I was growing up, that would have been considered the appropriate, even obligatory response. But things had changed. Now it would be seen as assault, no matter the provocation, and while Ward was usually on the wrong side of the cops, I had no doubt that he'd go running to them if he could fuck me over. There was also another level of caution. Punk though he might be, guys like him were packing all kinds of shit these days—not just guns, but truncheons, pepper spray, swords, fucking crossbows.

Outweighing all that was the heartsick, cold-sweat memory of a night last September when I'd gotten crosswise with a man in a way that had started out almost frivolous, but ended very differently. Something in me had declared, never again. It wasn't a conscious decision, but a certainty that had announced itself.

"You've had plenty of chances to clear your stuff out of here," I said to Ward. "If you left something else, too bad. Now disappear, and forget you ever knew this address."

He gave me his hard stare again.

"I got a legal claim to this place," he said. "You're trespassing, dude. So do me a favor, and *you* forget this address."

Still, I found myself wondering whether the assault charge would stick if I just sort of helped him move his car out of the way so Renee could leave.

Then Madbird came sauntering past me, a movement that seemed casual until, with sudden speed, he slammed the driver-side door shut so hard that the huge vehicle rocked. Ward's eyes bulged as round as quarters.

"We got a couple hundred pounds of rat shit over there," Madbird said, jerking his head toward the pile of trash from the study. "What I hear, it belongs to you. How about you take it home with you right now?"

That turned Ward's expression to flat-out alarm. His fingers darted to the ignition key and the car lunged backwards, cylinders rattling and smoke pouring out of the mangled exhaust pipe.

"You'll be hearing from my lawyer, bitch," he yelled at Renee. He peeled on out, tires spraying the residue of gravel left by the winter's sanding trucks.

Renee stared after him, looking like she was slightly in shock. I put my arm around her shoulders and gave her a quick squeeze.

"If he comes by again, call me," I said.

"If he comes by again, he's gonna find out I ain't kidding about that rat shit," Madbird said. Then he gripped his throat and cleared it with a dramatic hacking sound.

"Weren't you on your way someplace?" he said to Renee.

That broke her little trance. She smiled and started walking toward her car again.

"I'll hurry, I know it's desperate," she said.

When she was gone, Madbird gave me a sly glance.

"She's a sweetie," he said. "You ought to check that out."

I snorted, emitting a little explosion of powdered plaster.

"She's way too high on the food chain for me," I said. "Anyway, she's engaged."

"Yeah, well, she could get unengaged. I seen that happen before."

We waded back into the carriage house. The dust had settled somewhat, but it didn't take us long to get it moving again.

CHAPTER 9

A SIZABLE HEAP OF BUSTED-UP plaster and two beers later, Renee called to us from the doorway again, saying that some friends of hers had dropped by and they'd like to look around.

When we stepped outside this time, the sun had broken through a pocket in the clouds. The bright shock to my dust-filmed eyes made them tear up, blurring my glimpse of the two people with Renee. All I could tell was that she was standing beside another woman, with a man a little ways behind them, and that something about Renee seemed different. When I knuckled my vision clear, I realized that she was wearing a buff-colored leather shearling coat that she hadn't had on before. It was brand-new, with tags still hanging off a button.

She introduced the couple as Evvie and Lon Jessup, old family friends who lived a few miles south of Helena. Evvie was forty-plus, somewhat plain but elaborately groomed. Her hair was tinted a brittle red-orange that almost glittered. Lon was a sturdy, bearded guy several years older, who looked like he'd be at home working the land.

"Look what they gave me," Renee said, smoothing the coat's front with her hands. "Isn't it beautiful?" It was, indeed—at least a couple hundred bucks' worth of beautiful. And yet, there was something almost helpless about the way she spoke, like she was more embarrassed than pleased.

If Evvie sensed the same thing, it didn't show. She had a slow smile that crinkled the corners of her eyes, and when her smile deepened, so did the crinkles.

"Little Renee hasn't lived here in so long, we weren't sure she'd have anything warm enough to wear," she said.

Renee rolled her eyes. "'Little Renee.' You can tell we go back a long way."

"So many happy memories here," Evvie said with a sigh. "Such a beautiful house." Then she extended a hand to indicate the pile of rat trash. "But this *mess*. You poor dear." She gave Madbird and me a glance that seemed faintly accusing, as if we'd caused it.

"Evvie's in real estate," Renee said. "She's interested in handling the sale. Is it okay if we go into the study?"

So, there was a little more to this visit than a friendly call. Maybe more to the expensive gift, too—intended to make Renee feel obligated.

"It's not dangerous, just dirty," I said. "I'd take off that new coat, if I was you."

"We don't have to go inside, hon," Evvie told her. "I just need a peek." She stepped to the doorway of the carriage house and gazed in.

Lon Jessup had stayed in the background, not speaking except to say hi, but now he walked over to join his wife.

"You're brave men for taking this on," he said to Madbird and me as he passed. "We appreciate you helping Renee out." He leaned in the doorway beside Evvie, with his thumbs hooked in his belt. He was probably familiar with construction; most ranchers were, along with a wide range of other skills.

"Why are you cutting into the walls?" Evvie said. "I thought you were just fixing the damage."

Renee glanced uneasily at Madbird and me. I groped for an answer that would disguise our real purpose.

Madbird, ever quick on his feet, said, "Rats could of got inside them, too. We're making sure there ain't something left in there that'll stink."

Evvie didn't respond. Instead, a few seconds later, she swung around to face us.

"So how long's it going to take you?" she demanded, suddenly peremptory.

This put her first question into a context that I'd learned to recognize over the years, as had Madbird; his lips curved in a faint smile. The maneuver was one that was used by speculators, designers, and other players who were peripheral to the main construction on a project. It was intended to put tradesmen on the defensive and drive down their prices—suggesting that they were dogging it, doing unnecessary work, and/or overcharging—while at the same time demonstrating that the questioner knew all about such shenanigans and would fiercely defend the clients' best interests.

I had developed a number of responses, including some rude ones if the individuals really irritated me. But usually, I just let them know that unless they were signing my paychecks, I was going to tell them zip minus shit.

"That's up to the lady who hired us," I said. "What-all she wants done, and if she wants us to do it."

I could just about see Evvie trying to decide whether I'd sidestepped her on purpose or out of sheer dumb misunderstanding.

"I've hardly been able to think about it," Renee said. "I've been so overwhelmed."

"Of course you have, hon," Evvie said, stepping to her and giving her arm a comforting pat. "Has anybody else looked at the place? An appraiser?"

Renee shook her head. "I haven't even gotten that far."

"Good. A little word of advice—don't talk to a soul until the rat mess is all taken care of. Maybe nobody will ever need to know." Evvie winked slyly.

Renee looked doubtful. "Really? Aren't those kinds of problems supposed to be disclosed?"

"It's like a lot of other things—there's wiggle room. If the repairs turn out okay"—Evvie glanced meaningfully at Madbird and me—"I don't see why it should matter."

Right off the top, it would matter because cleaning out the pack rats' digs wasn't going to get rid of them. As long as Madbird and I were working in the carriage house, they'd hole up in their outside dens, but they'd be back as soon as we left. We could try to protect against them, but once they moved into a place, it was extremely tough to keep them out.

Evvie might not have known that, but as a licensed Realtor, she'd sure know that failure to disclose such a problem wasn't only unethical, it could leave the homeowner open to lawsuits. "Wiggle room" wasn't much of a defense.

"We better be going, Ev," Lon Jessup said. I wondered if he was embarrassed by her and wanted to hustle her away before she went further. Maybe he was used to it.

"We'll see you tomorrow at the ceremony, dear," Evvie said to Renee—the Professor's funeral, which was shaping up to be a big deal, with a lot of the prominent local community and various other dignitaries slated to attend. "I know how hard it must be, but you'll feel so much better when it's over." We all told each other that it had been nice to meet, and Renee walked them to their car.

"This isn't exactly my business," I said when she came back. "But that riff about hiding the rat damage—you could get sued for that."

Her mouth twisted unhappily. "Don't worry, I'll make sure everything's straight up. I don't *want* her in on this. But she caught me flatfooted—called and said they'd like to drop by, and a few minutes later, she came barreling in and acted like it was a done deal. Gave me that coat to nail it down."

"Yeah, I caught that."

"She's not *bad*, she just sees everything in terms of what she wants and how to get it." Renee's voice dropped confidingly. "They're not really old family friends, she just wants to think that. She and Astrid knew each other growing up, and then Lon met Astrid and Daddy somehow—I'm pretty sure it was Astrid who introduced him to Evvie, that's how they got together. But they were never around when I was growing up, even though she acts like I'm her long-lost daughter."

"Can't say I envy you there."

Renee sighed. "Anyway, I'm going to keep putting her off, and hope she'll get the message."

She walked on into the main house, and I went back to join Madbird.

"Starting to seem like a lot of people got their eye on this place," he said.

There was more of that to come.

CHAPTER 10

WE FINISHED OPENING UP THE walls with no results. Then there was nothing left but the crawl space, which deserved its name. It was just deep enough for us to squirm under the rough old two-by-twelve joists if we wanted to. We didn't. Doing that kind of thing was bad enough anyway, and this ground was thick with rat dung. We decided to take up a couple of floor planks and look in from the top.

That was cleaner but not easy. The rusty old twenty-penny nails, four inches long and thick as a pencil, weren't about to pull free. We had to lever up the planks enough to get a recip saw blade under them and cut the nails as we worked our way along. By now we were only speaking to growl curses at the metal and wood that fought us back. We were tired, and sweetie though Renee might be, we'd had our fill of this.

When we'd made a channel wide enough to hang our heads down into, we each took an end and started scanning the crawl space with flashlights.

Almost immediately, Madbird said, "Well, kiss my ass and call me howdy."

I rolled onto my other side so I could follow his flashlight beam. It was focused about ten feet from where he lay, on top of the foundation wall inside the rim joist. I could glimpse a few small dull metallic glints, the color of gold or brass, along with some paper scraps strewn around.

I heaved myself up, waddled over to Madbird on my complaining knees, and dropped down beside him for a better look.

I still couldn't tell what the metal was, but the other bits were fragments of photographs, with the same faded flesh tone as the ones of Astrid.

I felt like a well driller who'd finally hit water that he hadn't really believed was there.

Getting to it still wasn't any piece of cake. Professor Callister had been an expert bird hunter and had loaded his own ammunition—we'd found chewed-up plastic bottles of black powder, wadding, and other materials when we'd cleaned—and the spot was underneath his heavy old workbench. We had to unbolt that from the wall and drag it away, then cut another chunk out of the floor.

There, blocked from our earlier view by a mid span girder, we found something even better—a cloisonné jewelry box. It had an intricate pattern of deep red enamel inlaid with gold and a lid that rested inside the rim. Maybe the rats had clawed at it trying to get the gold—even without the flashlight, enough daylight filtered in through the floorboards to give that a faint glint—or maybe there'd been some perfumed object or sachet inside that they'd smelled. However it had happened, they'd managed to nudge the lid aside and pillage the contents.

Without doubt, this was the cache of photos that Renee had hoped for. There must have been a stack of them to start with, and there were still a few at the bottom that looked more or less intact.

The box must have also contained jewelry, no doubt dragged off into rat lairs in the woods, where it would be all but impossible to find. But a single earring remained, spared by the marauders because its hook had gotten caught in a splintered patch on a joist. At first glance, it looked like a spinner for big game fish like musky or northern pike; it was a good two inches long and one inch wide, in the shape of the letter S with an arc cupping its bottom like a rocker on a rocking chair. It appeared to be made of silver and was encrusted with blue stones, probably sapphires, that looked like real ones. If so, it was worth a fair chunk of cash. But it was so garish it was almost laughable; it suggested Roy Rogers and Dale Evans, fringed buckskin, cowboy hats with chin strings.

Exactly the kind of outfit that Astrid was sporting in the photos—along with earrings that looked a lot like this one.

"I can't say it looks like good news," I said.

"We don't have to tell her. Your call."

I rocked back on my heels, stood, and walked to the door to get a faceful of fresh air. Evening was coming on, and the lights of the main house exuded a cheerful warmth.

But inside there, an anxious woman was waiting, hoping to learn that her father had not been a vicious murderer.

I tried to weigh the factors. The photos were damning enough to Professor Callister. Jewelry, a classic killer's souvenir, was more serious still. And yet, there it all was, a reality that couldn't be denied.

Maybe settling the matter would be best for her—would bring closure, as the buzzword seemed to be these days. Then again, maybe that was bullshit.

I turned back to Madbird. "I guess I feel like we can't keep it from her," I said. "We don't have the right."

He lifted his chin in a way that told me he wasn't just going along, he agreed. That meant a lot.

I went to get Renee.

CHAPTER 11

SHE KNELT AND STARED DOWN at our find with her face alight with excitement—but wary, too, as if something might leap out and bite her. That wasn't so far from the truth.

"The earring was hers," she said.

"Is that what she was wearing in the photos?" I asked.

She nodded, her hand moving toward it.

"We better be careful about touching this stuff," Madbird said.

I'd gotten so jacked up about making the find that I'd lost sight of the implications, but his words brought them into focus. In spite of Renee's reluctance about the police, this development just might wind its way in that direction. They would not be pleased if we'd gone pawing around first.

"Oh, right," she said unhappily. "I hadn't thought of that." She pointed at the earring with her forefinger, tracing its shape in the air. "That's the Seibert brand, quarter-circle S"—the logo of the family ranch where Astrid had grown up. "They had a place where they mined sapphires. No, not mined . . ." She held her hands apart as if she was gripping something, and shook the imaginary object back and forth.

"Screened," Madbird said.

"That's it. Her grandfather collected them over the

years—not to sell, just for fun—and he finally decided to do something with them. He had a belt buckle made for himself and these earrings for his wife. They got passed down to Astrid."

"What about the jewelry box?" I said.

Renee shook her head. "I never saw it, so she probably didn't have it at this house."

I could see how Astrid would have hidden it in the privacy of her own cabin, a sort of bad-girl stash for the photos and trinkets of her sexy secret life.

Renee kept gazing silently at it.

Then, with sudden fierceness, she said, "Daddy wouldn't have kept things like this. He *wouldn't*."

Madbird caught my eye and nodded toward the door. He was right—she was deeply preoccupied, and we were in the way.

"We're going to take off," I said. "We'll come back and straighten up whenever you're ready."

She rose to her feet, dusting off her knees. "Thanks so much, you guys. Oh, wait, I have to pay you."

"Let's worry about that later."

"It ain't like we don't know where you live," Madbird rumbled. That won a smile from her.

He said good night and split off to his van. Renee walked with me to my truck. I hated the thought of leaving her there alone, especially to pore over those grim relics.

"Do you know anything about checking for fingerprints?" she said. "I know I blew it with that first batch. But these—if there were someone else's prints besides Daddy's . . . " She let the sentence hang unfinished. "I looked on the Internet. A lot of places sell kits."

"I don't think it's any job for amateurs, Renee. Especially with something like this."

"I looked for laboratories, too, where I could pay to get it done. But I didn't see anything."

It didn't strike me as likely that she could just box the stuff up, send it away someplace, and get back a neat little report.

"Have you thought about a private detective?" I said, although that might entail a larger-scale investigation than she wanted, and would definitely be expensive.

"It crossed my mind. But this is so sudden, and there's so much else going on. I'm just groping around right now—trying to find out what the options are."

Another possibility had crossed my own mind. I'd kept my mouth shut because it was dicey in several ways. But it made sense in others. My wish that I could do something more to help finally pushed me into voicing it.

"Renee, if there's one person around here who'll know more about this case than anybody else, it's the sheriff, Gary Varna," I said. "He and I have, uh, been acquainted for a long time. If you want, I could see if he'd be willing to talk this over and keep it off the record. Maybe he'd even do the fingerprinting. And, you know, act on it if something new came along, and forget about it," I finished lamely, "if not."

"That's very sweet. Let me think about it. I want to look those photos over before I decide anything."

"I thought we decided to leave them alone."

"I won't touch them with my bare hands. I have a hemostat I can use."

"You carry a hemostat?"

"My fiancé gives them to me. Instead of tweezers, you know? They work a lot better."

I factored in her fiancé's gift of surgical implements along with her expensive engagement ring. The word "doctor" took shape in my mind.

"Are you coming tomorrow?" she said.

I winced inwardly. I hadn't planned on attending her father's funeral, and she was probably only asking out of politeness.

Still, I said, "Sure."

"I'll be glad to see you there. Thanks again, Hugh."

I drove home accompanied by unwanted images that I couldn't keep from sneaking into my thoughts—the dignified, acclaimed man whom I'd known as Professor Callister, snaking his way on his belly across the dank earthen floor of that crawl space to the trophy he'd created out of murdering his beautiful young wife. Gloating over the photos, fondling the jewelry, using them to indulge in a solitary vice sickening beyond words. Or maybe he'd just hidden them and then left them untouched, satisfied with knowing they were under his feet.

But my mind, emotions, or whatever unit they formed found that a very hard sell.

I had only been around him when I was quite young, not often and never closely. But I remembered that between the ages of, say, five and ten—after I'd gotten old enough to have a sense of the world I was in, but before various forms of training had started me thinking in the ways they dictated—I had often seen into adults quite clearly: whether they were genuinely well intentioned toward me, or hostile under a nice veneer, with their teasing disguising cruelty. As an adult, when I looked at those same people, my early impressions were by and large borne out.

I didn't know if that was common among children—I didn't have any of my own, and I hadn't dealt with kids much in my later life. But even if it was, they couldn't process their feelings rationally, and the harsh, evident truth was that those kinds of warning sensibilities were easily buried by adult manipulation or force.

John Callister, though, had never paid any attention to me except to give me a grin and a friendly word, treating me humorously but sincerely, like an equal. I had never gotten the slightest hint of unkindness or creepiness lurking under a façade.

But if he was innocent, the real killer had gone free, and might even be close by.

PART II

CHAPTER 12

I GOT TO DARCY'S NEW apartment about seven-thirty next morning to help Madbird move the couch he was giving her. The place was in a complex near the Fairgrounds, one of several that had been built in that area in recent years. He was already there, parked at a building entrance, leaning back against his van sipping coffee. The couch was in the rear, protruding out a couple of feet with the doors roped tight around it.

There was no sign of Darcy, or of her boyfriend, Seth Fraker. Whether either would show up remained to be seen. When I'd talked to Madbird last night, the situation stood like this:

He'd called Darcy to ask for Fraker's help moving the couch. Predictably, she'd tried to deflect him, but he was firm. A lengthy negotiation ensued, the more complicated because Darcy was in the middle.

Fraker replied that he'd be glad to work with us, but his schedule was jam-packed.

It would only take a few minutes, Madbird pointed out, and Fraker could choose any time.

Fraker couldn't think of a single available slot. He was at his office every morning by eight o'clock sharp, he was booked for lunch and dinner meetings, and he worked late into the evenings.

And so on, until Darcy decided she didn't want the couch after all. She—meaning Fraker, who had probably whispered this to her—would buy a new one instead and have it delivered.

Madbird then informed her—and my mental ear could hear his patience-worn-thin, Marine drill instructor voice—that the couch was already loaded in his van and he was damned if he was going to take it out again. We'd bring it to her place at seven-thirty next morning; if Fraker wasn't around to help, we'd leave it on the sidewalk, and it was her problem from there. That was the last I'd heard.

I knew this was no longer about Madbird wanting to meet Fraker. Now he wanted Fraker to meet him. There would be a message delivered—that if Fraker thought of Darcy as a play doll, she was a doll that came with a very unsettling attachment. It wouldn't involve anything crude like threat or overt menace; it would be conveyed mostly through Madbird's sheer presence.

I drove on into the parking lot and pulled my truck up beside his van.

"Need some of this?" he said, holding up his coffee cup.

I nodded thanks. I usually brought my own, but my routine had been thrown off by Professor Callister's funeral. I'd had to shower—I usually waited until after work to wash off the day's dirt—and then root around to find some decent clothes, which I hadn't had the foresight to do last night.

Madbird handed me his steel thermos, which had been dropped off buildings, used as a hammer, and run over by trucks, and looked every bit of it. I rummaged in my front seat for a cup, blew the sawdust out of it, and filled up. The coffee was fragrant and strong, and if the old thermos didn't exactly keep it scalding, it was still a nice hit in the gray morning chill.

"I came a hour early to scope it out," Madbird said.

"Fraker's rig was here. I parked down the block and watched. He snuck out about twenty minutes ago."

"No flies on him."

"Maybe he's just putting on a act like he ain't sleeping with her. Let's give it a couple more minutes and see if he comes back."

We unroped the couch, an old but handsome piece with plum-colored upholstery, and set it on the pavement. In truth, it wasn't all that heavy; Madbird and Hannah had loaded it into the van, and he and I could have got it up the stairs without too much sweat.

Instead, we sat down on it to finish the rest of his coffee, like a couple of old-timers settling in to pass the day by watching the world go by.

"Kind of feels like when I was hitchhiking around after the service, sleeping on park benches," Madbird said.

"Anybody who sees us is going to be thinking, *There goes the neighborhood.*"

"Yeah, well, they ain't got all that much to brag on here."

We'd both put in a fair amount of time working on apartment complexes like this one and the others around it—long two- or three-story rectangles with low-pitched gable roofs, the rough-sawn plywood siding known as T-one-eleven, and equally generic interiors. But they were comfortable if they were decently kept up, and no doubt it was a dream come true for Darcy. She'd been living at the Split Rock Lodge, in an aging bunkhouse where employees could rent rooms for next to nothing. But it was bare bones and cramped, with shared facilities and no privacy beyond the thickness of a door.

"You know what the nut is here?" I said.

"Darce wouldn't tell me, but Hannah found out. Seven twenty a month, not counting utilities."

In other areas that wasn't much, but by Montana standards, it was steep. With utilities, cable, and phone, it would be close to a grand. She wasn't making much more than that.

Seth Fraker had to be covering it, and there was clearly more, or less, to his generosity than pleasing a girlfriend. He couldn't very well have shacked up with Darcy in her bunkhouse room. I didn't know what his own living arrangements were for the legislative session, other than that his family wasn't with him, but whether he rented or owned a house, his neighbors would know who he was. A lady visitor like Darcy would be highly visible. But in an anonymous place like this, he could come and go unnoticed with both the comforts of home and the pleasures of philandering.

"Looks like we're on," Madbird said. We stood up.

Darcy was hurrying down the building stairway toward us, closing the cover of her cell phone. She was an eyeful even this early in the morning—wearing a bright red nylon workout suit, the kind that looked like neon pajamas. She gave us her big beaming smile and hugged Madbird. The dynamic was clear—she'd lost her fight to keep this from happening, so now she was working on damage control.

"Thanks for doing this," she said. "Seth will be here in a second."

Right on cue, Seth Fraker's pickup truck came rolling in and parked beside us. He opened his door and jumped out briskly, wearing an outfit that astonished me even more than Darcy's—brand-new Carhartt overalls. I wondered if he'd bought them for the occasion.

He was in his mid-thirties, six foot plus and athletically built. He came at us with a comradely grin and firm handshake, projecting sincerity, although the impression was somewhat undercut by a baseball cap pulled down low and wraparound sunglasses that looked like the Darth Vaderized windows of his truck. I couldn't see much of his face except his very white teeth.

I'd been betting he wouldn't show, but Madbird had gauged him correctly. He could justify his evasions up to this point, but this one would have been a flat-out admission of cowardice. His ego and confidence in his status had won the day.

But behind his glued-on friendliness, he was still nervous, and pissed that he'd been maneuvered into this.

"I've sure been hearing a lot about you," he said to Madbird, with a trace of blustery challenge.

"Surprised you had the time to listen," Madbird said. Ignoring Fraker's fading grin, he stepped to a corner of the couch. "Let's do it."

He and Fraker took the upstairs end, harder because they had to climb backwards. Fraker made a show of lifting more than his share, and Madbird let him. Darcy stepped in beside me, and she was a strong young woman; with the four of us, we had the couch up the stairs and inside her apartment in no time.

Our physical effort had momentarily set aside the real business of this event, but once we dumped the couch, unease hung in the air as loud as gunfire. Darcy was still smiling, but there was no offer of coffee and donuts. She wanted us out of there.

But Madbird started prowling, poking around in the chaos of half-unpacked boxes that littered the floor.

"You still got that set of china Gramma Maude give you?" he said to Darcy.

She hesitated, then said, "Sure."

"I'm asking 'cause I don't see it."

"It's somewhere." Her voice was taking on an edge. "Look, I've got stuff all over the place. I can't carry everything around with me."

"You ever hear from her?" Madbird said, still picking through the boxes.

"Gramma Maude?" she said warily. "What are you talking about? She died."

"Yeah, I know. I put her ashes in a elkskin bag and hung it in a tree."

Darcy spun around, hurried into the bedroom, and shut the door hard. Madbird walked out of the apartment without a glance at Seth Fraker, who had watched the exchange like he was frozen in place, except for his mouth opening slightly.

As I started after Madbird, Fraker recovered enough to turn to me.

"Is he a little crazy?" he said.

"He's a lot crazy."

"You work with him, right? He must make sense to you."

"More than I make to him."

"Hearing from a dead grandmother?" Sarcasm was creeping into Fraker's tone. He wanted to get back what he felt he'd lost, and I was a safer target than Madbird.

"He was talking about people messing around where they don't belong," I said. "Not knowing jack shit, but thinking they do."

His face, from the little I could see of it, took on a haughty look. It warned me that guys like him had all the juice, but that kind of shit also angered me almost as much as it did Madbird.

"I don't care for the way you put that," he said.

"Must be close to eight. Time to lose that bunny suit and head to your office."

The corners of his mouth turned down in a way that suggested he could be really unpleasant.

"You've got quite an attitude," he said. "That why you got your face smashed?"

In fact, the purple crescent scar under my left eye had come from a light-heavyweight boxing match years ago. Attitude hadn't figured in at all.

"It's a private story, Congressman—only for friends," I said, and walked on out of the apartment.

CHAPTER 13

MADBIRD AND I HAD ALREADY agreed to blow off going out to our job at Split Rock today. My time was going to be chewed up by the funeral, and we both had chores that we hadn't been able to get to yesterday.

There was also the chance of fallout from the photo cache we'd found—especially if Renee took me up on my offer to talk to Gary Varna. I was anxious to see her, find out how she was feeling and what she was thinking. But this would be a particularly hectic morning for her, so I held off calling and spent the next couple of hours running errands.

The funeral was held at St. Thomas Presbyterian Church, a grand old red brick structure built in traditional style, with ten-foot wooden doors and a high arched nave. I got there at a quarter to ten, wearing the one sport coat I still owned—a Harris tweed that looked tolerable because it had spent most of the last ten years hanging in a clothes bag. The other dressy vestiges of my former life, suits and slacks and the like, had long since gone to the Goodwill store. I'd kept one necktie, but decided not to wear it; while it was fine hand-painted silk, its image of an eagle plunging with outstretched talons didn't seem appropriate for this occasion.

As I walked up the building's stone steps, I caught sight

of Lon and Evvie Jessup approaching—the Realtor-rancher couple who'd dropped by Renee's yesterday. I hesitated, thinking it might be impolite not to wait and say hello to them, but not really wanting to. I raised a hand in greeting. Lon waved back, but Evvie looked right through me. That jibed with what I'd sensed yesterday—that she'd judged within the first few seconds whether Madbird and I were worth knowing, the answer was no, and, essentially, we no longer existed. I went on inside.

St. Thomas, one of the town's biggest churches, was nearly full. I made a quick estimate of more than three hundred people. I decided I'd be more comfortable standing than shoehorned into a pew, and I'd also be able to duck out if there were too many long-winded speakers. I found an unobtrusive spot in a rear corner, settled back against the wall, and scanned the crowd.

The most prominent guest was Professor Callister himself, reduced to the contents of a brass urn on a table in front of the altar.

I picked out Renee by her dark brown hair and slender shoulders, sitting near the front. I didn't recognize most of the people flanking her. At a guess, they were Callister relatives from far eastern Montana. I recalled that the Professor had grown up on the family ranch there, but those ties hadn't stayed strong. Besides the long physical distance from Helena, that area tended to be very conservative, and his politics had separated him further. Still, they were the kind of salt-of-the-earth people who wouldn't have dreamed of disrespecting him by not attending.

The Seibert family, Astrid's side—who believed that he was guilty of the murders—was conspicuously absent.

The rumors of other prestigious guests hadn't been overblown. Along with the mayor and a slew of dignitaries and prominent citizens sat Montana's brash young governor, Riley

Winthrop. He was currently riding a wave of popularity and using that to implement an agenda of progressive reforms, although it remained to be seen whether his ass could cash the checks his mouth was writing.

More surprising was the sight of U.S. Senator Bart Ulrich, in a pew at the very front and center. He certainly hadn't been any friend to John Callister—he had opposed environmental protection measures as determinedly as Callister had backed them. I guessed that he was here today to counter that image, and no doubt he'd be stumping at the reception afterward; he was up for reelection and it wasn't looking good for him in spite of a lot of big-money backing, most of it from out of state.

Ulrich was popular among some factions in Montana because he took care of wealthy constituents, loudly proclaimed what people wanted to hear, and brought home a lot of pork. But he hadn't done much for the nation as a whole, and it was substantiated by now that his heels were among the roundest in the Congress. Without doubt, a certain amount of influence peddling went with the turf, and even was necessary for political survival. But he'd gone way over the line, with his ballot on the block for just about anything—which explained why lobbyists and special interest groups that had nothing to do with Montana were anxious to keep him in D.C.

While that was injury enough to citizens and government, he piled an infuriating insult on top of it—he was also an appallingly cheap date, at a price of a few thousand bucks per vote. With pols from other regions pulling down five and six figures, it made our great state look like a two-dollar whore.

Then I realized that I was slipping into a familiar old cynicism, a holdover from my newspaper days that surfaced without fail when I started looking at politics. I tried to clamp down on it; at a funeral, it had to be bad karma.

My spirits lifted a minute later when a familiar figure

stepped into the church—Tom Dierdorff, a good friend since we'd gone to grade school together. He spotted me and walked over to join me in leaning against the wall.

Tom was powerfully built, with a strong Teutonic face— he'd been a formidable wrestler—and a dry, sharp sense of humor. He came from one of the area's big ranching clans, but he never played that up—or the fact that he'd gotten a degree in electrical engineering from Northwestern. That could have taken him just about anyplace he wanted to go, but he'd realized that he was unwilling or unable to leave the land he'd grown up on. He'd come back to Montana, gone to law school, and now divided his time between his legal practice and ranching.

I'd made a similar decision some years back and, while Tom had handled his far more gracefully, that still enhanced our common ground. He'd helped me out in a couple of minor legal situations; no way could I afford him, but the way it worked was that he'd forget to send me a bill, then I'd drop by his place and find something that could use a repair, and I'd spend a few days evening the score. In terms of dollars per hour, the arrangement favored me by a factor of ten to one, but this was on a different kind of clock, and he'd made it clear that that was how he wanted it.

We exchanged a quiet greeting. Then it occurred to me that he might be a good source of information about the Callister case. He'd been living here at that time, and he was well connected on the levels that counted.

"Tom, I know this is out of place, but I have a good reason for asking now, not just morbid curiosity," I said. "Do you have any take on the murder story, behind the scenes?"

Tom was also a guy who considered his words before he spoke, the more so if they pertained to something weighty. His face didn't change for half a minute.

"I know some things that weren't made public, but that's

because I represented a client in a spinoff case—a nasty little situation with that Dead Silver Mine," he finally said. "I don't want to be coy, but there are confidentiality issues, sealed evidence, that kind of stuff. On the other hand, it's ancient history." He raised one eyebrow. "If you told me about this non-morbid curiosity of yours, I might have a better notion of how much leeway I've got."

The organ music was starting, the rustlings and murmurings of the crowd dying down.

"I'll give you a call," I said.

"You got it."

The minister was a spare, gentle-seeming man who nonetheless ran the show with authority and precision. Everything was solemn and tasteful. There were no lengthy testimonials, just a couple of brief statements about the positive aspects of the Professor's life and accomplishments. No mention was made of the tragedy that had ruined him. The ceremony lasted just an hour.

Renee was escorted out first, in the company of the people she'd been sitting with. She looked pale but poised, wearing a simple black dress that was very becoming.

But I was startled to see that instead of a strand of pearls or other tasteful jewelry, a large silver pendant hung around her neck.

I only got a glimpse, but I was just about certain that it was Astrid Callister's earring.

CHAPTER 14

THE RECEPTION WAS HELD AT the Gold Baron Inn, a classy older place not far from the capitol grounds. The funeral guests filled the big convention room, and I didn't have a chance to talk to Renee right away; she was busy greeting one person after another. Understandably, they wanted to pay their respects to her father, and she was the natural recipient.

But I confirmed that her pendant was that earring. She must have looped a chain through it. I could practically see some people trying to ignore it, while others gave it sidelong glances.

Now that the solemnity was over, this was pretty much like any other big party. The buffet line was doing a brisk business; people chatted over food and wine, the buzz of conversation punctuated by the clinking of silverware. The governor, known for his peripatetic schedule, either hadn't come or was already gone. Senator Ulrich was working the room like the pro he was, all smiles and handshakes. If there'd been any babies present, he'd have been unstoppable.

I stayed on the fringes of the crowd, waiting until Renee broke free. Eventually, I noticed that she was waving her hand and looking at me, beckoning me over to her. She was talking to another well-wisher, a bland, smooth-faced, fiftyish guy named Travis Paulson. I recognized him from the occasional big commercial jobs I'd worked; he was some sort of planner for the state. When Renee introduced us, we agreed that we'd seen each other around. But while his handshake was hearty, I didn't think I was imagining that he wasn't happy about my joining them.

"Travis saw the mess outside my house," she said.

His gaze shifted nervously. "Just happened to be driving past."

"I told him you were getting rid of those awful rats." She gave my sleeve a comradely little tug.

"Yeah, they put in a lot of work," I said. "Wish I could find laborers like that."

Paulson responded with a quick, tight smile: *nice try, pal, but not funny*.

"If you get in over your head with it, give me a call," he said to Renee. "I know everybody in the business around here—all the best people."

"We could sure use somebody to haul that trash away," I said. "You got a recommendation?"

He glanced at me coldly. "I only deal high end." Then he swung back around to Renee and stepped between her and me like he was cutting in on a dance, enfolding her in a lingering hug.

"I'm there for you anytime, honey," he said. Without another glance at me, he took his leave.

She sighed. "Sorry about that. I really hardly know him."

"From what I've seen of him, he mostly deals with the high end of sitting on his own fat ass. Renee, what are you doing with that earring?"

"I found something else last night," she said, dropping her voice, but excited. "I couldn't get to sleep, thinking about it. That's why I look like shit."

"You look terrific. What did you find?"

"You're a liar, but sweet. There's a pile of wood chips a few feet away from the jewelry box—with gunpowder mixed in."

I blinked. "Gunpowder?"

"It's hard to see because of the rat gunk."

"There was black powder all over the floor," I said. "Your dad had it in containers and the rats chewed them up. It probably just sifted down through the gaps."

She shook her head emphatically. "This was deliberate. Go take a look."

"Where are you going with this?"

"Suppose the gunpowder caught fire. It would burn those wood chips, and that old dry building would go up like a torch. The firemen would find the jewelry box. That wouldn't burn because it's enamel, right?"

She watched me anxiously while I thought it over, but I ended up having to shrug. "I still don't get it."

"It's like I've been saying all along. Daddy didn't put the box there—he didn't even know about it. The real killer did. He set things up so he could start a fire that would seem accidental. Then when they found the jewelry box, it would make Daddy look a lot more guilty."

I rubbed the back of my neck, trying to get my mind around the implications.

"So how come he never lit the fire?" I said.

"Maybe he didn't need to. He was waiting to see if the police got suspicious of him. Then he'd use it to throw them off, turn them back on Daddy. But they never did."

I could only judge by the way it sounded, and that was that she was clutching at increasingly thinner straws.

But I said, "Okay, I'll go look. Now let's get back to why you're wearing the earring."

"What if he's still around—maybe here in this room?" she said heatedly. "He knows Daddy just died. He's going to be paying attention to what's going on. If he sees the earring he'll recognize it and it will shake him right down to his boots. For instance." She pointed unobtrusively toward Travis Paulson, the man we'd talked with a minute ago. "He stares at it every time he thinks I'm not looking."

"He's not the only one noticing it, Renee."

"He's *really* noticing. Watch."

She turned casually away from him. I followed her cue, but kept him in sight peripherally. His restless gaze did keep returning to Renee, and it did seem to be aimed below her face—although I guessed it was her breasts he was staring at.

"Is there anything more solid to connect him?" I said. "Like a motive, or being a suspect back then?"

"I don't know. I'm going to start looking into all that. But I'm not just talking about him. Whoever it was, they'll want to find out how I got the earring, how much I know, what I'm going to do. So maybe they'll come around prying."

First I was flat-out stunned, then angry.

"You're trying to *lure* the guy? Jesus, Renee, this isn't Nancy Drew—we're talking a double murder. Take that thing off and put it away."

Her eyes turned defiant. "I'll wear it whenever I want. And don't you dare bark orders at me."

I was starting to realize that sweet, shy Renee had a stubborn streak.

"Sorry," I said. "Will you *please* take it off?"

"Me too. And no."

Several people were hovering nearby, waiting with polite impatience for their chance at her. It was time to cut this short.

"I'll go check out that gunpowder," I said.

"You mentioned bringing this up to the sheriff—would you still do that?"

I hesitated, but nodded.

"I should be able to break free from here in a couple of hours," she said. "If you're going to be around."

"I'll be around."

I made my way through the crowd to the exit, pointedly keeping several people between me and Senator Ulrich's glassy smile and glad hand. My concern about Renee was getting both deeper and broader. Now it was starting to seem like she was seeing tigers lurking behind every tree.

And yet I paused inside the door and watched Travis Paulson for a minute. The interaction here had strengthened my impression that he had a severe case of self-importance. He'd bustle around job sites waving blueprints and talking imperiously to the supers, who tolerated him only because they had to. I'd seen him driving with that same aggressive impatience, cell phone pressed to his ear, in a Seth Fraker–style pickup truck, a big new rig that had never hauled a scrap of anything.

He did seem to fit the model that Renee had described. His gaze was still flicking furtively toward her, like a nervous tic he couldn't control. He'd "just happened" to drive by her house and notice the trash pile. He'd pressed an invitation for further contact with her.

On the other hand, Helena was a small enough town that you easily could just happen by someplace, and it would be normal for a friend to take an interested look. I couldn't fault him for wanting more of her company. And above all, I just couldn't take him that seriously. Behind his swagger, he seemed too ineffectual to have committed such a harsh, resolute crime.

I hung around for a minute longer, watching the other men in the room. I didn't see any more signs of furtive fascination with the earring, and by and large, they were a distinguished-looking group.

But I was no judge of what might lie beneath the surface. Many of them had known the Callisters for years back into the past, and I could have been looking at a long-buried dispute or obsession that had driven one of those distinguished fingers to pull a trigger.

CHAPTER 15

I STILL HAD THE KEY that Renee had given me to her carriage house. Stepping into the cold, torn-up building was a familiar sensation, never uplifting and with nothing here to improve on it. I changed back into my work clothes, got a trouble light, and hunkered down where we'd found the cache.

The top of the masonry foundation wall, about a foot wide, had become a rat highway; with the caked dung and debris, the surface was hard to see, and we hadn't examined it closely yesterday. But as I moved the light beam, I spotted the pile of wood chips in a corner where rim and floor joists met, under the wall plate and studs—all dry old wood with plenty of updraft, a perfect place for a fire to start.

Shavings like that got scattered around during construction, although there was no apparent reason for this buildup. But a heavy sprinkling of a dark substance was mixed in, mostly congealed now but still finely granular in a few spots. I touched a fingertip to one of those and sniffed. It gave off the unmistakable acrid smell of gunpowder.

I made an effort to believe that this was just happenstance with a touch of freak coincidence, and that imagining anything else was buying into a folie à deux with Renee. But she was right. The powder hadn't just sifted down through the floorboards; there was too much of it, and no gaps directly above the spot.

Before the rats had turned the volatile black powder sodden, a single spark could have set it flaring. Flames and firefighters' hoses would have obliterated the setup; if any traces were found, there'd have seemed nothing strange about its presence in an area where a man had reloaded shotgun shells.

But the enamel jewelry box would have stayed more or less intact, with the fire mainly above it—the contents maybe heat-damaged, but still recognizable.

And investigators would swiftly have reached the conclusion that Professor Callister had hidden it there.

So had he? Or was Renee right again—that the real killer had established this slick ruse to divert suspicion from himself? The fire-resistant jewelry box seemed a notch fortuitous. Maybe he had provided it himself to fit his scheme, figuring that people would assume it had belonged to Astrid. Had he just stumbled across the photos somehow, maybe ransacking her cabin after the crime? Or had he known about them, and planned in advance to use them this way?

I poked around the study for a few more minutes without accomplishing anything, then admitted that I was mainly just stalling my visit to Sheriff Gary Varna.

As I walked across the yard to my truck, my gaze was caught by a vehicle a couple hundred yards uphill, in the woods behind the Callisters' house. That seemed like an odd place to stop. There were no houses or anything else nearby. It wasn't even a turnout; you'd have to pull off of Montana Avenue and drive a ways through the trees to get there.

The vehicle started to move immediately, pulling away and disappearing. All I could tell was that it was a mid-sized SUV, dark blue, several years old. They were a dime a dozen around here.

No doubt there was a perfectly reasonable explanation for its presence. That spot being an excellent vantage point overlooking this property, hidden from passing traffic and most other eyes, and the driver taking off as soon as I came into view, was all just coincidence.

CHAPTER 16

THE LEWIS AND CLARK COUNTY courthouse was a somber gray stone building that had seen its fifteen minutes of fame when the just-caught Unabomber was photographed on the steps outside. Besides housing the Sheriff's Department, it was also the old jail, and you couldn't fail to feel the gravity of that.

I'd been nervous about my offer to talk to Gary Varna ever since I'd made it to Renee. It was true that Gary was a longtime acquaintance of mine, and I could even call him a friend. And I thought he'd probably agree to an off-the-record look at what we'd found—not as a favor to me, but because he wanted to know what was lying under every rock, and he hated loose ends.

What worried me was that he suspected, correctly, my involvement in the disappearance of two men a while back. That had been the occasion for my last visit to the courthouse, handcuffed and flanked by deputies.

Now my relationship with him was a lot like Captain Hook's with the crocodile. Gary patiently kept an eye on me, following the tick of my inner alarm clock, confident that one of these days, the little raft of phony alibis that I'd patched together would hit a reef. I was equally sure that he was right.

There was some comfort in knowing that if he really

wanted to push it, he long since could have. In fact, I had reason
to believe that he had even run interference for me during that
investigation. But I couldn't help suspecting that was because I
was a morsel he was saving for later.

Meantime, we got along fine, although if I happened to
glimpse him unexpectedly—and at six foot five, Gary stood
out in a crowd—my blood pressure arced.

He was in his office, a cubicle as spartan as a Marine bar-
racks, wearing his usual unofficial uniform: blue jeans pressed
with a razor-sharp crease and a button-down oxford cloth
shirt. He looked the part for his job—tall, lean, light brown
hair just starting to gray. He was friendly as always, but as
always, the gaze of his slate blue eyes started my mouth going
dry. We chatted for a minute, until he paused expectantly.

"It's about John Callister," I said.

"John Callister," he said musingly. "There's a name that
brings up memories. I was sorry to miss his funeral, but I
couldn't get away."

"His daughter Renee's in town. She was cleaning up his
study and she found some photos and a piece of jewelry. She
thinks they're related to those murders, and I'm starting to
think maybe she's right."

He didn't move or speak, but his eyes focused a click.

I told him the story, adding that Renee hoped to keep this
confidential. And while I cringed at snitching, I felt compelled
to confess that she'd handled the items—and that she deliberately had the earring on display.

His displeasure was clear. "That kind of thing don't wash,
Hugh. I seem to recall you and me having a talk about it once
before."

"What was I supposed to do—physically restrain her?
Come on, Gary. She's being naïve, sure, but she's been carrying
that weight all these years, and now this new jolt. It's got to be
killing her."

He still didn't like it, but he nodded curtly. "Put that stuff someplace safe, and for Christ's sake, don't mess with it any more."

"Yes, sir."

He leaned back in his chair, head tilted to the side.

"Well, I guess I'd agree to keep it quiet, at least to start with," he said. "I got my own reasons for that. Most of the people who were involved would piss blood about reopening it. Makes them look bad, and real bad if they're proved wrong. And there's technicalities I don't want to deal with, like the city police ought to be called in. But if something serious turns up, Miss Callister's just going to have to take what comes."

"I'm sure that'll be fine with her," I said.

"She don't have any choice," Gary said patiently. "You better explain that to her."

His big-knuckled fingers started drumming the desktop. I interpreted that as sort of like a cat's tail twitching—something was brewing.

"That case sticks in my craw about as bad as any I ever came across," he said. "I pretty much had to watch from the sidelines. Didn't have any jurisdiction up there in Phosphor County, and those fellas weren't overly cooperative. I don't like to break bad on my esteemed colleagues, but a fact's a fact." His face and voice stayed bland, but if there was anything that pissed Gary off, it was being kept out of the loop.

"How so?"

"Oh, it was one of those situations where there was a bunch of factors involved and they snowballed into a hell of a mess. Dave Rucker was the sheriff back then, getting on toward retiring, and he figured this was his last chance for the limelight. So he tried to handle it himself, and he botched it right from the get-go, and then he stonewalled to cover. Some dirty politics going on, too."

That reminded me that Astrid had been embroiled in

some antagonism over the Dead Silver Mine. And Tom Dierdorff had mentioned it at the funeral, and also implied a hidden backstory.

"Can you tell me your opinion, just between us?" I said. "About the Professor?"

Gary grimaced like he was in pain, and I knew it was real. He was ironclad in many ways, entirely willing to manipulate people and even ignore the letter of the law. But he still cared deeply about its spirit, and when he couldn't enforce that, it ripped him up.

"I've never been convinced he was guilty," Gary said.

Coming from him, that was pretty strong. I'd expected a more noncommittal response. But before I could phrase another question, he glanced at his watch.

"I'm afraid I'm going to have to move you along—I got another appointment," he said. "I'll stop by the Callisters' as soon as I can. Not today, I'm swamped—I'll try for tomorrow."

I thanked him and rose to leave.

"Hugh?" he said, as I got to the door. "Is Renee staying in that house alone?" Now he was leaning forward with his forearms on the desk and his gaze intent.

"She has been, yeah."

"I'm not sure that's a good idea," he said. "Why don't you pass that on to her, too."

I walked to my truck feeling newly unsettled.

Renee was out there trolling for trouble, and Gary took seriously the possibility that it might exist.

CHAPTER 17

I DROVE STRAIGHT TO THE Gold Baron Inn, but the funeral reception had broken up and no one on the staff knew where Renee had gone. I swung by her house; she wasn't there, either. Probably she was with her relatives. I knew she had a cell phone, but I hadn't thought to get the number.

I'd cooled down by then, anyway. Gary was talking about a commonsense precaution, not an emergency.

Although it was still unsettling.

I realized that Renee might not be back for some time, and I didn't feel like just hanging around. I decided to follow up on what my lawyer pal Tom Dierdorff had mentioned at the funeral.

Tom wasn't in his office, but his secretary patched me through to his cell phone and he picked up right away.

"I wondered if you might have a minute to chat anytime soon," I said.

"I think maybe this is in the stars, Hugh. Talking to you this morning got my ass in gear to do something I've been putting off. A guy's proposing a development up around Gates of the Mountains. There's opposition; it's going to court. I need to look the site over, and I'd be glad for a pro to bounce my thoughts off."

"You better get a real pro if you want an opinion that's worth anything. But sure, I'd be interested to see it."

He gave me directions, and I headed north on Interstate 15. The terrain rose in a series of long, deceptively steep hills, through rolling open ranch land that gave way to forested mountains. The Missouri lay a few miles to the east, then converged with the highway near Wolf Creek and they ran together toward Great Falls. It was a fine stretch of country, and so far, it was largely unchanged.

I found the gravel road that Tom had described, and after a couple more miles, I spotted his parked pickup truck. There was nothing shiny about this one; it was caked with mud, dinged up and scraped, the bed strewn with fencing tools, rolled barbed wire, and feed. I caught the sweet musty perfume of hay as I walked past.

He was standing on top of a rise fifty yards away, wearing the kind of quilted jacket that a lot of stockmen preferred. This time of year, the wind off the snowfields still carried a pretty good bite. You'd never dream that he was a big-shot attorney; he looked like he was scanning for lost cattle. I hiked on up there to join him.

The hilltop overlooked a meadow that was surrounded by forest and skirted to the north by a creek just starting to shed its skin of ice. A couple of big dozers and a backhoe were parked on the site, with their ridged tracks leading to spur roads they'd cut into the trees. But nothing was moving except the neon orange plastic ribbons on engineers' stakes, fluttering in the afternoon wind.

"Did somebody shut them down?" I said. This weather wasn't anywhere near bad enough to do that.

"An environmental coalition. For openers, the developer started work without all the right permits. When he got that straightened out, they claimed the septic system's inadequate, it'll pollute the water table and filter down to the river."

Which, adjacent to this spot, happened to be one of the finest, most popular trout fishing stretches in the world.

"He's fighting back, of course, and his money's talking loud," Tom said.

"What's the setup?"

"Eighty houses to start with. Medium-high end, average around three hundred K—couple-acre parcels, set apart in the trees. But there's already a bigger operation on the table, a mile back toward the freeway. Apparently our man started feeling guilty about outpricing the average working stiff, so he wants to put in a couple hundred cheaper units, complete with a bar-casino. And plenty of room to expand."

That hit another raw nerve—the prospect of sprawl like I'd seen during my dozen years in California. I'd drive a stretch of highway flanked by fields, and when I drove it again a few months later, shopping centers and housing tracts had appeared. Cities that had been miles apart became one long strip. But the hard-line stance of trying to keep out development altogether was untenable. The population kept growing and people needed homes and jobs.

"I can't tell you anything about the building quality without seeing some foundations or framing," I said. "But the things you mentioned aren't good signs."

The odds were slim that the developer had made an honest mistake in starting work without permits. More often that was an aggressive tactic that worked on a "possession is nine tenths" mentality. He knew that once ground was broken, that created a momentum which was hard to turn around. Regulatory agencies tended to bluster but then back off, at worst imposing slap-on-the-wrist fines which might or might not ever get paid.

But beyond the legalities, it raised a red flag with more tangible consequences. Those kinds of outfits were prone to cutting other corners, such as by using substandard materials and practices. The inadequate septic system was a prime example.

"That's what I figured," Tom said. "Glad to hear you agree."

"I suppose it's going to go through anyway?"

"I don't think there's any question. Just whether sooner or later."

"What's your stake in it?"

He smiled wryly. "That's what I'm mulling over—I've had offers from both sides. Part of me wants to dig in and make it tough for him. Another part says that's pissing in the wind, and smart money is to join his team and try to see that at least it gets done right. Then again, I'm sorely tempted just to stay the hell out of it. A cop-out, I know, but it's going to be loaded with the kind of heartache us old homeboys already got plenty of."

I didn't have any advice, and I knew he wasn't really looking for any. Maybe it helped him to have a sounding board.

"Well, that's my own little tempest in a teapot," he said. "I guess we could go sit in my truck and get the heater on. No point in standing here freezing."

We turned our backs to the chilly wind and walked down the rise.

"I heard a while ago that the sheriffs were real interested in you," he said.

"I came within an ace of calling you. Turned out I didn't have to."

"So this is a different situation?"

"I'm afraid it is, Tom," I said. "And it's starting to take on weight."

CHAPTER 18

TOM'S CONNECTION WITH THE DEAD Silver Mine had come about by way of a radical environmentalist group, a few of whom had snuck onto the site and were caught damaging equipment. But before they could be tried, Astrid's murder took place, making the Dodd Mining Company leery of more bad publicity—this time, really ugly. They backed off taking all the defendants to court and instead chose a scapegoat, a young man with no money or clout, figuring they could railroad him to a long prison term. Tom knew his family and offered to represent him pro bono. He used the company's reluctance as leverage, threatening not just a trial, but a very noisy one. In the end, he was able to plead the sentence down to three years; the kid actually served less than half that.

In the process, Tom had learned a very interesting piece of information.

Astrid had belonged to that same radical group, and she had talked seriously about blowing up the mine itself.

That news had surfaced in Phosphor County at the time of the equipment-damaging incident and made its way around the rumor mill, stepping up antagonism toward Astrid. But then her death gave it a reverse spin, because it strengthened suspicion that the killer was a local resident or mining company employee. The gossip quieted, the Sheriff's Department ignored it, and it never played a part in the investigation.

I thought about it all through the drive back to Helena, but by itself, it wasn't much to go on. Maybe it was an important factor that could play a part in exonerating Professor Callister, maybe just another complication.

But it underscored one of the saddest aspects of situations like that, where the conflicts themselves weren't intrinsically violent, but got people riled up to the point of hatred—sadder still because the majority just wanted to improve their lives and would gladly have come to a peaceful compromise. It tended to be extremists who barred that and created bitter polarization, with each side roundly blaming the other.

Most environmentalists were well intentioned, but easy targets for dislike because they often took a moral high ground—including groups like Astrid's that felt justified in destruction. There were also wealthy interests that wanted to close off wilderness and make it their private playground, and used conservationism to disguise their real object. They had a lot of money and knew how to work the system. The result was a gridlock of litigation that blocked even the most sensible proposals, like salvaging fire-damaged timber that would otherwise rot. Sometimes it seemed like a lawsuit got filed every time somebody walked into the woods and opened a pocketknife.

At the other end of the spectrum were corporations contemptuous of both the land and its residents, resorting to barefaced lying and manipulation to gouge fast bucks out of a place, then leave it bleeding and move on. The landscape had plenty of those scars from companies that had flagrantly violated regulations and defaulted on promises of cleanup, then stonewalled authorities or simply dissolved. Mines like the Dead Silver project were particular offenders. There were several thousand abandoned mines in Montana alone and several hundred thousand in the nation that had been polluting for decades. The cost of detoxifying a typical site ran well into the millions; the overall amount was staggering and would have to come mostly from taxpayer money. Not much of that had been found for the purpose.

Caught in the middle of the conflict were the working people who had depended for generations on resource extraction industries. As they lost their way of life and sank into unemployment and poverty, it was only natural that many blamed the environmentalists, especially affluent outsiders. The hovering business concerns weren't shy about fueling the fire, knowing that would put pressure on politicians and intimidate activists.

I'd once harbored a naïve belief that most of those issues could be resolved if the money interests would take a step back from the trough; the purists would admit that everything they ate, wore, lived in, traveled via, and so on came from natural resources; and both sides accepted the fact that the people who did the hard, dangerous work of obtaining those resources should be paid and treated fairly. Encouraging breakthroughs came along once in a while, but in general, the bulb of reasonable compromise wasn't giving off much light.

CHAPTER 19

WHEN I DROVE UP TO Renee's house this time, her car was parked in the driveway.

But Ward Ackermans's big green rust bucket was right behind it.

The two of them were on the porch facing each other, along with another man standing beside Ward. Renee, still wearing her black funeral dress, had her back to the doorway like she was protecting the place.

My adrenaline started pumping. I pulled over to the curb, jumped out of the truck, and strode to the house.

Their faces turned toward me, and I recognized the second man as Boone Ackerman, Ward's father. Years ago, he'd been peripheral to amateur boxing circles—not in any official capacity; there were always guys like him who were just around. I suspected that he remembered me, too, although he didn't give any sign of it.

If ever I'd seen living proof of the old adage about the fruit not falling far from the tree, those two were it. Boone was around fifty, about the same size as Ward and with the same generic look. He also had a rap sheet, more impressive than his son's, as befitted his seniority. Boone was craftier; he'd mostly been involved in small-time financial fraud, and he was capable of emitting a snaky charm. But under that I sensed real menace, much more disturbing than Ward's tough-guy act. I didn't know for a fact that he'd ever been involved in violent crime, but it sure wouldn't have surprised me.

"I see you brought your lawyer," I said to Ward.

Boone's cool gaze flickered, just enough to tell me that the words had scored. If he'd ever opened a law book, it was in a prison library.

Ward strode to the top of the porch steps and jabbed a forefinger down at me. No doubt he'd been simmering about our run-in yesterday, and was emboldened now by having an accomplished felon to back him up. At a guess, alcohol and meth were also in the mix.

"The only thing I got to say to you is, get off this property," he said harshly.

"Funny—I was just about to say the same thing to you. Again."

"This is family business. Stay the hell out of it."

Renee folded her arms and spoke firmly. "You are *not* my family in any way that counts, and you're not welcome here."

"You've crossed a line, Ward," I said. "Harrassment, stalking—police turf. Next step's a restraining order."

Then Boone Ackerman raised his hands placatingly.

"Let's just everybody hang on a minute," he said. "Sir, I don't know exactly how you figure into this."

Sir—the slick, respectful con. He waited for me to explain myself. When he realized I was just going to let him wait, he went on.

"Well, my son's right. We got a legal claim to this place, and you tearing it up—" he pointed toward the carriage house—"that's trouble. But if you pull off right away, we'll be inclined to let it go."

"The only trouble here is you giving this lady a hard time."

"We didn't mean to upset her," he said quickly. "I'm sorry to hear she feels the way she does. I always thought highly of these folks—and her father *was* my second cousin."

"By a half-brother," Renee said.

"That may be, ma'am. Still, it's a blood tie that can't be denied."

"I'm not denying it. It just doesn't have anything to do with this."

"With all respect, that's not so. Ward stewarded this property to aid his kinsman, who lay stricken by affliction," Boone said, working a little jailhouse preaching into his act.

Renee's eyes widened in outrage. "Stewarded! We let him live here free for years and even paid his expenses, and he thanked us by turning it into a dump. You people never lifted a finger to help us—just schemed to get something out of us."

Boone put on a rueful smile and shook his head.

"I could give you plenty of examples where that ain't true," he said. "Now, we're only asking for what's rightfully ours. It may not say so on any piece of paper. But if you search your heart, you'll—"

She slapped her palms to her temples. "If you start in like that again, so help me God, I'll scream."

"Time for you guys to leave," I said. "Any more hassles, and you better believe the sheriffs will come calling on you."

Boone sized me up with his reptilian gaze, looking sour, like he'd run into an unexpected obstacle that had derailed his smooth maneuvering.

"We'll respect her wishes, of course," he finally said, with the phony dignity of those who sought profit by proclaiming themselves wronged. "Come on, son."

When Boone walked off the porch, I saw that he'd developed a limp. It might have been genuine, but I suspected it was manufactured for sympathy. He sure hadn't gotten it from any work-related accident.

Ward stomped down the stairs after him and headed straight toward me, a schoolboy bluff to make me step aside. With equal immaturity, I didn't. At the last second, he side-stepped, but gave my shoulder a hard bump with his.

"This time it ain't two on one against *me*, is it?" he sneered.

Letting it go hurt even worse than last time.

Boone stopped walking briefly, maybe figuring he'd need to step into the fray and blindside me or supply a few kicks. When I didn't take the bait, he started toward their car again, but this time he forgot to limp.

I was tempted to make a comment, but I let that go, too. With any luck, this situation was now at a stalemate where it would rest.

Sure it was.

CHAPTER 20

As Ward roared away with his signature spray of gravel, I started to shake, like I always did in the aftermath of a confrontation—sort of like an engine dieseling when it was switched off while overloaded with gas.

Renee came down the porch steps and surprised me pleasantly by giving me a kiss on the cheek.

"I think we deserve a drink," she said.

"I could use ten."

"It just so happens I bought you a little gift. Come on."

She led me into the kitchen, where the gift turned out to be a bottle of John Power & Son—a rough-edged Irish whiskey that I savored as an occasional treat.

"I love this stuff," I said. "How'd you know?"

"I asked Madbird. Tell him I got him one, too."

She had a bottle of chilled Clos du Bois sauvignon blanc for herself. I poured her a glass of it, then a healthy splash of the Powers over ice for myself. It tasted like the nectar of the gods.

"The nerve of those men," she said wryly. "Their pitch today was that they've decided to let me sell this place, but they want half."

I was almost amused. You couldn't fault them for thinking small.

Then Renee frowned, looking puzzled.

"That reminds me, I didn't see Evvie and Lon at the reception," she said. "You know, the couple that were here yesterday? She's the Realtor who wants to handle the sale?"

"They were at the funeral. I saw them going into the church."

"Huh. I can't believe she'd miss a chance like that to bond with me."

"Probably something came up," I said.

"I'm sure I'll hear. Anyway, thank God I didn't have to deal with her. Not a polite thing to say, but true." She picked up her wineglass and started toward the living room. "I'm going to run up and change. I'll only be a minute."

"You better stash that earring while you're at it. Sheriff's orders this time."

She paused and turned to me anxiously. "You talked to him?"

"I'll tell you about it when you come back."

Renee hurried on, leaving me, I had to admit, with tantalizing images flashing through my mind. Did mourning apparel mean black underwear? Was there some secret female code that dictated those things?

But my thoughts returned quickly to what had just happened. I walked outside and sat on the porch steps, aware that along with my anger and dislike of the Ackermans, guilt was creeping in.

At its core was an issue far broader than the personal one—a version of the old nature-versus-nurture debate, a complex calculus of being that involved the interaction of inherited factors and outside circumstances.

Ward, and probably also Boone, must have had a tough time in a lot of ways when they were growing up. Education and self-betterment were not priorities in their world. Their role models were lowlifes and outright criminals. God only knew what kinds of sinister doings took place in their warren of shabby dwellings. Whenever you saw a group of the younger clan members cruising around, it usually included a pregnant teenaged girl.

Then again, most of my friends had grown up without much—Madbird, for instance, on the Blackfeet reservation, a hell of a lot harsher than anything around here. My own father had spent his life as an ironworker, my mother as a grade school teacher. By and large, our household was no-frills and no-nonsense.

But my sisters and I knew that we could depend on them, that they'd provide for us and protect us, that their sternness came from concern for us—above all, that we were loved and wanted. To be a child who was neither, especially if mistreated besides, was a nightmare I couldn't fathom. And yet, so many parents kept bringing them into the world.

None of that resolved my feelings about Ward and Boone. They were still first-class shitweasels, who had made the easiest, most self-serving choices without hesitating to fuck people over. But thinking about the forces that had pushed them in that direction softened my animosity and made me face my own conceit.

Renee was a new kind of eyeful when she came out to sit beside me. I'd only seen her in around-the-house clothes and her black dress. Now she looked like a hometown girl, wearing tight jeans and a sweatshirt. And she seemed energized, even happy. With all her other problems that remained, getting done with the funeral must have been a huge relief.

The earring, I was glad to see, was gone.

"So what about the sheriff?" she said.

"It's kind of a good news–bad news situation. Gary doesn't think you should stay here alone anymore."

Her eyes changed and her mouth opened. "Are you serious?"

"He doesn't want you to be scared. Just careful."

"I'll only be here two more days."

"I can just about hear him say, 'Humor an old cop.' I'd feel better, too, Renee."

Her mouth twitched. "I hope that's the bad news."

"It's both. The good is, he agrees there's a chance your father wasn't guilty, and the real guy's still out there."

She stayed quiet for a moment, absorbing that—and probably thinking again about how she'd shown off the earring.

"I have another favor to ask you," she said. "I guess I should say, 'yet another.'"

"For this kind of whiskey, I'm all yours."

"I'd like to see the place where—this is hard to say. Where Astrid was killed. Her cabin. I've never been there, never wanted to go. But now I feel like I have to."

That idea hadn't even occurred to me. But I was curious, too.

"Sure, that's no problem," I said. "I could take you now, if you know where it is."

"I don't, dammit. I was hoping you would."

I shook my head. "Just the general area."

"Well, no big deal," she said. "I'll try to find out tomorrow." She smiled, but I could tell she was disappointed.

"Let me try Madbird," I said. "He just might have a line on it." He possessed an astonishing amount of that kind of information, and if he didn't know something, he usually knew somebody who did.

I went into the house and called him. He said he'd never been there, either, but his girlfriend, Hannah, had worked in that area.

"She just come home, hang on." Half a minute later, he was back. "She ain't ever seen the cabin; it's in from the road. But she's driven by there plenty of times. When you want to go?"

"Actually, now would be good."

"Well, hell, let's call it a road trip," Madbird said. "We'll come by and get you."

CHAPTER 21

MADBIRD AND HANNAH ARRIVED ABOUT half an hour later in Hannah's ride, a late 1980s Dodge Ram that she'd bought used through her job. A lot of government rigs got beaten to death in the backcountry, but this one had stayed in good condition. She'd had it painted a deep metal-flake blue and redone the interior herself. It was a sharp ride, and held the four of us comfortably.

Like Darcy, Hannah was a Blackfeet reservation girl, but a contrast to Darcy's brassiness and high visibility—petite, beautiful in a way that bypassed pretty, and possessing a sultriness the more powerful because it was contained. She was quiet but very tough—the proof of that being that she held her own with Madbird—and very smart. She'd made her way in the white world, going to college at Montana State, then advancing up the ranks in the Forest Service.

It was just about an hour's drive to the Phosphor County line, and Hannah said Astrid's property wasn't far from there. The landscape started feeling lonelier and wilder soon after we left Helena, and as the evening deepened, so did the sense of being at a dreamlike remove from everyday time and space. The road was narrow but mostly bare except for occasional sunless curves where patches of black ice lurked. Madbird was driving and spotting them was second nature to him, but they racked up a fair number of victims every year, usually unwary folks in SUVs who thought that going into four-wheel drive meant they were flying on a magic carpet.

"Any word from Darcy?" I asked.

"Nah, she'll still be pouting," Madbird said. "We figure just leave her alone for now. But that Fraker. You know what you told me about him being on that island and a woman drowned?"

Renee gave me a curious glance. I hadn't mentioned any of this to her.

"Yeah?" I said.

"Hannah started asking around about him. Tell them, baby."

Working in local government circles, Hannah was privy to a lot of gossip—a much richer source of information than the Internet.

"People say he's always played around on his wife," she said. "It's an open secret. A couple of the women ended up afraid of him. I guess he can be a mean drunk."

"Yeah, that fancy gin will do that to you," Madbird said with a humorless grin.

I explained the circumstances quickly to Renee, and then the conversation moved on. But Hannah's news left an unsavory little residue.

The last daylight was fading as we got to the town of Phosphor—with several hundred residents, the metropolis of a large area that was mostly rugged timberland. There probably weren't more than a couple thousand people in all of Phosphor County. The far-apart paved highways were narrow two-laners like the one we were on, and gravel roads tended to dead-end or loop back rather than go anywhere else. That eerie quality seemed concentrated here, fitting our purpose of visiting the site of a double homicide.

The town's main drag was a three-quarter-mile stretch lined by a dozen stores, a couple of gas stations, and several bars. Then we drove on into rural solitude again, punctuated by occasional lights and plumes of smoke from woodstoves. I'd grown up with that piney fragrance and loved it, but here, tonight, it didn't offer its usual comfort. Road signs were shot up and mailboxes bashed in, the sport of young men out drinking and letting off steam.

Abruptly, Renee swiveled to point at a mailbox mounted on a sagging fir post, beside a forlorn dirt track leading into the trees.

"Oh my God," she breathed. Madbird hit the brakes and backed up so we could see it in the headlights.

The name scrawled in crude black letters above the box number read: A SINNER.

I had no trouble believing that a private purgatory lay at the end of that gloomy lane.

The entrance to Astrid's property was unmarked, with no tire tracks or other signs of activity. The gate was closed with a lock and chain so we couldn't drive in, and Renee didn't have any real outdoor clothing, just her expensive street boots and the shearling coat that Evvie and Lon Jessup had given her. But at this altitude, the snow was frozen hard enough so that walking wasn't bad. We climbed the fence and started in on foot, Madbird leading with a flashlight.

The cabin was a quarter-mile farther, nicely situated on a rise overlooking a vista of pristine forest. But I could tell as soon as it came into sight that there was something wrong with its shape. The reason became clear when we got there. About two-thirds of the roof was gone, rafters and all, leaving a big gap open to the sky. Apparently somebody had started tearing it off, then quit. The remainder, without the support of the ridge, had collapsed under snowloads into a ragged-edged pile of cedar shakes and sheathing. The door and windows were also gone, now just dark rectangles that gave the look of a discarded jack-o'-lantern.

We followed Madbird inside and walked around, our footsteps crunching on the snow-crusted floor. It was large and nicely constructed, with walls of thick, uniform, squared fir logs that had carefully dovetailed corners. A big masonry fireplace was obviously the work of a real craftsman. Cabins built for function, like my own, were much rougher—often the work of one man with occasional help, using crude tools and smaller, easily handled timber. But Astrid's family had never lacked for money.

The last room we came to, though empty of furniture like the rest, had to have been the bedroom—the exact spot where Astrid and her lover had spent their last minutes of life. We stood in the doorway while Madbird shined the flashlight around. Its beam found nothing but barren walls and the empty socket of a large window overlooking the pretty meadow sloping down to the creek. I turned away without stepping inside the room or speaking. So did everybody else. As we walked back outside, Renee stayed a little ways off to herself.

Then Madbird said, "We got company."

I caught the sound, the deep rumble of a diesel engine. A few seconds later, a vehicle came into sight, a backwoods redneck's wet dream—a big older-model Chevy or GMC pickup, jacked up so the floor was damned near three feet off the ground. The tires would have carried a semi and the body looked like it had plate armor welded on, including bumpers like sections of railroad track. A winch was mounted on the front and a heavy brush screen covered the grille.

The driver fit the picture to a tee; he was spare, lantern-jawed and handlebar-mustached, wearing a peaked hunter's cap, a threadbare brown duck jacket, and logger boots. He got out carrying a rifle, a lever-action carbine like the Winchester that Chuck Connors had made famous in *The Rifleman*. He held it the same way, with the barrel pointed down but ready to raise fast.

"You get one warning about trespassing, and this is it," he said in a hard voice.

My first reaction was that he must have bought the property at some point during the past several years. Infuriating though it was to be treated like this, especially with the bullshit prop of the gun, he was within his rights to run us off. Then it dawned on me that there couldn't have been a sale without Renee knowing. Her father's marriage to Astrid would have entailed a title search to clear any claim he might have, and Renee had had his power of attorney since he'd fallen ill.

She was right on top of that, and she came back at him just as combatively.

"This place belonged to my father's wife," she said. "Astrid Seibert."

That obviously startled him. "You're related to *her*?"

"I just said so. Who are you?"

He recovered enough to swing the weapon's barrel in a short arc toward the road, a commanding gesture like a soldier would use herding prisoners.

"Somebody that don't like trespassers, that's who. Now get on out and don't come back."

"What right do you have here?" she demanded. "I know the Seiberts, and I don't recognize you."

"They got me watching the place."

"I'll find out." She took a pen and paper from her purse, marched over to the big truck, and wrote down the license number.

"The Seiberts give you a key to the gate?" Madbird said. "Or maybe that's your own lock you put on there."

The rifleman swung to glower at him. "You look like you belong on the rez. What you doing around here?"

Madbird neither spoke nor moved—just locked gazes with him.

The guy's mouth opened to speak, then closed. A few seconds later, he tried again. Still, nothing came out.

Madbird finally turned aside and spat into the snow, releasing his invisible choke hold. He put his arm around Hannah's waist and they started walking toward the road. I did the same with Renee.

"That ain't something to be proud of," the rifleman yelled after us—probably meaning Renee's relation to Astrid. We kept going and there was no more sound from him.

But Christ, did my skin crawl from imagining those rifle sights on our backs.

As we drove away, Hannah said, "I've heard about that guy. He's just got a little place but he acts like he owns everything around it, and he's obsessed with keeping strangers away. He's threatened Forest Service workers on federal land. He parked a backhoe across a county road to block it off."

We talked for a few more minutes about him and the sad condition of the cabin. Then we fell quiet, with Madbird unusually so. That happened when he was seriously pissed.

Like my father, he'd never told me much about his military experiences. I knew he'd been a Marine forward observer in Vietnam—one of those men who slipped far behind enemy lines, alone, to radio back firsthand reports on the accuracy of artillery and air strikes. A lot of Native Americans had gravitated to that sort of particularly hazardous role; it fit with the skills that many had grown up with and the temperament that many possessed, including an unconcern for danger and even an enjoyment of it. That wasn't a trait I shared with them.

But once in a while, usually in the context of hard drinking, Madbird would let something out. Tonight's encounter made me recall one of those incidents, on the troop ship carrying his unit overseas. A couple of Merchant Marine officers had also been aboard. On a single occasion, he had thought-lessly failed to salute one of them—not out of insolence, he just hadn't been paying attention, and the merchant seaman's appearance hadn't punched the same automatic buttons as a regular military officer's always did.

Maybe the guy was a martinet or just a prick; maybe bigoted; maybe he'd had a hard-on about being surrounded by combat Marines on their way to war. He'd gotten Mad-bird thrown in the brig for the duration of the voyage—eight days in a tiny stifling cell, where he'd been chained around the waist and forced to stand at attention sixteen hours out of twenty-four.

"Few years after I got back, I heard that guy was living in San Diego," Madbird had said.

That was the end of the story.

CHAPTER 22

WE ARRIVED BACK AT RENEE'S around eight o'clock, although it felt later. She invited everybody in for a thrown-together dinner, but Madbird and Hannah wanted to get on home and I figured I should do the same. They took off, leaving Renee and me standing in front of her house. I reminded her that she should check into a motel, and offered to help her find a room and escort her there.

"I've been thinking about that," she said. "Why don't you just stay here?"

There wasn't any pressing need for me to get back to my place. The tomcat was fine on his own; he foraged for himself, and I always left an open sack of dry food where he could get at it. I'd be spared the long drive there and back to town next morning.

"Well, if you're sure," I said.

"I'm glad for the company."

I was, too. Especially after seeing Astrid's cabin, the thought of a solitary night in my own was not appealing.

"Hang on a second," I said. I went to my truck, got my .45, and slipped it into my coat pocket. I'd intended to go inside with Renee anyway and look around to make sure nothing was amiss, and I figured I might as well have the pistol with me. Like with the bobcat, I felt slightly melodramatic. But between the Ackermans and the rifleman up in Phosphor, I was well reminded that criminals and sociopaths weren't all that hard to find.

When we walked through the house, she didn't notice anything out of place and the rooms and closets all seemed clear. But the signs of Ward's tenancy were painful to see—cracked plaster from objects being swung or thrown, scars on the floors, bathroom linoleum buckling from a sink that must have leaked for years. All the bedding and upholstered furniture was ruined; she'd had to buy a new mattress for her stay here, and had found a used Hide-A-Bed couch and armchair just so the living room wouldn't be too bleak.

We finished our tour and ended up back in the kitchen. "I'm starving, and you must be, too," she said. "I'll see what I can rustle up. Let me just see who called."

I poured us drinks while she checked the anwering machine—which she'd also had to replace, along with the phones, since Ward and his buddies had ripped off or destroyed the originals.

"Hi, Renee, it's Travis Paulson," a man's voice said briskly. "You know, we really didn't get to talk much, and I feel like we've got a lot of catching up to do. I'd love to take you to dinner." He left three phone numbers, starting with his cell.

Her face showed her distaste. "He must be kidding," she murmured.

The machine's beep signaled a second message.

"Hi, sweetie. Are you there?" a different man said. He paused, as if expecting her to pick up. "Okay—it's six-fifteen here. Give me a call." This voice wasn't pushy, but it carried a quiet authority. I didn't have to wonder who it was.

"I'd better return that one," Renee said apologetically. "It might take a few minutes."

"Actually, I'd appreciate a shower." It wasn't that I'd gotten dirty working today, but freshening up sounded good, and it would get me out of the way while she talked to her fiancé.

"Of course," she said. "Use the upstairs bathroom, it's decent. There are towels in the cupboard."

I'd only glanced into the bathroom on our walk-through, just the same quick once-over I'd given the rest of the place. But when I stepped in this time I was hit on all sides by feminine presence, charming and intimate—the fragrance of soap and perfume, a mélange of cosmetics and lotions, an aqua-colored razor on the bathtub's rim.

I hadn't lived with a woman since my divorce, just about ten years ago.

The hot water felt wonderful, reaching deep into my flesh to ease the chill that lingered in this kind of weather. I gave it plenty of time.

Walking back downstairs, I inhaled the aroma of frying beef and onions. Renee must have started cooking while she was on the phone, but she was done with the call, just adding a jar of store-bought spaghetti sauce to the ground beef. A pot of pasta was boiling beside it and rolls were warming in a toaster oven.

"It's nothing much, I'm afraid," she said.

"It's a feast. And you're right, I'm starving."

I'd noticed a small stash of firewood out back that the human rodents apparently had been too lazy to burn. I brought in an armload and got a blaze going in the living room fireplace. Then we dished up; Renee sat cross-legged in the living room armchair with her plate in her lap and I settled on the couch. It was so homey I was slightly embarrassed.

Except for the proverbial elephant that took up most of the room—Astrid's murder and the specters that had raised. Coming up with light conversation was tough.

But Renee gave it a brave try. "Are you glad you came back here, after California?"

I didn't even have to think about it. "This is where I belong."

"The reason I'm asking is, it's been on my mind. Moving back into this place instead of selling."

That stopped me with a bite poised on my fork. "The hell. I thought you were—you know, had things pretty well planned out."

"Yes and no. Ian—my fiancé—and I do fine together. He's an internist, I've got a great job, it's a life most people would kill for. But—I know this sounds crazy, but it almost seems too sensible."

"There's a lot to be said for a sensible life," I said, although my own efforts at it had failed roundly. "I suppose, uh, Ian, could find work here without any trouble."

She lowered her gaze. "If that was what we decided." The words hung there for a few heartbeats before she sighed in exasperation. "Dammit, I feel like I haven't talked about anything but my own problems."

I finally got a notion of something to say that might be helpful.

"You don't need to entertain me, Renee. Go off by yourself whenever you're ready."

She set her plate aside, and I saw that her eyes were damp. So much for helpful.

"Christ, I'm sorry," I said.

"It's not you, it's the situation," she said, dabbing at her eyes with her napkin. "All those years, I kept it at a distance, and now I can't let it go. Or it won't let *me* go."

"I'm glad to talk about it if you want. Believe me, I'm plenty interested."

"Are you sure? I could use a reality check."

"I'm sure."

She finished off her wine and stood. "I could use another glass of this, too."

I took my own plate to the kitchen and poured myself a little more whiskey.

"Here's how wacko I'm getting," she said when we were settled again. "I keep thinking of more people who could have done it. Like that guy at Astrid's cabin. Remember what he yelled about 'nothing to be proud of'? Whoever he is, he didn't like her."

"I already decided we should tell Gary about it, and give him that license number."

"Then that got me going about Ward and his father," she said. "Boone's the same kind of nasty redneck—he just tries to hide it."

"I'm with you there. Anything more specific?"

"When I came home this afternoon, the two of them were over at the carriage house looking in the windows. If Boone was the one who put the photos in there, he'd be worried about the work going on, right?"

"So then you showed up, wearing the earring. Any reaction from him?"

"He gave it a hard look, that's all. But he'd seen where you tore up the floor, so he'd be prepared, and he's very cool anyway."

"All right, let me try a reality check," I said. "Suppose they looked in the carriage house because they were using the work to prop up their bullshit claim. And Boone was beyond cool and prepared—he was completely wrapped up in the song and dance he gave us. If the earring had meant something to him, he'd have shown it somehow."

"I guess," she said, slightly crestfallen. "I thought about a motive, too, but it's a stretch. Say he'd had his eye on this place for years, hoping he could scheme his way in when my parents got older. Then Daddy married a woman in her twenties and Boone was furious."

"It's an interesting stretch," I said, remembering my earlier thoughts about secret antagonisms among people who'd known each other a long time. Renee's guess might be off the mark specifically, but point at something closer. "I'm not saying I'm right about those other things, either. I think Boone definitely belongs on the suspect list. Who's next?"

"Travis Paulson. He couldn't take his eyes off the earring and all of a sudden he's my long-lost best friend. I'll bet you anything he wants to take me out so he can try to pick my brain."

"He might have another agenda in mind," I said.

"I'm sure not going to find out. As it was, he asked me where I was staying, if anyone was with me, how long I'd be here. I didn't think anything of it at the time, I was too distracted. But now it seems creepy."

"People try to be sympathetic and those are just the kinds of things they ask," I said, although I had to agree that I didn't like the sound of it. And Paulson, like Boone, had pointedly noticed the carriage house work. "So what about his motive?"

She shook her head. "Like I said, I barely remember him—just that he'd stop by once in a while, and I had the feeling my father wasn't all that happy to see him. It was like Travis was glomming on, maybe because Daddy was famous."

Then she raised her hands palms up in a wry, helpless gesture.

"But I'm just babbling about all this," she said. "I don't know who the police suspected—I'm realizing I hardly know anything. I was living in Seattle when it happened, and my mother kept me insulated. I never talked about it with my father—I only saw him twice more before he had his strokes."

That brought sadness back to her face.

"Time for you to crash," I said. "You must be wiped out."

"I am," she admitted.

"Go ahead. I'll take care of the dishes."

"You really don't mind?"

"I really don't." I was compulsive by nature, driven to impose order on chaos, but my scope was limited. Cleaning up a kitchen was just right.

"I'll make up the couch bed," she said, rising from her chair.

"It's fine like it is."

"Oh, come on. You'd be a lot more comfortable."

"I don't want to be too comfortable. I'm on guard duty, remember?"

"All right, macho man. Can I at least get you a pillow and blankets?"

"Sure. I don't want to be too *un*comfortable, either."

She got the bedding from a closet, then started upstairs to her own room. On the way, she paused to give me a glance.

"I used to have a terrific crush on you, back when," she said.

I stared after her as she climbed on out of sight.

CHAPTER 23

THAT GOT MY THOUGHTS SPINNING in a very different direction from where they'd been most of the day.

Of course, that crush was a long time ago. Renee was barely a teenager then.

I headed into the kitchen to clean up. It wasn't much of a job; she was a tidy housekeeper, and there were only the dinner dishes.

The more I learned about her and the circumstances surrounding the murders, the more I sympathized with her psychological quagmire. Now I was starting to see the heavy burden of guilt she must be carrying. She'd never had a chance to talk to her father about the event that had ruined his life. No doubt she'd harbored resentment and jealousy toward Astrid, the interloper who'd stolen him away, broken up their family and home—and was closer in age to Renee than to him. Then came the nightmarish crime itself, probably bringing the irrational fear that her anger was somehow to blame.

All that was seething beneath the surface, along with the tangible troubles crowding in on her. She was holding up a hell of a lot better than I would have.

As I finished up in the kitchen, drying the dishes and swabbing the counters, I was aware of the sound of the shower running upstairs. Then that ceased, and the old house was quiet.

Until I heard Renee's voice say, "Ohhhhh"—almost a groan, faint and far away but still conveying horror.

I went up the stairs three at a time and ran to her open bedroom door. She was wearing a bathrobe, her hair damp— backed up against a wall, arms drawn tight against her chest and fists clenched, staring at her open lingerie drawer.

Inside it was a dark bristly mass that looked loathsome even from fifteen feet away—a big pack rat, shot through the body.

I pulled the quilt off the bed and wrapped it around Renee, then held her for a minute, trying to calm her shivering and my rage. There was no doubt in my mind that this was the work of Ward Ackerman. I hadn't even thought about him still having a key to this place, but of course he would. Maybe he'd killed the rat somewhere else, maybe in the woods right here; after living in this house for years, he'd know where their dens were. In fact, he was probably on a first-name basis with them.

The only time he could have done it was while we were in Phosphor. I wondered if he'd just been driving around and realized we were gone, or if he'd been watching more actively. The Ackerman clan certainly might own an SUV like I'd seen up on the overlook earlier today.

Or maybe it was Boone who was watching.

The corpse had leaked blood and fluids on some of the garments; others might have been salvageable.

"You want to keep any of this?" I said.

"I—couldn't."

That was what I'd figured.

I carried the drawer downstairs, wrapped the rat and garments in a plastic trash bag, and took that out to the garbage cans. Then I just stood there, with my gaze searching the dark, suddenly hostile surroundings.

I had to let the sheriffs handle Ward, and stay out of it myself. I had to.

Back in the kitchen, I scrubbed the drawer out thoroughly with a Brillo pad and dried it with paper towels, making sure there wasn't so much as a hair left from the rodent's hide. I took it back upstairs and fitted it in place.

Renee watched me, sitting on the edge of the bed still huddled in the quilt. It struck me that she had that solemn expression I remembered from when she was a little girl.

"Will you hold me again, just for a minute?" she said.

I was more than happy to.

But the minute stretched longer, and when the holding turned into shy kissing and then went on from there, I swear it wasn't entirely my doing.

PART III

CHAPTER 24

I WAS LATE FOR WORK at the Split Rock Lodge next morning. When I got there, Madbird was sitting on the steps of the motel cabin we were currently remodeling. That was not at all like him. His style was to hit the job running, and if you wanted to talk to him, you ran with him.

He scrutinized me critically. "You look like you ain't slept much."

"I never sleep good on Sunday nights."

"This is Tuesday." He watched me for a few more seconds, then jerked his thumb toward the cabin's interior. "We got a problem."

I exhaled. I didn't want a problem. I didn't want to be there. I'd been reluctant to leave Renee, but she'd gently shooed me out, reminding me that she had to go shop for underwear and didn't need my help on that. It was clear that she wanted some time alone. Even so, I had only come to work to tell Madbird I was going to take off again.

When I walked inside the cabin, that jerked me down to reality fast. All of our most expensive power tools—compound miter and table saws, his Hole-Hawg and our cordless drills, compressor and nail guns—were gone.

I came back out and sat down heavily beside him. We

both knew what most likely had happened. We'd left the place locked and there were no signs of a break-in, but at Split Rock, anybody could have a key to anything. We probably wouldn't have to look far for the perp.

"Let's see what we can find out," Madbird finally said. We walked across the parking lot to the main lodge. The residents here didn't tend to get active until later in the day, and the place looked like a ghost town, with nothing moving across the vista but last year's dead underbrush sticking up through the melting snow and swaying in the fresh breeze. A couple dozen vehicles were scattered around, most of them in perilous condition and many looking like they'd never move again.

I spotted Darcy's car among them, parked around the side of the lodge. So she was here working. I wondered if Madbird had seen her arrive or if he'd talked to her, but he didn't say anything.

Split Rock's owner, Pam Bryce, was in the kitchen setting up the lunch menu. Pam was a pretty earth mother with a big heart; she was pushing fifty but possessed an enduring youthfulness, with hennaed hair in a Little Orphan Annie mop, big hoop earrings, and enough bracelets for a gypsy caravan.

Her goal in operating the place wasn't profit, but to provide a home for fifteen or twenty lost souls who had nowhere else to go and few skills for surviving in straight society—drunks and small-time dopers, old hippies, a couple of vets who were disabled physically or mentally, and other such castaways. They helped out here and there and paid Pam what they could, and while there was incessant squabbling, everybody got by.

The operation had been tottering along for years, but finally there were so many plumbing and electrical malfunctions that something had to be done. Pam, saddled with mountains of unpaid back rent and bar tabs, was in no position to hire a mainstream contractor. She'd asked Madbird and me for advice. We didn't have much else going on then and it would be a decent way to get through the winter. So we'd offered to do it for rock-bottom wages—straight time and materials, cash under the table. Pam could manage that, although our payday usually came late. We didn't like lowballing other contractors, but the alternative was for her to lose the place, which would have meant her clientele being pushed out into a world where they couldn't cope.

When she saw us come in, she took on a sassy look and put her hands on her hips. The bracelets tinkled like mini-wind chimes.

"I told you guys, one at a time," she said.

Madbird grinned. "Careful what you wish for."

"What fun would that be?"

"Good point." He lifted a coffeepot off its burner, poured two cups, and shoved one at me. "Anybody around here get rich in the last couple days?"

Pam's face turned serious. "Uh-oh."

"A bunch of our stuff's gone. We ain't out to bust anybody's balls, we just need it back."

She sighed. "Artie drank in the bar until late last night, and bought two cases of beer when he left. I'd had him cut off because of his tab, but this time he paid cash."

That synched in precisely with the scenario. Artie Thewlis was a longtime Split Rock resident who more or less redefined the term "loser"—a shifty little guy who ran endless petty schemes to buy, sell, or swap stuff that he hauled around in his beater pickup truck. As often as not, the deals fell through completely or segued into something else that would.

Our expensive tools would have been a sore temptation for Artie, and he'd probably convinced himself that he could lie his way out of it.

"If he's not in his cabin, try Elly May," Pam said. "They left the bar together."

I thanked her and started to leave.

But Madbird said, "Darcy around?"

"She's setting tables." Pam pointed at the swinging doors that led to the dining room.

Madbird walked to the doors and shoved them apart theatrically, like a gunfighter in an old Western going into a saloon. Darcy was standing over a table, taking silverware from a wheeled cart and laying it out. Her head was bowed, and even in that brief glimpse, I got the sense that she was moving very slowly.

"Hey, pretty girl," Madbird said. "How about I buy you a drink later?"

She kept right on with what she was doing, never so much as glancing at him.

He stood there another fifteen seconds. Then he stepped back and let the doors swing shut.

"Let's go take care of our bullshit," he said to me.

CHAPTER 25

WE STOPPED FIRST AT ARTIE'S cabin and looked in the uncurtained windows. The mess inside would have given the Callisters' pack rats a run for their money, but there didn't appear to be any humans embedded in it.

Then we walked a ways farther to the home of blowsy, unnaturally blond Elly May. I was reasonably sure it wasn't her real name, but I had no idea what that might be. She was sweet-natured and not overly bright, which made her popular, and she got a monthly allowance from her parents, which made her even more so. Her windows were covered so we couldn't see in, but they had to be here. If they'd been drinking hard and late, they wouldn't have gotten any farther.

Madbird raised his fist to pound on the door, then hesitated.

"I kinda hate to do it," he said.

I knew what he meant. These kind of transitory unions weren't uncommon out here, but Elly May was a plum, especially for Artie. Lucky days like this were a long time apart in his life.

"Well, the course of true love never runs smooth," I said. "Fate's bound to test it, and we're just the delivery boys."

Madbird nodded and let the door have it, a half-dozen blows that sounded like he was using a sledge. We waited. Nothing happened. He pounded again, and I stepped to a window and gave it a sharp tattoo with my knuckles.

"Drop your cock and grab your socks, Artie," Madbird yelled.

The curtain of my window twitched, and I thought I glimpsed an eyeball peering out before it fell back into place.

That left us without much in the way of options. Forcing our way in would have necessitated damage. They'd have to come out eventually, but as long as they had beer, that could be a while.

"How long you figure those two cases will last them?" I said.

"Long enough to fuck up our day. But that just gave me a idea, if we can get in there."

I studied the cabin's exterior for possible points to breach. After a minute, it struck me that the door opened outward, with the hinges exposed; the pins could be removed from the outside. Security hinges to prevent that were available, but around here, back when this place had been built, nobody would have dreamed of such a need.

"Be right back," I said, and went to my truck for a hammer and nail set. It took us about thirty seconds to knock out the hinge pins and set the door aside.

Elly May was sitting up in bed in the classic pose of a woman caught in flagrante delicto, with the sheets clutched to her ample bosom. But instead of seeming scared or outraged, she looked interested.

"Wow, I didn't know you could do that," she said.

Artie was backed up against the far wall, wearing a fluffy pink bathrobe too big for him; it must have been hers. He looked so doleful that my ire evaporated. Madbird kept a stern face, but I could see that he was working at it.

"I hate to tell you this, Artie, but that ain't exactly your color," he said.

"You got no right to come busting in here," Artie quavered.

"Where are they?"

Sudden innocence crossed Artie's face. "Where are what?"

Madbird shook his head in exasperation and walked through the cabin to the kitchenette at the back. He opened the refrigerator and pulled out four six-packs of Schmidt beer and a few singles. Then he popped a top and upended the can over the sink, emptying out a frothing amber stream.

Artie stared at him in shock, then rushed to the kitchenette doorway.

"What the fuck are you doing?" he yelled.

"Party's over," Madbird said. He tossed the can aside and opened another one.

Artie turned agitatedly to Elly May. "Make him stop."

"*You* make him stop."

"This is your place."

That impelled her to get out of bed, wrapping a sheet not very effectually around herself.

"At least leave us a couple to get started on," she said pleadingly.

Madbird shook his head. "Sorry. This is a take-no-prisoners mission."

I glanced outside and saw that Pam was walking across the parking lot toward us. There was something ethereal about the sight, like a '60s album cover with a pretty hippie chick drifting across a symbolically stark landscape.

When Pam arrived, she paused to gaze at the displaced door.

"Don't worry, we'll put it back," I said.

"What's going on?"

"Artie's playing hard to get. Would you try talking to him? We just want to know what he did with our tools."

She stepped inside and paused again, this time at the sight of Artie in his flamboyant pink bathrobe, the Junoesque, bed-sheet-draped figure of Elly May, and Madbird calmly emptying beer down the drain.

"Artie, why don't you just tell these guys," she said.

"I don't know what you're talking about, man. Make them leave our beer alone and get out of here."

Pam folded her arms and glared like a scolding mother.

"Honest to God, you are so hopeless. We know you blew a wad of cash at the bar last night. Do you think we're that dumb?"

I could just about see Artie calculating through his half-drunk, half-hungover state whether it was worth trying to keep up the bluff. Finally, he lowered his head in remorse.

"I only hocked them," he said. "You guys weren't around yesterday, I thought you'd be gone a while longer, and I got a deal set up to sell some car parts. Then I was going to buy them back."

Right.

"Where?" Madbird said again.

"Bill's Bail Bonds."

I turned away, shaking my head. Wouldn't you fucking know it.

We rehung the door on its hinges and headed for my truck. But when we got there, Madbird kept on walking toward the restaurant.

"Hang on a minute, huh?" he said. "I better find out what's going on with Darcy."

That didn't take long; it seemed like he'd hardly gone inside before he came back out again. His face had an expression I only saw occasionally. It told me he was unhappy, but satisfied that things had turned out as they should.

"Fraker pulled the pin on her," Madbird said. "Told her he couldn't afford to have crazy motherfuckers like me lurking around. That was the way he said it—'lurking.'"

"Well, that's got to be tough for her, but I know you're not sorry to hear it."

"Things only would of got worse. But it's all my fault, of course."

"I guess she has to blame somebody."

He nodded curtly. "Hannah will start working on her and smooth her out."

"You're probably going to need help moving that couch back out of her apartment."

I was glad to see him grin.

"I think the two of us can handle it this time," he said.

CHAPTER 26

BILL LATRAY, PROPRIETOR OF BILL'S Bail Bonds (*Got Jail Trouble? Help on the Double! Call 445-BILL*), also operated a pawnshop out of the same storefront—a convenient accomodation for clients who couldn't raise the cash for a bond, but could lay hands on something valuable. Bill would acquire items for a fraction of their worth—nominally, he took them in hock, but very few were ever reclaimed—and resell them at a tidy profit. He was known for never asking where the merchandise came from. By his lights, that wasn't his concern.

Guns, jewelry, guns, musical instruments, and guns were his top moneymakers. But power tools in good condition were also welcome, and ours were on display when Madbird and I arrived at his shop. They weren't supposed to be on sale for the duration of the pawn ticket, another twenty-nine days, but Bill was also known for being flexible about that sort of thing. At least we'd gotten there before somebody beat us to it.

Bill was tending the glassed-in counter, where he kept pistols, rings, and other expensive items that might be easily pocketed. A rack of rifles and shotguns lined the wall behind him. At the room's far end, there was a small office where he ran his bail business. The rest of the space was filled with tables of used merchandise. Everything reeked with the smoke of the rum-soaked Crook cigars he favored and his brand of cologne, which would have broken up a riot faster than tear gas.

"How's it going?" he said, lumbering over to give us hearty handshakes. He was mostly Indian, built like an oil barrel on a pair of tree trunks, with a scarred, pitted face and a stare that made you want to shrivel down into your socks. In his younger days, he'd been the kind of barfighter that the toughest guys would take care to avoid—even now when he walked into a place, things tended to get noticeably quieter—and he'd done a couple years in Deer Lodge for assault. He even made Madbird nervous.

But he'd become my new best friend several months ago, when I'd done a little business with him. Since then, the situation had been somewhat like with Gary Varna. Bill made a point of being genial because he expected that one of these days, I was going to be in the market for another, much more expensive, bail bond, and he had his eye on my property as collateral.

"You guys looking for firepower?" he said. "I just got in a real sweet Glock forty-caliber. Just one owner, he hardly used it, and he ain't gonna be needing it again."

"Actually, Bill, the reason we're here—it's a little delicate," I said, and pointed at the tools. "A guy named Artie, you probably know him—he sold you those yesterday?"

Bill hesitated a beat, no doubt already seeing where this was going.

"Yeah?"

"They weren't exactly his to sell."

"Now, ain't that a bitch." He took a pack of Crooks from his shirt pocket, shook one loose, lit it in his thick cupped hands with an inhalation like an elephant sucking water into its trunk, and blew out a cloud of smoke that visibly darkened the room.

"Well, if I'd known it was you guys, I'd of kicked his ass

and called you," he said. "But the way it is, I'm a businessman and I got an investment to protect. Plus handling, shelf space, all that."

"What'd you give for them?" Madbird said.

"Hunnert and forty," Bill said, with a touch of pride. I winced. Replacement value would be close to two grand, and he could sell them for at least half that.

"How about we cash you out and call it even?" Madbird said. "That way, you ain't lost anything."

"Yeah, but I ain't made anything, either."

"Come on, Bill, those tools are our living," I said. "We can't afford new ones, or even to buy them back from you."

He gazed thoughtfully out the window.

"What the fuck," he finally said. "Call it seventy, we'll split it. Just remember, Bill LaTray gave you a break."

We assured him we'd never forget, dug the seventy bucks out of our wallets, and schlepped the tools out to my truck. A chunk of cash and half a morning pissed away recovering our own property, but we felt like we'd won the lottery.

As Madbird and I drove away, I confessed my disloyal intentions.

"Let's get some lunch, but I might skip out on the job while Renee's here."

"You know, I wouldn't mind a couple days away from Split Rock myself," he said. "I ain't exactly Mr. Popularity out there right now."

CHAPTER 27

WE CELEBRATED THE RECOVERY OF our goods and the riddance of Seth Fraker by getting cheeseburgers to go at an ancient drive-in called Al's, one of the few non-chain places left in town and the venue of choice now that the legendary Gertie's was gone. These were the great old-fashioned kind of burgers that came wrapped in greasy white paper, big as a saucer and half an inch thick, with an aroma that filled the cab of my truck. High roller that I was, I bought an extra one to take to Renee.

When we got to her place, Madbird said, "I'll start picking up tools," and headed off to the carriage house to leave her and me alone. He was no stranger to the morning-after-the-night-before scenario.

She and I hadn't talked about what might happen next, and I was on edge about it. But as I climbed the porch steps, she came out to meet me like she had the first time, and she made the awkward moment easy—gave me a quick kiss and embrace, looking genuinely glad to see me. There was no hint of regret or blame.

When I offered her the cheeseburger, she pressed her hands to her heart and went wide-eyed.

"For me?"

"The sky's the limit, kid."

"It looks wonderful. I'll get plates."

I took hold of her wrist lightly. "We'll handle this however you want. I'd like to be with you, but if you're uncomfortable, I'm out of here."

"I don't know what I want," she said, turning her face aside. "But there's something I need to tell you."

That took a bite out of my brief gladness, but I tried to get her joking again.

"Another skeleton in a closet?"

She stayed serious. "Kind of. I don't want to just blurt it out."

"Sure. Let's go ahead and eat," I said, and went outside to get Madbird.

In fact, I suspected she intended to tell me that our little fling had already run its course. I wasn't naïve enough to think I'd been anything more than a temporary comfort for her, at a time when she was frightened and in need. I didn't expect anything different, just as I hadn't expected it to happen in the first place, and I sure had no complaints. I'd never spent a sweeter night.

The real problem was, it lit up a big neon arrow pointing at a void that had deepened in me over the past years. It didn't stem just from living alone, but from a composite of that and other absences that could start you wondering why you were living at all. Most of the time, I managed to ignore it.

I stepped into the carriage house and informed Madbird that luncheon was served. He glared at me with wounded dignity.

"You expect me to come inside and eat with you white people?" he said.

"Renee does."

"Well—since she don't know any better, plus she's pretty, I'll do it this once."

"We have an invention called ketchup, that goes pretty good with the onion rings," I said.

"*Wahss*. First you get us hooked on firewater, now this new shit. Any of them beers left?"

Wahss—I didn't know the right way to spell it, or even if it could be spelled—was something I heard him say often. As near as I could tell, it meant bullshit, fuck you, *c'est la vie*, uff da, *oy vey*, and other such sentiments all rolled into one, along with an edge of its own.

"Yeah, if I can keep you from pouring them down the sink," I said.

CHAPTER 28

AFTER LUNCH, MADBIRD AND I went back to the carriage house to finish collecting our tools. I still wasn't sure what Renee had in mind or how long that would take, and he needed to get going, so we decided he'd drive my truck to the job and swap it for his van. She could give me a ride out there to get it.

We gathered our gear quickly, with the unconscious precision of having done so countless times before. But this time I hit a minor snag. The five-sixteenths socket from my set, about the size of a cigarette filter, was missing. I was sure I'd left it on the workbench, and at first I thought it must have rolled off. It was bright chrome and should have been easy to spot, but I checked the area carefully with no luck.

"You didn't see a socket lying around, did you?" I said, in case Madbird had put it someplace else.

He shook his head. "You check your tool belt?"

It was true that we often pocketed things like that without realizing it. I dug through the belt's worn leather pouches and spread their contents on the workbench—a couple of pounds of nails and screws of a dozen different kinds, chalk box, utility knife, much-nicked chisel, twenty-five-foot tape, nail sets, lumber crayon, pencils, a handful of sawdust and plaster chunks, and a bottle cap from a Mickey's Big Mouth beer. I couldn't figure out how the hell that had gotten in there—I hadn't drunk Mickey's Big Mouths since high school.

But no socket. Not that this was a big deal; I had a couple of others somewhere, and I could buy a new one for a few bucks. There was just something peculiarly annoying about losing a tool. It would nag me for weeks, and I'd be looking for it subconsciously everywhere I went. I scanned the room in exasperation, trying to think of other spots where I might have stashed it.

Then I heard Madbird's deep rumbling laughter. My annoyance level rose. I didn't see how this was all that funny.

"What you want to bet that thing got drug off where the sun don't shine?" he said.

When his meaning hit me, I had to laugh, too.

Those motherfucking pack rats were still on the job.

CHAPTER 29

I'D DECIDED TO INSTALL DEADBOLTS on the doors of Renee's house, so I kept the tools I needed for that. We were loading the rest of the gear into my truck when she came hurrying out to us.

"Sheriff Varna just called," she said. "He's on his way over."

Madbird paused. He didn't cotton to authorities, especially of the law enforcement variety.

"I'd like you to be here for this," I said. "But if you want to book, I understand."

"Hell, I'll stick around. He ain't the *kind* of cop puts a hair acrost my ass."

Gary pulled over to the curb in his sheriff's cruiser a couple of minutes later. Watching him climb out was always a little disconcerting. He just kept on rising.

"Renee, I'm sorry we have to meet under these circumstances," he said, exending his cordial handshake to her.

"Thanks so much for doing this," she murmured.

"I wish I could promise it'll help. All right, let's see what you found."

"I've been keeping the things inside," she said, and went to get them. Madbird and I took Gary to the carriage house.

He crouched over the crawl space with his forearms on his knees, studying the jewelry box and pile of gunpowder. I gave him a rundown, ending with Renee's suggestion that the killer had planted this damning evidence against Professor Callister and set up a seemingly accidental fire to expose it, but never followed through because the police hadn't gotten close enough to him to be a threat.

Gary nodded noncommittally, letting me know he'd heard me, and that was all.

Renee came in with the photo fragments of Astrid and the earring, which she'd transferred to a metal cash box. Gary stood up creakily, with the failing knees of a man in his fifties, and opened the box on the Professor's workbench. He scrutinized the items with that same intensity, not touching, just looking.

"I can tell you right now these pix are high-quality—professional or good amateur," he said. "But that kind of print paper's common as dirt, besides trying to trace it back a dozen years."

"But you'll start looking for suspects who were into photography?" she said.

"That did cross my mind." His tone had a touch of irony, but also respect. She appeared to be making another conquest, and not an easy one.

"Did the police know about these things—that Astrid had them and they went missing?" Renee asked. "Did my father ever say anything about them?"

"Like I told Hugh, I wasn't in the loop much. I'll try to find out."

Then Madbird said, "I think maybe I'm seeing something here."

He was still standing beside the open crawl space. The rest of us walked over there to join him.

"If a fire starts, the firemen want to find a reason for it, right?" he said. "It looks like it just come out of nowhere, they're going to get suspicious. So this guy didn't want to just light a match."

I passed my hand over my hair, adding that to the long list of things that had never occurred to me.

"Go on," Gary said, with sharpened interest.

"Old place like this, the obvious thing's the wiring. But he's got to make it happen when he wants." Madbird swung around to me. "We got any Romex? Be easiest if I show you."

"Some scrap in the truck," I said. "How much you need?"

He held out his hands two feet apart. I went to my pickup to rummage in one of the side toolboxes that lined the bed, where I kept a mélange of handy odds and ends, fasteners, shims, hardware, and the like. I found a partial roll of sheathed 12/2 cable—commonly called Romex by tradesmen even though that, like Sheetrock, was technically a brand name—clipped off a couple of feet, and took it to Madbird.

First he used it as a pointer to tap a pair of old black knob-and-tube wires, about two inches apart and strung on porcelain insulators every few feet, that ran along the floor joist where the wood shavings were piled.

Knob and tube was considered dangerous stuff these days. Electricians were required by code to cut out and replace any of it they found. Besides being ungrounded, it aged badly, with the insulation cracking, fraying, and leaving bare spots that could create fire hazards.

Which was exactly what could have happened here. An insulator had broken; they were brittle, it could easily have been cracked during construction with no one noticing, and years of settling and vibration from people walking above eventually jarring a chunk loose. That had freed the top wire to sag so it almost touched the bottom one, and the sharp edges of the porcelain had nicked them so glints of bare copper showed through. Any contact between them would cause sparks. Those kinds of fires were common, sometimes smoldering for days or even weeks before they took off.

But this one only would have taken seconds, because the sparks would have hit the gunpowder.

"That takes care of the fire guys—they'll figure it was a accident," Madbird said. "But really, he's the one broke the insulator and nicked them wires. Now all he's got to do is make them touch."

With his pocketknife, he separated and stripped the Romex so he had a few inches of the bare copper ground at one end, and bent that at a right angle. Then he pushed it at the knob and tube strands again, using the prong to connect their frayed spots.

A sharp little *pop* brought a shower of sparks.

"Only take him a few seconds to crawl in and do that, and a few more to get back out," Madbird said. "By the time anybody spots the fire, he's long gone. Had it all set up ahead of time so it was ready to go if he got spooked."

Gary looked bemused. "Well, I ain't necessarily saying I buy it. But on the other hand, I'm tempted to offer you a job, Madbird."

"Appreciate it, Sheriff. But I already done three years in uniform, and I got a feeling a new one would fit pretty tight."

"Yeah, I admit I get that feeling myself sometimes."

"I better tape them wires up. Okay with you?"

"Give me a minute to get some photos first," Gary said. "I want to take the things you found, too, including that jewelry box. I've got an evidence camera and containers in my car—I could use a hand with them."

As we started out to get them, he paused to look at Renee.

"My dear, I hope like hell there's something to this. I'd love to see your father cleared, and if I can nail whoever's guilty, I'll die a happier man." But while Gary's words were kindly, his face was concerned. "Let's just keep in mind that if we are looking at somebody else, he's not just dangerous. He's really slick."

CHAPTER 30

BEFORE GARY LEFT, HE STEPPED firmly into sheriff mode and let us know what he expected of us, starting with Renee.

"Did you spend much time with Astrid and your father?" he asked her.

It took her a beat or two longer to answer than I would have thought.

"Not a whole lot, but some," she said. "It took a while for things to simmer down after he divorced my mom. There was a lot of anger. But then I started visiting here sometimes on holidays."

"Did you and Astrid get along?"

There came another measured pause.

"Yes. I mean, she wasn't really a *warm* person, and I was programmed to hate her at first. But she was nice to me, and fascinating because she seemed so glamorous. Expecially because I was such a mouse."

"Okay, here's what I'm getting at—and understand, this is still just speculation, all riding on that big 'if,'" Gary said. "First off, let's throw out any notion that her murder was random, or a crime of opportunity. He planned it carefully, and that tells me he had a strong reason. Finding that reason just might find him.

"So, Renee, I want you to remember everything you can about Astrid. Who she spent time with, quarrels or rough spots or if she seemed to be hiding something—every little detail you think of, even if it don't seem important. And, sorry to say this, but be careful to keep your father in mind. You might unconsciously tend toward leaving him out."

She looked uncomfortable and I understood why. The task would be emotionally bruising.

But she nodded and said, "I'll start making notes about it. And some things Hugh and I talked about last night, if you want."

"I'm glad for anything you can come up with. Now I need a word with you two gents."

He walked Madbird and me over to his car, hooked his thumbs in his belt, and eyed us with an authoritative stare.

"Being as how you're in on this, whether anybody likes it or not," he said, with the none-too-vague suggestion that he himself didn't, "you might do some quiet nosing around. If you run into anything, you will *not* act on it yourselves. You'll call me immediately, twenty-four seven."

He scribbled briefly on a notepad, then tore the sheet in halves and handed one to each of us—his office, cell, and home phone numbers.

"I'm not crazy about amateur help, but a lot of people will open up more to somebody who's not a cop," he said. "And you guys have impressed me with your talent for—let's call it 'disinformation.'"

That gave my pulse rate a boost. It wasn't anything that all three of us weren't well aware of, but I didn't like hearing him say it out loud.

But Madbird, unshaken, grinned. "'Disinformation.' I ain't heard that word since Nam."

Gary's face also creased in a smile, wolfish in its own way.

"It means pretty much the same thing now as it did then," he said.

After Gary left and Madbird took my truck with our tools to Split Rock, I went to the house to find Renee. She met me at the door as usual, but this time with a brittle politeness that radiated pique.

"So I'm open to the public, but you guys cozy up in private?" she said.

That had been Gary's decision, not mine, but I was still chagrined for not realizing that she was upset.

"We weren't talking behind your back, Renee. It didn't really have anything to do with you."

"This *all* has something to do with me. Why couldn't I hear it?"

That wasn't an easy question to field. Now wasn't the right moment to tell her about my criminal career, and I couldn't think of any partial explanations that didn't make me sound even worse than I'd been.

"Gary was reminding us that we owe him," I finally said. "And he can call in the marker anytime."

"Owe him for what?" she said, still skeptical, but with the edge fading.

I stepped closer to her, just enough so our forearms brushed.

"Maybe we could trade secrets later," I said. "When you're ready to tell me that one of yours."

She leaned against me lightly and spoke into my shoulder. "I'm getting there. It's a raw nerve, and Gary jammed his finger right on it, asking me to think about Astrid. Kind of spooky."

"Well, that's the issue right now. And let's face it, it's your issue."

"I know. Sorry I snapped at you. I started feeling outnumbered by you guys."

"I make a pretty good punching bag," I said. "I've got a lot of experience."

"Can I ask you to take me for another drive?" Her face was still pressed against me, her voice muffled.

I decided the deadbolts could wait. She was only going to be here one more night. If she had something on her mind, that came first.

"Sure, if we can use your car," I said. "Where to?"

"You live out in the country, right?"

"Yeah?"

"Is there a place we could shoot your pistol?"

Jesus, Mary, and Joseph.

CHAPTER 31

RENEE'S CAR, A TIGHT, TOUGH little Subaru Outback, easily handled the mud and ruts of the road up Stumpleg Gulch. When we got to my cabin, I made a quick check around the premises. Everything seemed fine in my little world, including the black tomcat, aside from him being pissed about my absence and loudly letting me know it.

Then I led Renee through the woods to the back part of the property. Like at Astrid's cabin last night, she wasn't dressed for the outdoors—she was wearing the same street boots and shearling coat—so I took an indirect route to pick the driest and easiest going.

But she didn't seem concerned about that or even to notice her surroundings, except to glance occasionally at the .45, which I was carrying in its gun belt, slung over my shoulder. She'd been quiet, her focus inward, all during the drive here, and had said just enough for me to glean that whatever unsettling revelation she was about to make was connected to Astrid and to firing a weapon.

Her capacity for keeping me off balance hadn't diminished, that was for sure.

As we walked, I kept an eye out for signs of my new neighbor bobcat. I didn't see any, but I was far from expert at that sort of thing and fresh tracks would be hard to pick up, anyway. The snow was still ankle-deep in spots but there hadn't been any recent fall, and while the surface melted slightly during the warming days, it froze to a crust again at night, with the underneath staying grainy. The result was that feet, paws, and hooves left clumsy outlines to begin with, which quickly blurred into vague depressions.

If he was around, he wouldn't be for long—as soon as Renee started blowing a window through this peaceful afternoon and into her past.

The landscape opened up when we came to the steep mountainside that formed my northeast border. It was a perfect backdrop for shooting; my father had set up a range with target stands and distances marked up to two hundred yards, which we'd used both for recreation and to sight in our rifles for hunting.

I set up one of the paper targets I'd brought along, a standard two-foot square with concentric rings. I decided to start Renee close in. The .45 could be reasonably accurate in skilled hands, but it was designed to knock a man down if the slug even touched him rather than for precision. I walked to the ten-yard marker, hung the gunbelt on a pine stob, and while I always kept the chamber clear until I was ready to fire, I did a routine check to make certain.

"Ever shoot a pistol before?" I asked her.

"Some, growing up. Daddy had a twenty-two he used for teaching my brother and me."

"I assume he talked about safety?"

"Over and over again. Assume it's always loaded. Never let the barrel point at anyone. Make sure everybody's behind you before you shoot."

"That's a good start. Did he show you a stance?"

She moved slowly, remembering body commands that had long since gone rusty, but she stepped into a correct firing range position—imaginary pistol in both hands, arms extended straight in front of her, feet shoulder-width apart.

"Good again," I said. "Next, this thing's a long way from a twenty-two."

"I shot a bigger one once—nine-millimeter, I remember."

"A forty-five's still got a lot more whack. Somebody as light as you, it's going to jolt you pretty hard, and the grip's made for bigger hands so it'll try to jump out of yours. Hang on tight, squeeze the trigger gently, and don't shoot again until you're fully under control. Oh, yeah, it's also loud."

I'd brought a packet of foam earplugs along with the targets and extra rounds. I dug it out of my shirt pocket and gave a pair to her. She brushed her hair behind her right ear and started to insert one. But she hesitated, then stopped.

"I don't want to dull this," she said.

That brought me out of my officious-instructor mode and back around to the weirdness of why we were here in the first place. I shoved the earplugs in my pocket. We wouldn't be shooting enough to risk long-term hearing damage—it would just be less comfortable.

"Okay," I said. "Step up to the plate."

She positioned herself facing the target. I placed the pistol in her hands, steadying them with my own, with the barrel pointed down and to the front. I jacked a round into the chamber and touched her thumb to the safety.

"As soon as you click this off, you're hot," I said. "You've got seven shots."

I let her go and stepped back. She raised the weapon and aimed for several seconds. I could see her hands wavering with its weight.

A *boom* ripped across the still afternoon and through my eardrums. Renee stumbled backwards into my hands, which were waiting to catch her waist. The barrel flew up to point skyward, but she held on and kept it in front of her.

"That's fine," I said. "Go ahead, you'll get used to it."

She fired the next six shots carefully, with increasing control. When she finished, she looked attractively disheveled—bright-eyed, flushed, breathing slightly fast. I took the pistol from her, cleared it, hung it in its holster, and went to check the target. She'd hit it five times out of seven, with two of the shots inside the dinner-plate-sized circle and another only a few inches away—pretty damned impressive for a novice who didn't weigh much over a hundred pounds.

I set up a fresh target and took the used one to show her.

"Annie Oakley would be jealous," I said.

Renee didn't speak. Her eyes still had that bright, almost glazed look.

"You want to go again?" I said.

She nodded.

I reloaded the pistol, wondering if it was time to try a couple of prompting questions that might start her talking.

As it turned out, I didn't need to.

"Stand behind me," she said. I hadn't expected the sound of her voice, and it startled me a little. It was subdued and shaky.

I stepped to where I'd been when I'd caught her waist.

"Closer. Right up against me."

Carefully, I pressed my chest against her back and put my hands on her waist again. I could feel her warmth through our coats, and the quick rise and fall of her breathing—even imagined that I sensed the tremor of her heartbeats.

She raised her hands and took aim at the target.

"That nine-millimeter pistol was Astrid's," Renee said. "She stood just like you are and touched my breasts while I shot it."

CHAPTER 32

WE SPENT THE REST OF the afternoon in bed in my cabin. Renee fell asleep before long, with the tomcat curled at her feet. He'd wasted no time in claiming her, and he was giving me looks that plainly urged me to get lost.

She had to be exhausted; she'd never gotten a chance to rest up from the stress and strain of the past days. The silence and the gray light through the windows were soothing, and maybe there'd been a catharsis in the secret she'd finally let out.

I was short on sleep myself, but too wired to drift off. I was entirely content to lie there, however, and I had a new blitz of information to process. In a way it was the most bizarre yet, but somehow it didn't even surprise me—maybe because it dovetailed into what I knew about Astrid. Just as she was a threat to Renee, the reverse was also true, so she had used seduction to establish control, the same as she would have with a man.

Or maybe it didn't surprise me because I was getting harder to surpise.

As Renee described it, the incident had happened during the summer when she was seventeen and visiting her father and Astrid in Helena. At first, the wicked-stepmother syndrome prevailed, but Astrid was shrewd about breaking through that; she treated Renee nonjudgmentally and like an adult, and was candid and amusing about herself. She was alluring, mysterious, exciting—irresistible.

Toward the end of the visit, on a day when Professor Callister was gone, Astrid confided that she loved to shoot. She showed Renee the nine-millimeter pistol and invited her to try it. Just the fact that she owned a gun was a little shocking, and for two women to go out shooting seemed almost improper. Their mood was conspiratorial, girlishly mischievous.

Astrid drove them to a wilderness area a few miles away. They hiked into the woods until they found a suitable clearing, away from any trails.

Then Astrid pressed up against her back. And cupped her breasts. The July afternoon was warm and sultry, Renee remembered. Feeling the voluptuous older woman touch her like that had made her almost dizzy.

She'd kept shooting until the clip was empty, then sagged back into Astrid's embrace. After a moment, Astrid released her. They went home as if nothing had happened and neither of them ever mentioned it again.

"I'm not hung up about the sex part. You know, because I was turned on by a woman," Renee had told me, talking quietly with her cheek on my chest. "I didn't want to be, I didn't not want to be. I just went completely docile—it was like she *owned* me. That's the problem."

"How so?"

"Because I loved it. It was so intense, so powerful."

"It's kind of supposed to be like that. Especially at that age."

She rose up on an elbow to gaze at me intently. "That's not what I mean. Ever since then, I've been craving somebody who overwhelms me like that—not a good, healthy kind of love where you give and take. I'm an emotional cripple. If somebody loved me, I don't know if I could really love him back."

That wasn't an easy thing to hear.

"What about your fiancé?" I said. "Does he know?"

"Not about what happened with Astrid. I've told him the other part—that I don't know if I'll ever feel what I should for him."

"He's okay with that?"

"He thinks I'll get over it. He's so *normal*, and he assumes that will rub off on me. I guess it has—I've been with him almost two years."

"I don't think there's any such thing as 'normal,'" I said. "Not on that turf, anyway."

"Okay, I'll settle for 'less screwed up.'" She made it clear then that she didn't want to talk about it anymore. After giving me a sweet, lingering kiss that suggested regret, apology, and maybe good-bye, she turned away and drifted into sleep.

As for me, I was left in a bittersweet confusion that was deeper than ever. No way was I the kind of man who might arouse that blind, consuming passion in her. And, taken though I was with her, I wouldn't have wanted that.

Yet again, there was a whisper in my head that said maybe, just maybe, I was seeing this wrong—that Renee knew she could never change in the way her fiancé expected her to.

So she was testing me to find out if I would accept her as she was.

CHAPTER 33

WE LEFT MY CABIN AROUND sundown and went to town to stay the night at Renee's. She was going to drive back to Seattle tomorrow, and she needed to pack and get an early start. She'd be returning in a few weeks; she still had business to settle in Helena.

But the question of whether we'd even see each other again remained in a silent limbo.

Her house was dark when we arrived there; neither of us had thought to leave on a light, not realizing we'd be gone so long. With no streetlamps nearby, the yard and surroundings were immersed in gloom, and the silhouette of the old mansion added a Gothic edge. I still felt a touch melodramatic climbing the porch steps with the .45 in my hand, but I was glad to have it. Finding the dead pack rat last night made the possibility of an intruder seem all too real.

I took the key from Renee, opened the door, flicked on the light switch inside, and stood there a few seconds, letting my eyes adjust. I started to step in, intending to take a walk around like we'd done last night.

Just as my foot crossed the threshold, I heard a sound come from the hallway ahead that divided bathroom, kitchen, and back bedrooms—a stealthy rustling, like a small animal might make. *Those rats* was the first thought that flashed across my mind—the little bastards had gotten in here, too.

Then came a distinct metallic click.

Along with it, the large figure of a man appeared in the hallway entrance, lunging into view from where he'd been hiding behind the wall. All I could grasp in that split-second take was that he was wearing a ski mask and combat fatigues, and that his hands were swinging up to point at me.

I threw myself back against Renee, knocking her out of the way as hard as I could, and tried to shout at her to get the hell out of there. The sound I made came out something like, "Gaaahhh!"

Gunshots exploded from inside the house and splinters from the doorjamb sprayed against my face.

I managed to chamber a round in the .45 and take rough aim at his shape, but I was still off balance and my vision was blurred. As I started pulling the trigger, he dropped into a crouch.

His next shot hit me like a sledgehammer to the right side of my ribs, spinning me around. I tripped over my own clumsy feet, crashed against the porch railing and down to the floor. For a couple of seconds I was too stunned to move. Then I rolled to face the door, forcing my body into position to again take shaky aim.

But the man inside the house had vanished.

I got hold of the porch railing, pulled myself up to my knees, and tried to stand. But Renee was beside me with a hand on my shoulder, firmly holding me in place.

"You just settle down," she said.

"Get out of here, he might still be inside."

"He ran out the back. I saw him."

I stopped struggling against her hand. "You sure?"

"Positive," she said. "And I called the police."

I coughed, or maybe wheezed. "He was running, huh?"

"Shhh."

"Not limping or anything?"

"No. Now shut up, dammit."

She helped ease me down onto my left side, as the first distant cries of sirens came to my ears.

PART IV

CHAPTER 34

JUST ABOUT TWENTY YEARS HAD passed since the last time I'd opened my eyes in St. Peter's Hospital. While I didn't have any clear memories of that experience, there was still a familiarity this time around—antiseptic smells, equipment hovering over my bed, tubes sticking out of me, and the feeling that my head was duct-taped onto my body.

Then I became aware of a Cheshire cat–like grin, floating in the vague distance across the room. It took me a few seconds to focus on the rest of Madbird around it, leaning against the wall with his arms folded.

"How's it going there, Hawkeye?" he said.

"You're just a bad dream," I muttered, and closed my eyes again.

"Must be the dope they been giving you."

"Have I been here long?"

"Overnight. It's Wednesday morning, about seven-thirty."

Several more seconds passed in silence.

"How many times did I fire?" I asked, with my eyes still closed.

"Four."

"Nothing?"

"I guess you took out a bathroom window and beat up on some plaster. But hey, it ain't all bad—if you'd hurt him, you probably would of got sued or thrown in jail."

"That was my plan all along. Just scare him off."

"Hell, yeah. Thinking on your feet like that, that's where you white guys got it over us. We'd shoot him, and then we'd be fucked."

But Madbird had far more important news than my marksmanship score. He had talked with Gary Varna.

Renee not only called the police while the shooting was going on, she'd stayed on the line and told them that the attacker had run into the woods behind the house. They'd arrived in time to cut off his escape, and found him hiding.

He turned out to be Travis Paulson. And it turned out that Paulson—who had never married, and lived alone—had a longtime hobby, which he'd kept carefully under wraps.

A search of his house revealed a sophisticated photography studio, along with an extensive photo stash of more than twenty women, ranging in age from late teens to forties, all posing nude.

The collection included a duplicate set of the prints of Astrid that we had found in the carriage house. Without doubt, Paulson was the photographer who had originally taken them.

Which went a long way toward explaining his fascination with Astrid's earring. The only other time he had seen it was sexually charged.

In the photos of Astrid, she obviously knew what she was doing and even appeared to be enjoying herself. That also seemed to be the case with most of the other women. But a few told a different story. In these, the models were obviously unconscious—and he was having sex with them.

He was insisting to the police that these encounters were also consensual—that the women had knowingly allowed him to give them a date-rape drug. But the cops knew that was bullshit, and it gave them a lot of leverage.

That was all the information that Madbird had at this point. But it carried a terrible, wonderful implication.

Although Paulson claimed to know nothing about the cache in Professor Callister's study—he insisted that he had given that set of photos to Astrid and never seen them again— the evidence now pointed at him as the one who had planted it there. He admitted that he himself was the photographer; he'd been friendly with Professor Callister and familiar with the layout of the carriage house.

From there, things fell into place. He'd known that Madbird and I had started tearing into the study, and when he saw Renee wearing the earring at the funeral, it was clear that the cache had been discovered. He'd tried to get Renee alone at dinner to find out how serious a threat this was. When she refused, he'd decided he couldn't risk letting it go any further, and he'd lain in wait to stop her.

Travis Paulson had stepped into the limelight as the murderer of Astrid and her lover.

CHAPTER 35

I DRIFTED IN AND OUT of sleep after that, occasionally aware of the monitors I was attached to and hospital personnel stopping in to check on me. The wound was a dull throb in my side; it didn't feel much different from broken ribs, although that was probably thanks to painkillers. I got a look at the front of it when a nurse changed the dressing—a ragged little hole where the bullet had entered, surrounded by a blackish purple bruise. The exit wound was worse, but I couldn't see that. Still, it wasn't too serious, she informed me; assuming I was able to get up and take care of myself, I might go home as early as tomorrow.

I drifted in and out of lucidity, too; it came in brief spells before the haze would creep back and put me under again. I recalled getting shot with detached vividness, as if I was watching a movie. I even did some thinking about the events leading up to it, and about where this was headed. And a part of my mind that acted on its own tried to make sense of it all, although I couldn't keep track of that very well.

Long ago, I'd started believing that everybody had a sort of cosmic bank balance where commodities like luck were stored up, and I had no doubt that I'd just made a heavy withdrawal from mine. Paulson's aim had been almost as bad as my own, and he'd used a .40-caliber pistol, popular with cops, which fired a fast powerful round. He'd clipped the lower right side of my chest, splintering ribs both on entry and exit. But the jacketed bullet had passed under my lung, barely grazing it, and had punched straight through instead of blowing out a big chunk like a .357 or my own .45 would have, or glancing off bone and turning inward as lighter ammunition sometimes did.

Then there was the real luck. A killer who'd gone free for twelve years—who had certainly committed rape in the interim, and maybe worse—was finally on his way to prison for good. Like a hidden viper, he'd been the more dangerous because nobody had known about him. That threat was ended, and so was Renee's personal nightmare.

As for me, I was going to have some time on my hands, and I wouldn't be able to fill it with the usual upkeep around my place. It would be a couple of weeks before I could take on physical work, and then only light tasks. I'd have other things to keep me busy, like dealing with the police about the assault and filling in the rest of the Paulson story.

But I was still going to be up against something I dreaded—a deep-seated reason why my life had ended up the way it had. I'd never been able to explain or quantify this, which was part of the problem. It was an inner absence, which brought a feeling along the lines of waiting endlessly at a bus stop, in a strange and bleak industrial city, on a cold night; a flaw in your being that darkened everything you saw, saddened everything you felt, slowly crushed the life out of an inmost part of you. It wasn't depression, it was the root of depression. For years, the single thing that I had craved most was oblivion, the complete annihilation of consciousness. But I believed that was something you had to earn, and I didn't know how to— only that I hadn't.

I'd tried to resolve the issue in various ways and failed.

With that frustration piled on top of the rest, I'd ended up running. That was a major reason for the job I'd settled into; it allowed me to keep moving hard through the days and wear myself out. Then when I got home at night, fatigue and, too often, alcohol reduced my worries to nothing weightier than getting my boots off and filling my belly. There was nothing commendable about that, but it worked.

Renee's fear of being an emotional cripple wasn't a one-way street. Even if she did offer her light to me, I wasn't sure I could ever be fair to her, either.

CHAPTER 36

I WOKE UP AGAIN AND spent the usual groggy moment figuring out where I was. The outdoor light filtering through the window blinds seemed stronger than last time I'd looked, but if there was a clock in the room, I hadn't yet located it. My sense of time was too out of whack for that to matter, anyway.

My throat was dry and scratchy, as it seemed to be every time I came to. Maybe it was the hospital air, maybe medications. I'd learned by now to maneuver water from the bedside stand without disturbing either the tubage that pierced me or my own torn flesh. I drank greedily; it was cool, soothing, and it freshened me like it was the first thing I'd really felt since I'd been here. I was stronger, even hungry. I decided that when a nurse stopped by again, I'd get myself disconnected and try to make it to the bathroom without weaving like a drunk while somebody held on to my arm. Then I'd see about scoring some breakfast, or lunch, or whatever they'd let me have.

But the next person who pushed open my room door wasn't a nurse. It was Renee.

She peered in cautiously. "I came by earlier and you were asleep," she said in a half-whisper. "I don't want to disturb you."

"It's fine."

"I'm so glad you're going to be all right." She came to the bedside and kissed me, a brief but intense touching of lips. Then she stepped back, looking anxious.

"Ian flew in this morning," she said. "He's here with me. He'd like to meet you."

"Ian?"

"My fiancé."

"Oh, right. Sorry, I'm sort of goofed out on the meds." I shrugged, attempting nonchalance, but it brought a stitch of pain in my side that made my mouth twist. "Sure, bring him in."

She leaned over me again and spoke close to my ear, this time in a real whisper.

"I haven't told him anything about us."

I nodded thankfully. At least his jealous anger wouldn't be in the equation.

I knew that Ian must be a decent guy, and I admired people who did the work of healing; that was a hell of a lot more demanding than anything I'd ever taken on. But from what Renee had mentioned, he was also sure of himself, maybe to the point of arrogance. I wasn't interested in dealing with that, particularly now.

But the man who stepped into the room was anything but cool. He had a rawboned build and a kindly face that was on the homely side, with jug ears and a big nose. He did give off quiet self-assurance, but it was the sort that stemmed from competence.

"This will sound dumb, but I don't know how to thank you," he said.

I started to shrug again, but caught myself. When it came to pain, I was a relatively fast learner.

"Renee's the one who took the chance—dangled herself on a hook till the sucker hit," I said. "All I did was get in the way."

She put her hands on her hips and gave me her teacher-to-bad-schoolboy look.

"There's a little more to it than that," she said.

"Yeah, I shot up your house, too." I took another sip of water. "Heard any more about where things stand?"

"I talked to Gary Varna this morning," Renee said. "Paulson still swears he didn't commit the murders."

"Big surprise. So how else does he explain waiting for you with a gun?"

Renee lowered her gaze. "He had something else in mind. It almost would have been worse." She turned away uncomfortably.

"He was going to force her to drink rohypnol," Ian said, putting his arm around her. "He had handcuffs, tape—and a camera."

At first I was stunned. Then a wave of rage swept over me, bristling my hair and heating my face. If I could have gotten hold of Travis Paulson just then, I'd have crushed his throat and savored watching his eyes dim out.

I realized that I'd risen up off my pillows. I settled back and took my best shot at smiling.

"Hey, Renee," I said. "It's over, and you cleared your father."

She smiled back, and Ian gave me a grateful look.

Before they left, they made it clear that they'd be glad to do anything they could for me. Ian had already talked to hospital personnel about my treatment; in his judgment, I was in good hands. He also insisted on paying any medical expenses that weren't otherwise covered. I had no intentions of taking him up on it, but it was damned generous.

The bottom line was, I was sorry I'd met him. The situation was complicated enough anyway, and now I was stuck with liking him.

CHAPTER 37

WHEN THE HOSPITAL SPRANG ME next day—technically against medical advice, but they agreed as long as I promised to come back immediately if I had trouble—Madbird drove me home in my pickup truck, with Hannah following. He'd invited me to stay with them until I was feeling spryer, but I told him I'd more likely want company after I'd spent a few days alone at my place. He knew what I meant.

They loaded me up with groceries and a couple of bottles of whiskey, and since my .45 was still being held as evidence, he loaned me his .41-Magnum Smith & Wesson, in case the bobcat showed up. The Smith was also a big pistol, with a six-inch barrel, and at least as loud as the Colt. I hoped I was right that the noise would scare the cat off. It sure didn't need to be worried about my aim.

Hannah stowed the groceries while Madbird built a fire in the woodstove. Then they took off, and I was on my own. For the moment, it felt good. I'd been comfortable at St. Pete's and the staff were great, but there was still that unavoidable sense of being in a hamster cage, helpless and pressing buttons for food.

I hadn't had another chance to talk with Renee in private, and I didn't figure I would before she and Ian left for Seattle.

I'd watched her face as she left the hospital room, hoping for some hint of affirmation, but it hadn't come. If anything, she'd seemed to avoid my gaze. But she had to be incredibly shaken and confused right now. All I could do was stay out of the way and let her decompress.

It was getting toward lunchtime, and my appetite was coming back. Hannah, angel that she was, had cooked me a beef pot roast and at least a gallon of mashed potatoes. I chunked some of both into an iron frying pan and set it on the stovetop to warm, moving slowly, letting my body teach me what hurt and what didn't.

While the food heated up, I thought about the conversation I'd had with Gary Varna yesterday. He'd come to visit me after Renee and Ian left, wanting to take a statement if I felt up to it.

I'd known that was going to happen, and I'd tried to prepare myself. The problem was that I didn't want to give up Renee's secrets—her mini-affair with me, and her sexual encounter with Astrid. Those issues weren't in play yet; right now, Gary's focus was on the assault. But as the case expanded to include Astrid's murder, so would the range of questioning. I had to assume that eventually, Renee and I would be asked to account for every minute of the past few days.

The last time I'd been under Gary Varna's scrutiny, I'd had to lie about a lot of things. But I didn't want to lie to him anymore. I hated doing it at all; I wasn't any good at it, even when I wasn't in a drug fog like now; it was dangerous and nerveracking, particularly with him; and above all, it was a dogshit way to treat this man who had done a hell of a lot for me.

I'd ended up deciding to compromise—to be straight about everything except Renee's sexual encounter with Astrid. That was up to her.

"Gary, before we start—I can't see that this even figures in, but you should know it," I'd said.

One of his eyebrows rose a few millimeters. "Go ahead, the tape recorder ain't on yet."

"Remember when I told you Renee found that dead rat in her dresser? Afterwards, she was . . . in a mood to be consoled."

"'Consoled.'" His mouth twitched in one of his crocodilian smiles. "Not bad, Hugh. I can't exactly say you're a gentleman, but you do take a stab at it now and then."

"The situation's kind of awkward. What with her being engaged."

Gary gazed past me for a moment, drumming his long fingers on the arm of his chair.

"Well, I appreciate your telling me," he said. "Personally, I agree with you, I don't see why it should matter. But you better realize, Paulson's defense will probably jump on it like a pogo stick."

"I know. I was just hoping it wouldn't come up for a while. Give her a chance to work things out with her guy."

"All right, I hear you. You ready now?"

When the formalities were over, Gary told me more about the situation with Travis Paulson. He hadn't put up much resistance to police questioning; if anything, there'd been a sense of sneaky bragging as he described his accomplishments.

When he wanted to photograph a woman, he'd start by flattering her, then maneuver her into cozy situations and work up to his proposition with a variety of pitches—what a shame if her beauty was never recorded before it faded; everyone had a right to a private side of their life; acting out a harmless fantasy was exciting and healthy; and so on. He'd assure her that his interest was purely aesthetic, that he'd give her all the prints and negatives, that it would remain forever secret. Most of the ladies refused at first, but a significant number soon let him know they'd like to discuss the matter further.

Paulson admitted that he'd traded on his acquaintance

with Professor Callister to get chummy with Astrid, and he eventually made his pitch to photograph her. In keeping with her brashness, she agreed readily. She wore the cowgirl outfit, including the garish earrings, because he encouraged all the women to indulge their fantasies with props or costumes.

He was fascinated with Astrid anyway, powerful and striking as she was. Then when he saw Renee wearing one of the earrings around her neck, he came unglued. He claimed that he had no idea how she'd gotten it, or how it figured into the murder; he only connected it with the thrilling couple of hours he'd spent photographing Astrid's nude beauty, and the many more hours he'd spent poring over the photos since then. Those factors had melded together into a driving compulsion to repeat the experience with Renee and take it to the next step.

By now, Paulson had also admitted to the police that the sex he'd had with unconscious women was not consensual. During the photo session, he would tell them they were tense, which impaired their natural loveliness, and he'd insist that they drink a glass of wine to relax. Of course, they didn't realize that it was laced with rohypnol. He wouldn't have dared to try this with Astrid or most of the others; he carefully chose victims who were naïve or passive. If they suspected afterward that something amiss had happened, he could convince them they were wrong, or coax and bully them into not making a fuss.

When Renee wouldn't give him a chance even to begin his approach, anger and frustration entered the mix in his mind. That was when he crossed a line. He believed that she was alone and vulnerable, and he'd gotten away with enough rapes to convince himself that he could again. He swore that he'd never used violence before and hadn't intended to this time; he'd brought the pistol only to frighten her into submission and get her to drink the rohypnol. He'd broken into her house through a back window and watched until he'd seen her car approaching, then hurried to hide; but with his haste and in the darkness, he hadn't seen me. When I stepped inside instead of her, he'd started to run out the back door, but panicked when he saw that I was armed.

That was the story that Travis Paulson had told so far. The police were searching for evidence to link him to Astrid's murder, including fingerprints from the cache we'd found in the carriage house. No motive had yet come clear, but the loss of control that Renee had caused him was telling. Speculation was that his fascination with Astrid, rage at his failure to possess her sexually, and jealousy of her lover had boiled over.

My nose told my belly that the meal I had warming on the stove was ready. I started to wash the dishes after I ate, but the cabin was filled with a pleasant warmth from the fire that Madbird had built, I was weak enough so that just getting from the hospital to here had worn me out, and I started feeling my ribs in a way I couldn't ignore. I washed down a Percocet with a shot of whiskey, and slipped into a delicious sleep.

Three hours later, I woke up feeling like shit.

I prodded myself into taking a slow walk around my property, and I was drawn to the firing range to relive yesterday's interlude with Renee. That was bittersweet at best—electric, disturbing, and now infused with the ache of loss.

But the chilly air and exercise helped my mind and body both, and I drifted through the evening dabbling with computer, books, and thoughts. When I crashed, I was tired again, relaxed, and ready for a real sleep.

Maybe I'd rested too much already. Again and again that night, I woke up in a sweat from wrestling with my dreams, if that was what they were.

CHAPTER 38

THE NEWS OVER THE NEXT couple of days wasn't so good.

No fingerprints from Travis Paulson or anyone else had been found on the items from the cache. Everything had been wiped carefully clean. More sophisticated tests were possible, but state and federal crime labs had years-long backlogs, and weren't likely to invest their time and resources without very compelling reasons.

Moreover, Paulson had successfully passed a lie detector test, and he'd been able to establish an alibi that seemed relatively solid. On the night when Astrid and her lover were murdered, he had been staying in the resort area of Big Sky, working on a consulting job. He had located two coworkers who confirmed that they'd had dinner with him in a restaurant that evening, then drank in a bar until about eleven. They remembered clearly because they had seen Paulson the next day after the news broke; he'd told them he knew Astrid, and seemed visibly shaken.

Big Sky was just north of Yellowstone Park, about two hundred miles from the crime scene. The drive was mostly over winding two-lane roads and took close to three hours even under optimal conditions, let alone on a wintry March night. And according to the coroner's estimate, the deaths had occurred before midnight.

There was still room for doubt. Lie detector tests were inconclusive almost by definition. With some lucky driving, Paulson could have made the round trip during that night, and the estimated time of death could have been significantly wrong. The bodies hadn't been discovered until the following afternoon, and as Gary pointed out, the forensics of the case had been handled abysmally.

But those things were all but impossible to establish. For the most part, the bungled investigation was a defense attorney's wet dream. Evidence had been lost or contaminated; what survived wasn't of much use; there was nothing that might have provided a DNA match with Paulson; records from the Phosphor County Sheriff's Department were sloppy, inconsistent, and failed to cover a lot of important ground; and so on.

A smoking gun might still turn up. The police were quietly but intensely working on the case, searching Paulson's property, reconstructing his movements around the time of the murders, interviewing his rape victims—digging for anything that might give them a pressure point.

But so far, the only fact that stood beyond doubt was his vileness.

Failing a breakthrough, prosecutors wouldn't be able to convict him of the murders and wouldn't try; they'd drop the matter and settle for the rape and assault charges. It was some consolation that those would send him to prison for years.

But that would still be a major letdown for Renee, and would leave the uneasy possibility that the real killer was still out there.

With that handwriting on the wall, Gary had started looking into other leads, but nothing promising had turned up there, either. The rifleman who had run us off Astrid's property, one Eustace O'Reilly, was indeed the xenophobic asshole that Hannah had described—a neo-fascist survivalist type who venomously hated government, yet lived on a combination of welfare and workers' comp from a minor injury he'd managed to parlay into a claim.

No doubt he had also hated Astrid as representing everything that his dim little worldview held to be wrong. But while he threw his weight around when he could, he'd never been known to actually harm anyone, and he had an even better alibi than Paulson for the time of the murders—his wife had kicked him out of the house, so he'd spent a few months living with his mother in Portland, Oregon. At a guess, his act hadn't gone over too well there.

It looked like O'Reilly was off the hook—although I had a feeling that Madbird was going to head up to Phosphor one of these days and twist his tail until he squealed. I just hoped I got to go along and watch.

Another scumbag still on Gary's radar was Ward "Pack Rat" Ackerman's father, Boone. But Gary had had many run-ins with him over the years, and found it hard to believe that Boone possessed the balls to commit those murders or the smarts to plant the cache. Vehicle records didn't support my notion that the SUV I'd seen watching Renee's house might have belonged to the Ackerman clan; of course, it could have been unregistered, borrowed, or outright stolen, and Gary was leaving the door open. But he'd held off searching the place or bracing them about the dead pack rat incident because he didn't want them aware that the cops were paying any attention to them. He assured me he'd come down hard on them as soon as the air was cleared.

The next two weeks continued without any measurable progress on those fronts. I drifted along, settling into a routine that helped to carry me. My wound healed well and I got stronger. I took long walks in the mornings and evenings, on the lookout for the bobcat. I didn't see him, and I found his tracks only once, in a dusting of fresh snow. Spring was gaining the upper hand over winter; there were more critters around, and it would be easier for him to cover ground and find deer.

Still, I always carried Madbird's .41 Magnum. The black tom usually went with me. He wasn't used to having me around so much but he adapted fast, seizing enhanced opportunities to extort beef and beer.

Every other day I drove to town and took care of necessary business—dealing with the police, getting a chest X-ray and my bandage changed a couple of times, and on my way home, driving by Renee's house. As near as I could tell, it was undisturbed. I went out to Split Rock a few times to check in with Madbird, timing it so he'd be finishing work and we could have a couple of beers. Things were fine there, too, and I always came away recharged by contact with his insane magic.

Early on, a reporter called from the *Independent Record*, wanting a story about the assault. Years earlier, I'd been in his shoes, and I'd have helped him out if I could have. I told him that the police had asked me not to comment, and he didn't push it. But the paper released a brief follow-up to their first account of the assault; this one included my name, and several old friends called to offer help. It was good to know that there were people concerned about me, even if I had to get shot to prove it.

Otherwise, the phone stayed quiet. Usually that was the way I liked it and it didn't bother me during the days, but the sound of a particular sweet voice sure would have been welcome as the evenings dragged on into night.

CHAPTER 39

THERE WAS MORE ACTION ON another front—the drama between Darcy and Seth Fraker wasn't over. She was still furious at Madbird, blaming him for the breakup and barely speaking to him. But she needed to vent, and both Hannah and Pam Bryce were adept at drawing her out; they quietly kept him in the loop, and I gleaned bits from him when we talked.

The affair had devolved into a familiar sort of aftermath, a running dogfight of sniping, recriminations, and pleas. Apparently, most of that was coming from Darcy—Fraker really did want out. As coldly as he had dropped her, at least he couldn't be accused of continuing to string her along.

More troubling, she wasn't just hurt. Her anger was escalating, and taking on an unattractive aspect. She had decided that Fraker owed her; on an emotional level, she had a case. But she'd started hinting none too vaguely that she was talking money. Whether this was for revenge or what she'd been playing for all along wasn't clear and didn't matter. It was edging into blackmail. Fraker had stopped taking her phone calls. She had started following him to confront him. He had threatened a restraining order and stalking charges. She was ready to tell the world the seamy truth about the golden-boy-happily-married-pillar-of-morality. And so on.

Madbird was back in a quandary. He couldn't stop Darcy from what she was doing. There was nothing illegal about Fraker's callousness; coming down on him in any serious way would only get Madbird thrown in jail. He'd already made Fraker nervous, and with any luck that would hold him in check. But the well-founded rumors that Hannah had heard about Fraker's unpleasantness toward women added to the mix. Once again, Madbird could only wait around worrying— not something he was good at.

Then a Sunday afternoon came along that was balmy enough so I couldn't stand just hanging around. Even though I didn't have any errands, I headed for town. I took it slow and for some time I cruised nowhere in particular, enjoying the drive and the weather, looking at things in a way that I hadn't for a long time. The air smelled good and people seemed happy. It was a nice interlude from the hovering trouble.

Toward dusk, I turned homeward, making my usual pass by Renee's house, then deciding to treat myself to a fancy dinner. I stopped at a supermarket and bought a good-sized chunk of wild salmon, linguini and Parmesan cheese, sourdough bread, an avocado, and vinaigrette dressing. Then I figured that as long as I was burning up a paycheck I hadn't earned, I might as well also pick up a bottle of Powers, so I swung into an establishment called Wild Bill's, toward the eastern edge of town.

Wild Bill's wasn't a place I frequented; it was newish, a combination liquor store-bar-casino with a faux western décor and a well-groomed clientele. But it was convenient, and I stopped there occasionally when other places were closed or I was short on time.

There were close to twenty vehicles in the parking lot, including several big pickup trucks. If I recognized one of them as being Seth Fraker's, it didn't register consciously.

But as I went into the liquor store, I passed an open doorway to the barroom and glimpsed him at a table in there with a couple of other people.

I would have ignored him and just bought my whiskey, except that he was laughing and I caught the flash of those perfect white teeth.

I walked through the doorway and down to an empty section of the bar, making eye contact with Fraker long enough to see his laugh freeze. Then I turned my back to him and ordered a Maker's Mark, intending to have only the one drink, and leave. All I wanted was to piss on his parade.

But a minute later he came over and leaned against the bar beside me, swilling his own drink a little too close to my face—not exactly belligerent, but letting me know who was top dog. He was unsteady and his breath smelled heavily of gin. No doubt it was Bombay Sapphire.

"Look, I've got nothing against you personally," he said. "But I'm sick of this loony tunes bullshit. She better back off, and I strongly advise you not to get in the middle of it."

"I'm not here on Darcy's account or anybody else's," I said. "Believe that or not, I couldn't care less. But as long as I've got the chance, let me ask you—you have any idea how she feels, the way you treated her?"

I assumed he'd get defensive in a nasty way. Instead, he scrunched up his face like a kid about to start blubbering.

"You have any idea how *I* feel because I can't help being like that? How much I hate myself for it?"

I almost laughed in disbelief. "You should get an Oscar for keeping your pain so well hidden."

"You don't know anything about it," he muttered. "You're an arrogant prick."

He raised his drink as if he was going to drain it. Then, without warning, he sloshed it into my face.

My open right hand came across the bar in a sharp hook and slapped the glass out of his grip. It bounced on the floor like a baseball, a hard one-hopper, bursting into a spray of shards.

The other customers in the room went still, leaving only the sound of the video poker machines bleeping and burbling their jingles in the next room.

Fraker stared, stunned, at his empty hand, then looked up warily at me and started edging backwards.

"Yeah, I am an arrogant prick," I said. "But I never gave myself the limp-dick excuse that I couldn't help it."

The bartender, a young woman who clearly wasn't accustomed to this kind of thing, had gone as silent as the customers. I pulled out the change left from the twenty-dollar bill I'd bought my drink with and dropped it on the bar.

"Sorry about that," I said to her. "Here's for your trouble."

I drove home braced for the wail of sirens in my ears and the flash of police lights in my rearview mirrors. They'd have had plenty of excuse to run me in; on top of everything else, I reeked worse of Fraker's gin than he had. But nothing happened, and by the time I got to Canyon Ferry, I couldn't help smiling. I'd broken my resolution about physical confrontations, but in a way I could easily live with. I'd come home without my whiskey, but no amount of booze could touch the way that slap had felt—fast, hard, and right on the money—or the look on his face.

This day was already one I would cherish in memory, and a couple of hours later it got impossibly better.

I was in my cabin, with water starting to heat for the linguini and the salmon marinating in a teriyaki barbecue sauce, ready to grill, when I heard the faint sound of an engine. That was highly unusual. There was almost no traffic up here anyway, let alone on a Sunday evening.

I opened the door and watched the approaching headlights. The vehicle was a small, dark-colored station wagon—just like Renee's forest green Outback.

I strode to my gate, not daring to believe it, and half-terrified that if it was her, that might mean something was wrong. But she got out of the car and stepped into my embrace, seeming weary but fine.

After a minute or so, she said, "Remember when Gary asked me to think back about when I spent time with my father and Astrid?"

"Yeah?"

"He was right—I started digging around in my head, and found something. Can I stay here a while?"

"As long as you can stand it," I said. "Come on, you're just in time for dinner."

I put my arm around her and walked her to the cabin.

CHAPTER 40

I EASED MYSELF OUT OF bed next morning, leaving Renee to sleep in after her long drive from Seattle. I quietly stoked the fire, boiled water, and made myself a cup of strong black coffee. Then I wrapped up in a down coat and sat outside on the cabin steps.

The early morning air was still crisp, but the real bite of winter was gone. The patchwork of bare earth and snow spread out before me turned darker every day; the trees were greening, with fattening buds. I was starting to hear songbirds, instead of just the occasional croak of a crow or screech of a magpie. In general, the land and sky felt softer. We'd still get hammered again a couple of times, but it was like a receding tide; each time a wave withdrew, spring had gained more ground.

It seemed that my own world might be changing, too, although I couldn't yet gauge how much.

Renee had taken a leave of absence from her research job. Her employers hadn't been happy about the short notice, but they had agreed, and the door was open for her to return. Whether she'd do so was up in the air, along with more.

She hadn't yet said anything about Ian. I decided I'd let her bring that up when she was ready to. But the engagement ring was gone from her finger, and we both understood that her staying here was, in part, a trial to see how things might work out.

But the main reason that had brought her back here, which she'd mentioned on arriving last night, was harder-edged and more compelling—the memory of an argument she'd over-heard between her father and Astrid. It had happened during Renee's last visit with them, only a few months before Astrid's death.

Renee had been aware that the tension between the two was rising, and by that time, the bloom was definitely off the rose. Professor Callister, mild and good-humored by nature, seemed prickly and even angry. Astrid's treatment of him was aloof, dis-dainful, and sharp. She was gone by herself a lot, sometimes until late at night, and she made no attempt to explain her absences. Infidelity wasn't mentioned outright in their exchanges, but the atmosphere was charged with that possibility.

On the evening of the argument, Renee had been out with friends and got home around eleven. Her father was alone, reading in the living room. He said good night to her with his usual affection, but she sensed that something had happened; he was almost grim, and later she heard him pacing around restlessly and even muttering to himself, a habit he'd never had. That kept her restless, too.

She dozed, but woke up around three in the morning to the strident voice of her father challenging Astrid. He seemed to be confronting her with an object—something that she had hidden and he had found.

"What the hell are you doing with this?" he demanded. He sounded more upset than Renee had ever heard him.

"What are *you* doing with it?" Astrid retorted, shrilly, with-out her usual cool. "How dare you go through my things."

"That's a brat's answer. You're acting like a little girl; you think you're playing a game."

"Oh, I know it's real—*you're* the one who does nothing but talk."

Then they lowered their voices and moved farther into the house; maybe they'd realized they might wake Renee. She only caught a few more words at the brief argument's end. As the Professor's footsteps stomped across the floor, Astrid called bitingly after him:

"Go ahead! I'll just get another set."

Renee heard the back door close, and went to a window. Her father was striding across the yard to his study in the carriage house, carrying a scroll or tube that looked like a rolled-up poster. A minute later, sparks rose from the woodstove chimney; at a guess, he was burning it. She watched for some time longer, but he didn't come out again.

Renee had thought hard about the incident, trying to reconstruct it in detail, and had connected some dots. First, she was almost certain that in Astrid's final taunt to Callister—that she would "just get another"—she had used the word "set." That was a term commonly used for blueprints, site maps, and general construction plans—which were usually carried in longish rolled-up scrolls.

Second, Astrid's lover, the one who had been murdered with her, was a manager in the Dodd Company—the backers of the silver mine that she had fought.

Third, Astrid had been involved with a group of radical environmentalists, and she had talked seriously about blowing up the mine.

Not much had ever been done with this aspect of the crime. While it was conceivable that her lover was the intended target rather than Astrid, nobody gave that much credence. There was a ton of hostility toward her but none toward him, at least that had ever surfaced. He'd just been unlucky enough to be there. The affair itself didn't seem to have any particular significance; it was assumed to be a case of sleeping with the enemy, with attraction prevailing over antagonism—if not exactly time-honored, certainly not unknown. He was close to Astrid's age, was more appealing physically than her twenty-years-older husband, and the forbidden-fruit aspect would have added spice.

But maybe lust and kicks hadn't been the only impetus for the affair. What if she had really seduced him to get information—such as a set of construction plans—to help her pinpoint sabotage targets? That was the kind of intrigue she had delighted in, and he wouldn't necessarily have known her real object.

Callister's fury at finding the blueprint-like scroll, and the fierce words that Renee had overheard, did lend credence to that scenario. And that opened up yet another labyrinth of possibilities, one even murkier than what we'd encountered so far.

Needless to say, Renee was determined to explore it.

I went back into the cabin to make breakfast—bacon, eggs scrambled with cheddar cheese in a little of the bacon grease, sourdough bread toasted in an iron skillet, and more of that rich coffee.

My gaze kept straying to the sight of the sleeping woman in my bed—her cloud of dark mussed-up hair, a glimpse of bare nape, the sweet curve of her hips under the quilt. It had taken some maneuvering last night to keep my ribs comfortable, but we'd managed quite well. My condition was definitely improving.

The tomcat had settled in behind her knees and was purring quietly, waiting for me to serve the meal. I was happy to oblige.

CHAPTER 41

RENEE ATE SITTING UP IN bed, wearing one of my T-shirts—we'd never gotten around to unpacking her car last night—with the cat and me flanking her on opposite sides. He could put away bacon like a black hole sucking down a galaxy, and she was a soft touch; he beat her out of damned near every other bite.

"I've decided to sell the house," she said.

I nodded, although that gave me a little pang. But it made all the sense in the world, and it didn't necessarily mean she wouldn't stay in Helena.

"What about the repairs?" I said.

"I'll get somebody to finish cleaning up—not you; don't even think about it. Otherwise, it goes on the market as is. I know that's a mistake, but I just can't deal with it anymore."

"That's not a mistake."

"Well, this probably is—I'm going to let Evvie Jessup handle the sale. She called me in Seattle when she heard about the shooting. All gushy about how glad she was that I was okay, but really, she was keeping her foot in the door."

"I don't see why it should matter," I said. "She's a professional. You might want to make sure she discloses the rat problem."

"It's just that I'm uncomfortable with her. But she knows

the place, I don't have to hassle finding somebody else and showing them around, all that."

"You're dodging a bullet, too," I said. "If you went with somebody else, she'd never forgive you."

"Amen," Renee said solemnly.

I stood up and reached for her empty plate, but she caught my hand and held it.

"I've already dragged you into such a mess," she said. "Are you sure you want to keep going?"

I'd said much the same thing to Madbird once; he'd answered much the way I felt now, and those words came to my mind. But they were a notch too colorful for this situation, so I toned them down.

"Ever hear an old song called 'Riot in Cell Block Number Nine'?" I said.

"No. It must have been before my time."

"There's a line that goes something like, 'Scarface Jones said it's too late to quit—pass the dymamite, 'cause the fuse is lit.'"

She smiled and gave my hand a grateful squeeze.

It wasn't yet eight o'clock, too early for Evvie Jessup's office to be open, so Renee called her at home. Evvie was surprised to hear that Renee was back in town, and thrilled to get the news about the house sale. She said she'd hurry in to her office and be there by the time we got to town.

I cleaned up the dishes and made the round of morning chores while Renee showered—I'd have lobbied to get in there with her but the space was small, and while usually that would be a wet soapy delight, an elbow to my ribs was inevitable— then took my own turn.

When that was all done, I tried Tom Dierdorff's phone. He answered with Monday morning grumpiness.

"Sounds like you're getting ready to sweet-talk a jury," I said.

"Sorry. I like to drink kerosene to get me going, but the doctor made me switch to coffee. Just doesn't have the same bite."

"Yeah, but you can start smoking again."

"Goddamn, I never thought of that. You're a fucking Pollyanna, Huey."

"It's a mick thing. Hey, I'll stop wasting your valuable pissed-off time. Any chance I can talk to that tree-spiker you defended in the Dead Silver deal? Some new twists have come along."

There came one of his considered pauses.

"I'll ask him, if I can find him. He was living in Missoula, but we haven't been in touch for quite a while."

"I'd really appreciate it, Tom. This is important."

"I'll get right on it. You still healing okay?" He was one of the friends who'd called to check on me after I'd been shot.

"Never better," I said, glancing at Renee.

I gave him Renee's cell phone number in case he got the information while we went to town to deal with Evvie. Then Renee and I packed overnight bags to take with us so we could head straight to Missoula without having to come back here.

Missoula was a hundred-plus miles west of Helena, on the other side of the Rockies and the Continental Divide. The division between here and there wasn't just geographical; it aptly symbolized a deep social and political rift in this state, and probably in the nation. Missoula was widely perceived as the Berkeley of Montana—home to the state university, and a hotbed of 1960s-type alternative lifestyle and activism. Some found the atmosphere positive and exciting; many others saw it as a cesspool of decadence and subversion. The two edges of that sword were getting sharper all the time. I had friends from there who had actually become nervous about driving in other parts of the state with license plates that began with the telltale number 4, which identified them as residents of Missoula County.

What a lot of people didn't know was that the original hippies there were mostly working-class kids from small
towns, ranches, and reservations around the state—tough,
hardworking, many of them war veterans—and that while
some were educated, they were far from effete intellectual
snobs. I'd always thought that the true underlying reason for
the establishment's wrath at them was that they refused to
walk any company line and they were very canny about seeing
through bullshit. In general, they had a lot more in common
with old-time people like my father than either group did with
the newer Montana that was springing into being.

I had always loved Missoula, and I'd had a lot of good
times there. The old bars—Eddy's Club, Charley B's, The Top
Hat, Luke's, The Turf, The Flame—were the kinds of places
where you might meet people who'd led lives you could hardly
imagine, fall in love, and get the shit kicked out of you, all in
the same night.

But my ambivalence about growth kicked in again every
time I visited. The funky old downtown had been gentrified
and was thronged with tourists in summer. The university—
once a modest, well-run operation that was mostly attended
by Montana residents—had doubled in size and turned into a
moneymaking venture, largely designed as a party school for
rich kids from out of state. The city itself was exploding at
the fringes with commercial strips and industrial parks, while
a policy known as "infill" had invaded quiet older neighbor-
hoods, with second residences shoehorned into back and side
yards, many of them cheaply built rentals. It was getting to
look more and more like someplace in California. But there
again, I had to recognize that all those elements would serve
more human beings in many ways; and personally, I didn't feel
that I had any claim to locational purity.

The drive from Helena to Missoula was about two hours.
It would have been sensible and politically correct for us to

take Renee's comfortable, economical Suburu instead of my truck. But I felt cramped in smaller vehicles, I liked sitting up high, and I liked having a lot of metal around me.

I stowed our gear under the pickup's seat, and we headed for town.

CHAPTER 42

EVVIE JESSUP'S OFFICE WAS A ground-floor suite in a mini-mall off Eleventh Avenue, toward the east edge of Helena. I wasn't particularly anxious to exchange small talk, so I pulled up in front to drop Renee off. I could see Evvie through the large plate glass windows, sitting at her desk. As soon as she spotted Renee, she rose and hurried to the door, waving excitedly.

I backed up and swung the pickup around in the parking lot. Just before I turned onto Eleventh again, I glanced automatically at my rearview mirrors. I was compulsive about that, checking them constantly even on deserted roads. My glimpse showed Renee stepping into the office, with Evvie embracing her.

A third figure had also come into view, a burly bearded man wearing tinted eyeglasses—Evvie's husband, Lon. He must have been in the rear of the suite and had opened the door to come into the main room. But a few seconds later, when a break in traffic allowed me to pull out, he was still standing there motionless.

A tiny tick registered in my brain. As often happened, it was gone before I could make sense of it. But I'd started learning to pay attention to those occurrences, and to remember where I was and what I was doing at the time. Sometimes they came to light later, with interesting results.

While Renee took care of her house business, I had a matter of my own to attend to. Having her around had opened my eyes to things I hadn't noticed for years. This had started when she'd chipped a fingernail unpacking, and realized that she hadn't brought a nail file. The only help I could offer was the tool I used to round off my own manicuring snags, an automotive file for cleaning the points in my truck's distributor.

My awareness had escalated from there. My twenty-year-old shaving brush had shed almost half its bristles; my only belt was worn thin and stained with construction glue; the shower caddy I'd cobbled together out of tie wire and welding rods was functional, but lacked an aesthetic je ne sais quoi; and so on. Most of my other possessions, clothes, and furnishings were in equivalent shape, but that was too much to worry about now. I figured I'd start by upgrading a few personal items and try to grow with the job.

Renee had given me her cell phone so she could call me to come pick her up. I was just getting downtown, on my way to DeVore's Saddlery to buy a belt, when it rang. That surprised me mildly—I hadn't thought she'd be done so soon. It also flustered me; I barely knew how to operate the things anyway, and I didn't dare to try while I was driving, so I steered the truck over to the curb.

But the caller was Tom Dierdorff, with the news that he had scored—located his former client, who was not only willing to talk about the Dead Silver incident but jumping at the chance.

"He's still got a hard-on about it," Tom said. "Sounds like if anything, you're going to have trouble shutting him up."

His name was Buddy Pertwee; he was still living in Missoula. I wrote down his phone and address—I recognized it as being on the north side, the core enclave of the old hippie scene and still home to a fair share of holdouts from those days—thanked Tom, and went on about my rounds until Renee called me to come get her, a half hour later.

I'd hoped I could just swing by the realty office and pick her up outside, the same way I'd dropped her off, and when I pulled up in front I stayed in the truck. But Evvie came out, too, and practically fluttered over to me; obviously, my stock with her had risen dramatically. She reached in through my window, pressed my face between her palms, and planted a kiss on my lips, eyes shining beneath her nuclear sunset hair.

"We are *so* grateful to you for saving our dear one," she said. She seemed as sincere as she was capable of being.

Lon Jessup shuffled outside, too, hanging back, as seemed to be his style. When Evvie let me go, he stepped in and offered a hearty handshake.

"Nice work, pardner," he said. "My hat's off to you."

Then Renee and I hit the road for the bright lights of Missoula.

CHAPTER 43

IT WAS STILL MORNING, AND we weren't in any rush to get there. Buddy Pertwee worked for a landscaping business and wouldn't be available until late afternoon. I decided to avoid the Interstate and take a longer route that was one of my favorite drives—all two-lane roads, first northwest to the Blackfoot River corridor, and then following the Blackfoot west to Missoula. There'd be hardly any traffic most of the way, and the landscape was a showcase of what I loved about Montana.

The day was typical for this time of year, with big billowy clouds that put a biting edge on the breeze when they darkened the sun, but then would part for a tantalizing burst of warmth. Canyon Creek was still iced along the banks but mostly rippled fast and free, so clear it made me thirsty. The forest thickened and the patchwork of snow became a solid quilt as we climbed the hairpin curves up Flesher Pass. From the top, the view stretched for miles, ended only by mountains or the horizon.

"I didn't sleep with Ian again, since us," Renee said. Her words came out of the blue; she'd hardly spoken for the last half hour, and she hadn't mentioned him at all until now. The Continental Divide seemed an odd place to suddenly bring him up. But then again, maybe it was exactly right.

I got one of those pleasant little tingles that I'd gotten with her before, a mix of emotions and physical sensation that brushed across my skin, or maybe rose up through it.

"I figured that was none of my business," I said. "But it's nice to know."

"I told him about you and me."

"I've been wondering about your ring."

"I gave it back to him," she said. "We didn't completely break the engagement. I just need to step away for a while."

"How'd he take it?"

"He was very understanding. Hurt, but he knows it's not about him. It's my own problems, that I've been having all along. Then on top of that comes this crazy situation with my father."

I was relieved. I had feared that Ian was the one who had broken the engagement because she'd confessed our affair or he suspected it, and that her regret might be growing.

"Does he still think you'll come to your senses?" I said.

"I guess so. He's the one who asked not to break things off. But he might change his mind. And let's face it, there'd be women standing in line for a nice young doctor."

"I hardly know Ian, but I suspect he's not going to change his mind unless he has to."

She gave me a quick grateful smile. "I hope I don't sound heartless. I feel guilty, of course."

I felt bad for him, too. But if I'd been him, I sure wouldn't have wanted to be on a marriage track with a woman who felt anxiety instead of anticipation.

Renee settled back and turned her attention to the road-side scenery, while I concentrated on negotiating the steep tight turns of the pass. Coming up it was one thing; going down was another, especially in an old rig like mine. This truck was built for work, and though it handled well and soundly, it didn't have the correction buffers built into modern vehicles. If you went into a curve a few miles per hour too fast or a few feet too far to one side, pulling out would be hairy at best. Then again, she was still running as strong as ever after forty years—well worth the extra effort—and she'd never let me down.

As the terrain leveled out the road continued to wind through a particularly lovely area approaching the Blackfoot highway. West of the Divide, the ground cover of snow mostly disappeared except in the distant higher mountains, and the crisp blue of the sky segued into a softer gray. The weather over here tended to be warmer and wetter anyway, and now it looked like a front was moving in from the Pacific. A fine drizzle began as we followed the Blackfoot, fat and roiling with spring runoff. The last few miles into Missoula took us through Hellgate Canyon, a narrow cliff-lined stretch that had been a favorite place for hostile Native tribes to ambush each other. According to one theory, this was the origin of the city's name—a Salish Indian word meaning "horrible."

We splurged on a good hotel, a sedate older place near downtown, and got a third-floor room with a little balcony overlooking the Clark Fork River. After lunch, we still had a couple of hours to while away before meeting with Buddy Pertwee. We decided to stay home and rest up—get ready for the reason we'd come here.

There's a special quality to a situation like that. With the door closed, the room was our sanctuary, cozy and private, and nobody knew or cared that we were there. We stretched out on top of the bed and bundled up together in the comforter, achieved a satisfactory arrangement of limbs, exchanged one brief chaste kiss, and slipped into a delicious trance soothed by the murmur of the river below and the fingers of rain streaking the hazy windows.

CHAPTER 44

I CALLED BUDDY PERTWEE JUST after five o'clock that afternoon; he suggested meeting at an old downtown bar called Knuckles. I was slightly hesitant about taking Renee there. I hadn't done much partying in Missoula for quite a few years, but back then Knuckles had been the watering hole of choice for local bikers and a lot of other hard-edged individuals.

But there were leavening elements of old hippies, blue-collar working people, college students, and other young folks groping their way up the perilous ladder of life, and rowdy as it was, real trouble was rare and usually happened later in the evenings when enthusiasm was running high. It was also a good-sized place, so we'd be able to get off by ourselves and have a private conversation. And I wanted Buddy to feel comfortable, on turf of his own choosing.

Downtown was only a few blocks away, so Renee and I walked. She carried one of those little traveler's umbrellas that she offered to share, but the rain had lightened to a drizzle and I enjoyed feeling it against my face. I liked rain, at least when I didn't have to stay outside working in it all day—maybe a throwback to my Celtic heritage, a gloomy, gene-deep love for a misty land where I had never gone.

Still, the damp weather enhanced the neon-lit welcome of

Knuckles when we stepped inside. The main room was a long rectangle, with an L-shaped bar running most of its length and a fine old hand-carved backbar. The first thing that struck you when you walked in was a unique and stellar portrait collection, by a renowned local photographer, of old-time cowboys, railroad men, and drifters who had frequented this place. The way that he had caught their faces was magic; their eyes, their creased, weathered skin, and their broken smiles were windows into their hard and sometimes desperate lives. A gold star pasted in a bottom corner meant that they were dead. There were a lot of those.

We paused to order drinks from the bartender, a pretty young woman with multiple body piercings. When she turned away and crouched to pull a beer out of a cooler, the scallop between her top and her low-cut jeans revealed what looked like a snake tattooed down her spine. It must have been a fairly big snake, a green one. In general, the body art motif spoke loud. I saw one guy shrug off his jacket and sling it over a barstool, and I thought at first that he was wearing a striped shirt. In fact, his arms were bare.

Renee leaned close to me and whispered, "I almost got a tramp stamp once, but I chickened out."

"Tramp stamp?"

"You know. A butterfly or something, up high on a girl's behind, so you can just see it above her whale tail."

"*Whale* tail?"

"Thong, The back part," she said, giving me her patient-teacher look again.

After several seconds, it registered. "Oh. Because that's the shape. Like the tail of an actual whale, sort of, uh, rising up out of the ocean of her womanhood."

She patted my hand approvingly. "What a quick study you are. Did you ever think about it? A tattoo?"

"I never had the money."

We took a booth toward the rear. The crowd was moderate—a few regulars who'd probably been there all day, several men bullshitting over their after-work beers, and a couple more playing desultory eight-ball—but there was a steady trickle of newcomers, mostly of the younger set. I watched them as they came through the door; I didn't know what Buddy looked like, but I'd given him a brief description of Renee and me, and she, at least, wouldn't be hard to spot in here.

When he did come walking over to us, I liked the immediate hit I got. He had the knobby look of a guy who was accustomed to using his body; banged-up hands and scraped forearms spoke to the landscaping work he did. His face had the kind of wary, tough look that came from taking some hard shots in life, like the time he'd done in the state prison in Deer Lodge.

I stood up, shook his hand, and told him the drinks were on me. He said my own setup, a bottle of Pabst and a shot of Knob Creek bourbon, looked pretty good. Renee sat him down beside her and turned on her quiet charm; as I waited at the bar, I could see her listening attentively and nodding. By the time I got back to the booth, he had lit a cigarette and seemed to be relaxing.

"Buddy used to live in Phosphor before he moved here," Renee said to me. "He was telling me about what happened to Astrid's cabin. Remember, the roof was half-gone?" She turned back to him inquiringly.

"What I heard was, her family wanted to get rid of it, so they found a guy who was going to take it apart and reuse the logs somewhere else." He spoke in a raspy voice, with his gaze constantly shifting. "But he walked off before he got too far. Didn't like the feel of it."

I had no trouble understanding that.

"And they just left it?" Renee said.

"Guess so. I haven't been over that way for a long time."
He took a swig of beer, then returned to his posture of hunch-
ing over the table with his forearms encircling his drinks. I'd
read somewhere that that protectiveness was a habit men
picked up in prison.

"Bad memories?" she prompted.

"Worse than memories. I'd get stomped." His quick gaze
flicked back and forth between her and me. "I was a rat. I'd
worked in the woods around there, and I knew a lot of the guys
who were on the mine project. I'd hang around in the bars and
bullshit with them like I was their friend. But I was really finding out what was going on up there and when nobody would
be around."

"You must have believed in what you were doing," Renee
said soothingly.

"Yeah, the noble cause," he said, now with a bitter tone.
"I told myself that for a long time, and some of it's true. You
watch places you love getting trashed so assholes in New York
or Hong Kong can get richer. But I finally figured out the real
reason I was into it—I was on a big power trip. I was the dude
who knew the secrets, I was pulling the strings. I thought I
was so cool, like an undercover agent." He shook his head
unhappily. "Now I can't believe I did it. I'm not some fucking
trustafarian—I grew up the same way as those people, they
were my friends."

His tough eyes had dampened. I reached across the table
and pushed his shot glass closer to him.

"Finish that off; I'll get us a couple more," I said.

When I got back from the bar this time, he looked like
he was feeling better again, no doubt under Renee's calming
influence.

"So how did this outfit work?" I said. "Was there an organized group? You, Astrid, other people?"

His gaze swung to me combatively. "Look, I'm glad to

talk to you guys, on account of Tom Dierdorff—he saved my ass. But I'm not naming names."

I realized I'd touched a sore spot. "Sure, I understand. That's not important," I said, although it might be. I'd worry about it later. "Keep going, please."

"It was half-assed organized. We'd have meetings, act like we were commandos. But the only thing that ever really happened was when a few of us fucked up that equipment."

"And the others walked, and you took the hit," Renee said.

Buddy nodded grimly.

I decided to cut to the chase.

"Buddy, we heard Astrid was planning to sabotage the mine," I said. "Actually blow up the construction. But it doesn't seem like the sheriffs ever really investigated that."

He snorted scornfully. "They never *really* investigated anything. Those guys were like *Reno 911!*—only not funny. The one thing they were good at was busting balls on dudes like me."

"Did Astrid ever talk about that?"

"She hinted around at it."

"You think there was anything to it?" I said. "For openers, it doesn't sound like your people had that kind of know-how."

"Not even close, man. But there was this rumor—like an urban legend, nobody knew where it started or if it was pure bullshit. Supposedly, she met some dude in Colorado who was righteous for the cause, and he was an ex–Special Forces ranger. He took her with him to raid a gyppo logging camp that was poaching old-growth timber. They didn't kill anybody, but one guy wouldn't back down and they shot him in the leg. Then ran them all off and wrecked their stuff."

Renee's gaze on Buddy was already intent, but now it turned to a stare.

"Was it Astrid who shot him?"

Buddy shrugged. "Same as the other deal—nobody knew for sure and it wasn't the kind of thing you asked her. Anyway, the buzz was that the Green Beret dude was going to come up here and blow up the mine—plant the explosives, all that. But I don't know if he was even real."

"Did you ever hear anything linking that to the murders?" I said. "Like somebody found out what she was planning, and decided to stop her? Maybe even somebody from the mining company?"

"Never anything solid. Of course, with the Keystone Kops in charge, who knows?"

Then his eyes narrowed, and he emphasized his next words with little jabs of his forefinger.

"But I can tell you this, man—there were people who thought she had it coming."

Renee flinched, and Buddy's face turned anxious with apology.

"Hey, sorry. I didn't mean that the way it came out," he said.

She managed a wan smile. "Don't worry, I'm learning all kinds of new things about her. So what finally happened with your group?"

He leaned back in his seat, almost flopping, like he was overcome by the thought.

"It was way weird. The last couple meetings, she was all of a sudden like a different person. That *fire* was gone—you could tell she didn't even want to be there. Then she told us all to chill for a while, she'd get in touch. But she didn't, and the whole thing just fell apart."

This was another surprising piece of news, with no ready explanation. The possibility that Astrid had simply lost interest seemed highly unlikely.

"What brought that on?" I said.

"Never found out." He groped distractedly in his shirt

pocket for another cigarette. "I tried to talk to her, but she turned real nasty—basically told me to fuck off. Other people said she was the same way with them. The feeling I got was, she was really pissed about something."

"Something?" Renee said sharply. "Because you and the others screwed up?"

He shook his head decisively. "If that was it, she'd have told us. She got right in your face about shit like that."

His restless gaze had kept moving all along, his head frequently swiveling toward the door. It went there again and paused, apparently on another young man who had just walked in and was scanning the room.

"I'll be back in a minute," he said, getting up.

I was sure that the newcomer also saw him, but there was no sign of recognition between them. Buddy headed down the rear hallway to the restrooms. The other guy turned around and left the bar.

There was an alley around the side of the building, and a back door at the end of the hallway, that both led to a parking lot. I suspected that in its shadows, some kind of illicit substance and a sum of money were about to change hands. It had crossed my mind earlier that Buddy must have a backup source of income for the winter months, when the lawn and garden business wouldn't cover the bills.

Renee wasn't paying attention to that or anything else around us; her gaze had gone unfocused. I touched a finger to her forehead.

"What's going on in there?" I said.

"I'm wondering where I've been all these years. Can you think of anything else in particular we should ask him?"

"I'd say let's just keep him talking."

That wasn't hard. When Buddy returned, he still had plenty to say. But after another half hour he started to run around the same bush, and he edged more and more into bitterness at his mistreatment by the Dodd Company and the local authorities. Tom Dierdorff's wry warning crossed my mind—getting him to shut up would be the tricky part.

But our patience was rewarded when he let drop another eye-opener.

Astrid's infidelity hadn't been one-sided. The young mining company manager who'd been murdered along with her had a girlfriend at the time—a local woman from Phosphor named Tina Gerhardt, whose family owned the town's small grocery store.

That news put Phosphor on our itinerary back to Helena tomorrow, a detour of about an hour. Tina might be long gone by now, and if she was still around, she might not want to talk to us. But the opposite could just as well be true, and like Buddy, she might even have an ax to grind. The grocery store was a local hub where everybody in the area stopped by frequently and gossiped, and she was connected to the crime. She very well might have gleaned information that had never officially come to light. It was definitely worth checking out.

As Renee and I were getting ready to leave Knuckles, I bought Buddy one more drink and set it in front of him.

"For what it's worth, seems to me you've carried that weight on your back long enough," I said. "Paid your dues, all that."

He looked surprised and pleased. "Thanks, man." But then his face turned almost plaintive, like he found the thought more unhappy than reassuring. "I keep telling myself I should go someplace new, get something else going. But it's hard when you got a record. And, you know"—his fingers opened and closed, like he was trying to take hold of words— "there's something about this town. It's got a drift you get caught up in."

I'd heard other people say that about Missoula, and I'd felt the tug myself.

CHAPTER 45

THE TOWN OF PHOSPHOR LOOKED a lot more appealing the next afternoon than it had when we'd driven through at night, a few weeks earlier. Yesterday's gray sky had cleared to blue, filled with billowing, wind-tossed white clouds, and flashes of sunlight gave a warm glow to the funky old brick buildings. Kids with bulging daypacks were wandering home from school, stretching out the interlude between the responsibilities at both ends. There was the sense that things were hard-used but wholesome, and even the western touches—a rack of antlers mounted above the door of the Elkhorn Bar, a big log lintel carved with a cattle brand at the entrance to a mom-and-pop motel—which would have seemed clichéed elsewhere were authentic here.

I slowed my truck to the main street's 25-mph speed limit and headed for the Phosphor Food Emporium, where Renee and I hoped to find Tina Gerhardt.

Last evening and during the drive here, we'd rehashed our talk with Buddy Pertwee from every angle we could think of. The importance of the new information he'd provided seemed to boil down to this:

If the story about the mysterious Colorado commando was true, it lent more weight to the premise that Astrid was serious about sabotaging the Dead Silver Mine, and had gone so far as to acquire construction plans and enlist his explosives expertise.

But then she'd shown an abrupt, astonishing behavior change. Her passion for the cause so dear to her had vaporized; she'd seemed angry, distracted, and had harshly rebuffed her former comrades. Buddy Pertwee was convinced that this wasn't caused by their group, but by an outside factor.

For sure, Astrid had worries. Her marriage was in trouble; she was despised by many of her neighbors; as time went on, her secret, Mata Hari life had probably gone from exhilarating to nerve-racking; and however dedicated and naïve she might have been, she had to realize that she was flirting with massive property destruction, possible injury and death to others, and a lengthy prison term for herself.

But all of those factors had been present over a long period of time. Maybe she'd finally bowed under all the pressures, but everything I knew about her told me she was determined to get what she wanted, and the more difficult that was, the more stubborn she became.

What had caused the sudden change? Had she been murdered because of it, or because she had changed too late?

The Phosphor Food Emporium, which you could have picked up and put down a dozen times in a supermarket, was in the center of town. We hadn't tried to call Tina in advance; we agreed that she'd respond better to Renee's physical presence than to a voice over a telephone, and also that Renee would have a better chance of breaking the ice if she went in alone, at least to start with. She wouldn't mention the developments that had led us here; she would use the semi-true pretext that she'd never learned much about that dark chapter of her family history, and her father's recent death had made her feel the need.

But when I pulled the pickup into an angled parking space in front of the store, she sat without moving, hands gripping her purse in her lap.

"Talking to other people hasn't been hard," she said. "But this time—I keep thinking about how hurt she must have been. And then a complete stranger walks in out of the blue, and drags it up again."

"That was kind of what happened to you, with those photos," I said.

"In a way, I guess. But that was a fluke. This is deliberate, and so personal."

"You don't have to do it, Renee. If you're uncomfortable, let's just leave."

"No, I want to. I'm trying to convince myself I have a good enough reason."

"How's this? It was no fluke that two people got killed."

She sighed. "Pretty convincing, I'm afraid." She popped open a compact mirror and nervously touched up her lipstick, then gave me a mock salute and stepped out of the truck. I stayed where I was, with the sour taste of hypocrisy in my mouth. That kind of shit was easy for me to say. I didn't have to walk in the door and chance facing the outrage or tears of a deeply wounded woman.

I didn't feel right just sitting there in the truck, so I got out. But Renee was back from the store immediately, with the deflated look that I had come to recognize when she absorbed a punishing disappointment. I met her on the sidewalk.

"Bad?" I said.

"Bad enough. There was an older woman at the cash register. I asked to speak to Tina. Turns out Tina was her daughter, and she was killed in a car wreck six years ago."

I winced. "Was she upset?"

"Just cold. She asked what I wanted. I told her. She said, 'Well, I guess Tina can't help you, now can she?'" Renee shrugged helplessly. "I apologized and left."

"My fault," I said. "I should have done some homework before sending you barging in. Something like that never crossed my mind." I opened the pickup's passenger door for her. "Time for you to kick back. I'm taking you to a rustic retreat in the fabled Big Belt Mountains. Log fire, bottle of fine wine, charbroiled filet mignon."

Her face softened toward a smile. "Sounds expensive."

"We can work out a payment plan."

As Renee was getting into my truck, another woman came out of the grocery store, hurrying toward us. She looked like she'd been working; she was wearing an apron and her hair was pulled back into a ponytail. She possessed a kind of faded prettiness that I'd often seen in these small hardscrabble towns, as if the people took on the same worn look as their surroundings. But she was probably about Renee's age—certainly not old enough to be Tina Gerhardt's mother. There was no hostility in her face; she seemed uncertain, anxious.

"I heard you talking to my mom," she said to Renee. "I could maybe tell you some things, if you want."

CHAPTER 46

HER NAME WAS JANIE GERHARDT; she was Tina's younger sister. She led us back into the store, past the unwelcoming gaze of her rawboned, bespectacled mother.

"Where you going? I need help," Mrs. Gerhardt called after her, although there weren't any customers.

"I'll send the girls out," Janie said. Both spoke in sharp tones that suggested a long-standing battle for control.

Then Janie exhaled dramatically, stopped walking, and about-faced.

"Come on, Mom, let's talk to these people. How can it hurt?"

Mrs. Gerhardt didn't answer. We followed Janie on through the Phosphor Food Emporium's short aisles of modestly stocked shelves. I was reminded of the pretty good grocery market in *Prairie Home Companion*—if they didn't have what you wanted, you could get along without it.

The building itself was bigger than it looked from the street, with a newer addition built onto the rear. As we came to learn, the extra space had been intended to expand the store, during the days when the Dead Silver Mine seemed a sure bet to jack up the local economy and population. After that failed, Janie's father had been forced to take a truck-driving job to make the payments, and was on the road much of the time. She and her mother ran the store. The family had closed off the addition and converted it into an apartment—cinder-block walls and concrete floor—where Janie now lived with her two teenaged daughters. Her husband was long gone. This was a female dynasty.

The daughters were home when we walked in—one at a computer desk, the other lying on the couch surrounded by a spread of books and papers, both with an eye on the TV screen, which appeared to be featuring young celebrities misbehaving. Competing music pulsed from an open bedroom door. They were about thirteen and fifteen, with a resemblance to their mother and to each other; both were wearing skin-tight lowcut jeans that exposed their navels, skin-tight lowcut tops that made the most of their striving young cleavage, and enough makeup to put on a stage production of *Grease*.

"Turn off the noise and go help Gramma," Janie said. The girls responded with groans and eye-rolling, but no complaints. While the power struggle between them and their own mother had doubtless started, kids who grew up like this understood from an early age that the family was in the sea of life together, to swim or sink.

Their glances at me were only mildly curious—I was a kind of guy they were used to—but they lingered on Renee, sizing her up carefully. She was dressed much the same as them except with less flesh on display, but I supposed there were signals telling of her worldliness—another facet of that mysterious chain of female communication that endlessly passed me by.

When they were gone, Janie stepped to a shelf with several glassed photographs, and touched one.

"This is Tina," she said.

Tina Gerhardt had been an attractive young woman, with a chiseled face framed by soft, thick, light brown hair. There was a touch of Barbie doll about her, although some of that came from the generic studio portrait,

Janie wiped her hands nervously on her apron. "Nobody's brought this up for a long time," she said. "What do you want to know?" She seemed slightly accusing now, like she was wishing she'd listened to her mother after all.

"About Tina and her boyfriend, mainly," Renee said.

"Brent?" Janie shrugged. "He was sort of full of shit—liked to hear himself talk. But all right, except for cheating on Tina."

Then another woman's voice said, "He wasn't all right, and neither was that Astrid. Weren't for their little game, Tina would still be here."

I turned to see the elder Mrs. Gerhardt walking into Janie's apartment. She waved Renee and me toward the dining room table.

"Go on, sit down," she said. "I'll make coffee."

CHAPTER 47

RENEE AND I LEFT THERE about an hour later. I couldn't say that Mrs. Gerhardt had warmed to us, but she'd opened up and told us a story of quiet heartbreak.

When Tina had gotten the devastating news that her boyfriend had been murdered—Brent Hoffey was his name—she'd suffered the additional shock of learning that he'd been cheating on her with the town's Public Enemy Number One. That created a huge wound in her life, and nothing arrived to heal it. She stayed in Phosphor and worked at the grocery store, with occasional new boyfriends who weren't going anywhere, either.

She started partying hard. The night came when she was out drinking with two guys, maybe going somewhere or maybe just riding around, and the driver misjudged a turn coming down a steep twisty road. The vehicle plunged more than a hundred feet down the almost vertical mountainside, with nobody wearing seat belts. Tina and one of the men were killed in the crash. The other died in the hospital soon afterward.

Blaming that on the affair between Astrid and Brent Hoffey was something of a stretch, but Mrs. Gerhardt's anger was entirely understandable. I'd also started to see that her initial rebuff wasn't either personal or political. Instead, it was another phenomenon I'd come to recognize as fairly common in places like this—a mind-set with quasi-religious tones. She was a proud, rigid woman, who viewed life in concrete terms. Everybody should fit neatly into pigeonholes, know exactly who they were, and do exactly what they were supposed to. That would keep the universe operating in proper order. When trouble occurred, it was because somebody had dropped the ball, and more often than not, the victims brought it on themselves.

Thus, along with the other heartaches that fate had brought to her and her family, she keenly felt a loss of dignity. Locking the door against any further intrusions was an attempt to salvage that; it gave her a measure of control.

As Renee and I drove homeward along Phosphor's main drag, the patina of charm that I'd imagined earlier was missing. Maybe it was only because the sun had dropped behind the mountains, and that sporadic warmth had given way to the cloudy, chilly reality of the late afternoon.

But there were too many weathered FOR SALE signs, and they had the hopeless air of scruffy hitchhikers that nobody would ever pick up, stranded in the middle of nowhere. The streets were empty of shoppers or moving vehicles, although the parking spaces in front of the town's two bars were full. The only customer at the little burger drive-in was a middle-aged man in a beat-up old station wagon, who appeared to be just sitting there.

A group of teenagers had clustered at the high school athletic field, but these had a different look than the daypack-toting crowd we'd seen earlier; they were sitting in their pickup trucks or leaning against them, some smoking, but otherwise inert. Maybe it was that same gunmetal sky that gave their faces a hard, hungry cast as they watched us strangers pass by. It seemed clear that they were well acquainted with having nowhere to go, nothing to do, and no expectations of anything better—easy prey for alcoholism, the new Black Plague of meth-amphetamine, and aimless rage that often led to violence.

The ripple effect of the Dead Silver Mine's failure was the single major point that I had taken away from talking with the Gerhardt women. They hadn't preached or even talked openly about it, but it had seeped out through their words again and again.

The mine's promise of prosperity had lured people to move to this area, buy and build homes, start and expand busi-nesses. Most were betting on the income and borrowing over their heads. When the economic house of cards collapsed, it fell hard. People simply packed up and disappeared. Store win-dows got boarded up and buildings abandoned. Banks were left holding dozens of properties they had no hope of selling. The tax base plummeted, taking support for schools and public services along with it.

The situation got still worse a few years later, with the closing of the sawmill that was Phosphor's only other main-stay industry. The cause involved the usual conflict—corpo-rate greed for quick profit versus environmental sanctions and lawsuits—complicated by murky political issues like lumber tariffs with Canada. The mill owners, longtime local residents, cut their own profit margin down to subsistence, but finally couldn't afford the soaring price of raw logs, and sometimes couldn't get them at all.

In practical terms, that seemed insane. The surrounding forests were full of trees ready for harvest, including large tracts damaged by fires or insects which would rot if they weren't taken soon. Phosphor Country was full of experienced loggers who would gladly do the work.

But, like the old joke went, you couldn't get there from here.

It was all too easy to understand the anger and frustra-tion—not just in Phosphor, but in other places all over the country with parallel situations—at being pawns in a giant Monopoly game, controlled from distant boardrooms and government agencies and universities, but played out on their turf and to their loss.

Renee and I had steered the conversation unobtrusively toward whether that might have motivated Astrid's murder, but the Gerhardts seemed to genuinely believe not. They knew everybody in the area and had heard every scrap of gossip. Without doubt, there were men around Phosphor who'd had both the motive and the temperament. But, like Buddy Pertwee, Janie and her mother had never made any solid connection. Tina had felt the same way—the killer was a stranger.

Of course, that didn't mean they were right.

CHAPTER 48

THE CONSTRICTIVE FEEL OF PHOSPHOR eased off as we drove home, through forest that gradually opened up into ranch land and then the miles-wide expanse of the Helena Valley, funneling into the apex of the old part of town rising up against the mountains to the south. We arrived in the last throes of after-work traffic. a joke by big-city standards, but it had thickened enough over the past years to become a nuisance. At least it had a healthy bustle.

Instead of going straight to my cabin, we detoured past Renee's to make sure everything was okay. That neighborhood was well removed from the hum of commerce, and the streets were quiet as usual. Her house seemed fine from the outside, but I wanted to go in and take a look around. There was no telling who else might know she was back in town.

I still had very clear memories of the last time I'd pushed open that front door, and getting met with a blast of gunfire—so clear that as I got out of my truck, I had to stop and hyperventilate for a few seconds.

But this time, I never made it that far. Instead, I had a different déjà vu, a tangible one. A couple hundred yards up the hillside, a dark-colored SUV was moving through the trees;

apparently it had been stopped there and was leaving, accelerating onto the street.

The spot was exactly where I'd seen a dark blue SUV do exactly the same thing, right after Professor Callister's funeral—as if the driver had been watching the house.

I couldn't swear that this was the same vehicle, but it sure the hell looked similar.

Renee was fussing with something in her purse and hadn't yet gotten out of my truck. She looked up, startled, when I swung myself back in and jammed the key into the ignition. The old rig rocked with torque as the engine caught, and we both rocked with it as I wrestled it in and out of her driveway in a fast three-point turn, then stomped on the gas.

"Watch the cross streets for that son of a bitch," I told Renee. "If we get close enough, take the license number."

"What son of a bitch?" She was staring at me, her left hand braced against the dash and the other clutching her door handle. I realized she didn't have any idea what I was doing.

"Somebody was watching the house. Blue SUV, medium size, few years old."

"O-kay," she said uncertainly, still clinging to her handholds.

Two blocks farther, her quiet street intersected with the broader route of Montana Avenue, leading up the hill where the SUV had been parked. A couple of cars were approaching on it. They didn't have a stop sign; I did. I blew right through it, flashing my headlights and leaning on the horn. Brakes squealed and other horns blared back, but we got through untouched. We came out of the skidding left turn headed uphill, and I rammed the accelerator to the floor again. The engine throbbed with the strain of the steep climb, rattling the windows.

When we got to where I'd seen the SUV, it had disappeared.

I kept going on Montana, hoping that the driver had done the same. The street continued more or less straight on into the hills; I could see quite a ways ahead, and while a vehicle might briefly be hidden in a dip or curve, it would reappear within seconds.

It didn't. Either he also had his foot on the floor or he'd turned off. Some of the intersecting streets eventually led back into Helena or out of town, but almost all of them wound through newer developments laid out in labyrinthine lanes and cul-de-sacs.

I slowed the truck and glanced at Renee. She shook her head unhappily.

"I never saw it," she said.

Maybe the SUV driver had known we were after him, and hauled ass. Maybe we just weren't due this particular bit of luck.

The blaring of a horn behind us jerked my gaze to the rear-view mirror. A car was coming up on us fast. It damn near rear-ended us, then whipped around to pass, with the very pissed-off-looking guy behind the wheel leaning across the seat to give me the finger. It must have been one of the vehicles I'd almost collided with, back at the stop sign. I didn't blame him.

Out of frustration and stubbornness, I cruised around a few more minutes, then pulled over where the SUV had been parked. As I'd expected, the vantage point was excellent, on a downhill slope, hidden from passing cars, with a clear view of Renee's house—including into her bedroom windows.

It was time to report in to Gary Varna.

CHAPTER 49

TWO HOURS LATER, JUST AS dusk was giving way to night, I drove back to my cabin, alone.

Gary had decided to take the wraps off this case and start his people working it actively. He had to assume that someone was watching Renee, and that that someone might be the murderer of Astrid Callister.

He had also fired me, politely but firmly, as Renee's bodyguard. From here on she needed a professional, and tonight that was going to be Gary himself—she would stay with him and his wife. First thing in the morning, he would take her to the airport and put her on the red-eye to spend some time with a friend from college who lived in Arizona. She might have to work out a plan to stay hidden indefinitely.

I was fervent with thanks to all the powers in the universe that we'd been alerted in time to get her to safety. She assured me she'd call as soon as she got settled, and no doubt we could work out a way to see each other if that was how things shaped up.

Still, she was gone from my life again.

PART V

CHAPTER 50

I TOSSED RESTLESSLY THROUGH MOST of the night, then got up early and spent a couple of hours drinking coffee and thinking things over, waiting for Gary or Renee to call and let me know what was in the offing. But whatever that was, it probably wouldn't involve me, and I wasn't sure of what to do next.

I'd made it clear to Gary that I'd be happy to help if he could use me, and he'd said he'd keep that in mind. But with the cops stepping in, amateur hour was over, and I didn't want to risk doing anything that might get in their way or muddy the waters. I was healed up well enough to start working at Split Rock again and I couldn't keep ignoring that job forever, but neither could I imagine trying to get back into it right now.

So I puttered around my place, mulling and fretting, until the phone finally rang about eight-thirty. For once, I jumped at it.

But the tense harsh voice that spoke into my ear was Madbird's.

"Darcy didn't show up for work," he said, with no preliminaries. "I'm at her apartment; I broke in. She ain't here but her car and purse are, and things don't look right. I need the cops, but I ain't sure they'll listen when I point them at Fraker. If you'd call the sheriff, that might get things moving."

"You really think he did something to her?" The opposite had flashed across my mind right off—that Fraker might have gotten horny enough to patch things up with Darcy. But Madbird would be way on top of all those kinds of possibilities. That he even considered calling the police was a measure of how concerned he was, and his next words iced that.

"He threatened her yesterday," Madbird said. "I just found that out; Hannah wouldn't tell me before."

Jarred out of my own little stew pot, I said, "I'll call Gary right now. See you as soon as I can get there."

CHAPTER 51

THE SCENE AT DARCY'S APARTMENT was official but low-key. With someone as prominent as Seth Fraker involved, this matter would be kept discreet, at least to start with. From the outside, it looked like a burglary or another relatively minor matter; the only signs of police presence were two Helena city units parked in the lot with lights off and a cop posted at the door. But several more men were inside the place, probably detectives and technicians.

I was grateful to see that Gary Varna had shown up in person. Nothing could make Madbird feel much better, but that would help.

Madbird and I talked quietly for a minute, and I learned the lead-up series of events. Yesterday, Darcy had told Hannah and Pam Bryce that she and Fraker had argued, with anger and frustration running high on both sides. Fraker spoke words to the effect that women had tried to pressure him in the past, and he knew how to teach them a lesson. When Darcy scoffed, he bristled and said, "One of them laughed just like that. She went swimming one night and never came back."

He had to be referring to the incident on St. Martin island when his lady companion had drowned—a chilling confirmation that there'd been something far more sinister involved than his supposed efforts to save her.

But no one had ever told Darcy about that, and she assumed that Fraker was just making it up. Pam and Hannah both knew about it, but decided not to tell Madbird because of well-grounded concern that it would push him into confronting Fraker, with predictable consequences. Instead, they worked on Darcy to convince her that Fraker might be dangerous and she'd better back off.

Then Darcy didn't show up for work this morning and Pam got scared. She contacted Hannah, who called Darcy's cell phone repeatedly. She had been answering Hannah's calls without hesitation, but now the phone just rang. Hannah finally confessed to Madbird about the threat. He drove immediately to Darcy's, jimmied the door—the deadbolt wasn't locked—and found the apartment empty, with her purse there and the cell phone in it.

The most likely guess seemed to be that Fraker had come by and talked her into going somewhere with him, maybe in a spur-of-the-moment rekindling of passion. With any luck, she was safe in a motel room and she'd turn up before long.

But there was also concern that he'd lured her out on some pretext—say, called her to come sit in his truck and talk to him—and then taken off with her against her will. It was hard to believe he was crazy or stupid enough to harm her, but then again, he was an ugly drunk.

Gary Varna came stalking over to us, looking as grim as Madbird, which was easy to understand. A twelve-year-old murder case erupting out of the blue was trouble enough. Now, right on its heels, came the disappearance of a young woman, with a highly visible politician implicated.

"Fraker went to work this morning same as ever," Gary said. "Claims he doesn't know anything about this, but he agreed to talk to us. I'm heading back downtown."

Of course Fraker would deny it and act like all was normal, while he came up with a cover story.

Gary wanted Madbird on hand to consult with. My own presence wasn't required; the police might interview me at some point, but I was far down the priority list. Still, I decided to go along and keep Madbird company. I knew that beneath his stoicism he was bristling with tension.

I went out to my truck, climbed in, and started it up. My windshield was misted from a new weather system that was bringing back wintry gloom. The temperature had dropped a good fifteen degrees since the recent couple of balmy days, and heavy wet clouds threatened rain or even snow. I turned the defrost to high; the old fan whirred and screeched—another of the endless repairs that I hadn't found time to get around to—and I had to click it on and off a couple of times to settle it down.

My thoughts were still with Madbird, and maybe it was that clicking sound that caused a sudden connection in my mind between him and something I'd forgotten but that had been hovering in my subconscious.

Right now Madbird was staying on the fringes of the buzzing activity, stony-faced, appearing detached. But that was far from the case; I'd come to recognize the same quality in a lot of Native Americans. They might seem to be absorbed in work, talk, drinking or playing pool in a bar, but behind that screen, they were intensely observant and aware of everything that was going on around them. Above all, they were watching people, gauging what was likely to happen in the immediate situation and whether somebody new would turn out in the long term to be a friend, enemy, or other.

The connection went back two days, to when Renee and I were about to leave for Missoula and we'd stopped by Evvie Jessup's realty office. I'd noticed her husband Lon in the background, where he usually seemed to stay. I'd put that down to the social awkwardness of a bluff, outdoorsy man dealing with people he didn't know.

But now, I was struck by the same sense I'd just gotten from Madbird—that Lon Jessup, behind his outward shyness and tinted glasses, was carefully taking account of everything going on around him.

Indians possessed that kind of wariness for good reason, but I'd rarely if ever seen it in the kind of man that Jessup appeared to be. Was it innate to him? The result of a harsh upbringing?

Or did it stem from circumstances that had come about later in his life—that had created a need for constant vigilance?

I realized I knew hardly anything about Lon—nothing at all about his past except Renee's mention that he'd been friends with Astrid and Professor Callister. It was a safe bet that he'd been inside the Professor's study and knew its layout. While Madbird and I were working there, he had dropped by and unobtrusively checked it out. He'd seen Renee wearing Astrid's earring at the Professor's funeral—and then hadn't come to the reception afterward, an abrupt and surprising derailment of what he and Evvie had obviously intended. And if the SUV driver had, in fact, been watching Renee, Lon was one of the few people who knew that she had come back to Helena within the past couple of days.

I felt my skin prickle lightly, the kind of sensation that old-timers used to say came from somebody stepping on your grave.

CHAPTER 52

INSTEAD OF HEADING DOWNTOWN TO the courthouse, I drove to Evvie Jessup's real estate office. Madbird and Gary wouldn't miss me for a while, if at all, and hanging around worrying about Darcy wasn't going to help her.

I pulled my truck into a parking lot across the busy strip of Eleventh Avenue, staying screened by other vehicles, and found a spot where I could see into the office plate glass windows without being noticed by anyone inside there. I didn't have a real plan—I just wanted another look at Lon Jessup, to watch him while I thought things over.

But Evvie was alone in the front room, sitting at her desk, talking on the phone, doing business or maybe gathering the gossip she was notorious for.

Another connection took place in my head. Through her, Lon had a direct pipeline into a lot of behind-the-scenes information in this town—maybe including police activity.

I'd never heard any mention of Lon as a suspect, including from Renee. I didn't know if he'd been looked at and vetted, or simply never considered. But I hadn't gone straight to Gary to ask because I didn't want to be the boy who cried wolf, especially when he was so busy with other concerns, and more especially when those were vital to Madbird. This notion of mine was nothing but a fancy, and probably a wildly unfounded one—I couldn't even call it speculation.

There was another reason I kept it to myself. The last time I'd been in a really serious situation I was overwhelmed, without a clue, scared shitless. Madbird had informed me solemnly that I'd stepped into a different world—one that had been there all along, coexisting and intertwining with the one I knew, but that I'd been oblivious to. Without his guidance I'd have been lost there for good, and very possibly would have died.

That hadn't turned around one hundred and eighty degrees by any means, but I no longer felt helpless. I'd become aware of an edge to it, an intensity, that brought me to life in an electric way. I couldn't truthfully say I enjoyed that like Madbird did, but it sure the hell was exciting.

Now I wanted to push it some—and this time I was the one hunting instead of the one on the run.

Over several minutes of watching Evvie's office, I didn't seen any sign of Lon. He might have been in the back, but I decided to move on and take a look at their home.

I remembered Renee describing the place as being off old Highway 282 near Montana City, a few miles south. Much of that area was former ranch land that had been carved up and developed fairly recently, and there was a maze of spur roads looping in and out.

But I didn't have to cruise long to find the Jesssups' mailbox; it was right on the highway, although they didn't sacrifice any privacy on that count. The property was pristine, meadowland in front that merged into timber, at least a couple dozen acres and maybe more. Their house was set so far back in the trees I could only see flashes of its blue sheet metal roof.

I wasn't about to go driving in there and risk Lon spotting me, but half a mile farther along, a gravel road turned off that side of the highway and led several miles into National Forest land. I'd driven it when I was a teenager, along with pretty much every other back road in this part of the state; I didn't remember it well, but it had to roughly skirt the Jessups' property.

I made my way along it, orienting myself by occasional glimpses of the blue roof, and found a suitable place to pull off into the woods. I rummaged through the assorted baggage I carried in the truck and dug out an old Bushnell rifle scope that I used for glassing game on hunting trips. If anybody came along and saw me, I'd shove the scope in my jacket and act like I'd stopped to take a leak. But that didn't seem likely, particularly in this dank weather; the landscape was deserted to the point of looking forlorn.

A short hike later, I came to a copse of aspen that offered a good view and I settled down with the scope. Now I could see that the house was a beauty, a big prow-fronted cedar home with a huge deck that included a covered hot tub. The interior was probably close to five thousand square feet. The going rate for something like that ran well over a hundred dollars per square foot. Depending on how much land there was, the overall property had to be worth a couple of million and maybe several. Evvie came from money and maybe Lon did, too. For sure, they weren't paying for this with a desultory real estate business.

There were no signs of Lon here, either, or any other life—no lights or flicker of a TV screen showing through the windows, no vehicles parked around, no dogs or cats. The rail fence that fronted the highway was built for looks more than function; there didn't appear to be any livestock to contain. The scene could have been the kind of sterile advertisement you saw in glossy magazines that sold the West.

Back from the highway, the rail fence gave way to older barbed wire, probably part of the original ranch. I got to my feet and followed it, maintaining a good distance and staying in the trees—curious as to how far the property extended and what else might be on it. There were no outbuildings or other structures that I could see. After about a mile, the fence ended in a little coulee.

Before I turned back, I stopped and spent a minute peering through the scope—and glimpsed what looked like fresh tire tracks across a patch of bare muddy earth.

They were hard to follow; most of the ground was thick with pine duff. But I picked up a couple more traces, running from the direction of the house toward the swale.

Well, there was nothing unusual about someone driving a vehicle on their property. Lon might have been cutting firewood, hunting varmints, or doing something else perfectly ordinary.

But I was far out of sight of their house by now and there still hadn't been a whisper of human presence anywhere around. I couldn't see any reason why it would hurt to take a closer look, so I kept on walking.

The coulee was only ten or fifteen feet deep, choked with brush and deadfall. There was no way to drive through it for as far as I could see, certainly not in the area that the tire tracks seemed to lead toward. But I noticed a big clump of debris in there, much thicker than the surroundings. Duff was piled on top of the brush in a way that didn't look like it had fallen there naturally.

Kind of like a giant pack rat nest.

I put the scope to my eye again. Inside the clump, I could just make out a few bits of metal, gleaming dully in the cold gray morning light.

I shoved the scope into my pocket and trotted the couple hundred yards to the spot.

Son of a bitch if the metal didn't belong to a dark blue, mid-'90s Ford Explorer, just like the SUV that had been watching Renee's house.

Madbird's attempts to educate me were bearing fruit. I'd started to learn that everybody had something to hide.

CHAPTER 53

I DROVE BACK TO HELENA as fast as I could make it, ripped up between adrenaline about Lon Jessup and worry about Darcy.

Finding the SUV was far from conclusive, but it fit in well. The immediate surmise was that Lon had seen Renee and me come chasing after the SUV, and he'd hidden it because he knew that connecting that vehicle to him would be enough to start investigators looking harder. He was already worried on other counts. Although the cache we'd found in the study was wiped clean of fingerprints, forensic technology now was so sophisticated that a single hair from head or body, a fleck of skin, or a bit of dried saliva could identify him. And this time he wasn't dealing with backwoods sheriffs who weren't interested in pressing the case—he'd have Gary Varna on his ass, along with shrewd, determined Renee.

Madbird was pacing in front of the courthouse when I arrived.

"Is Gary here?" I said.

"Yeah, him and his people are talking to Fraker."

"They getting anywhere?"

"I ain't heard much yet, but no surprises. He swears the

last time he saw Darce was when they had that fight a couple nights ago. Says the drowning story's bullshit, he was just trying to scare her." Madbird's eyes narrowed into his scrutinizing gaze. "What's going on? You look all amped up."

I felt almost ashamed for intruding on the concern about Darcy, but there was nothing else to be done.

"I've got news," I said. "Come on, I'll tell you both."

We went inside and I managed to convince Faith, the kindly but tough lady desk sergeant, to pull Gary from the interrogation.

"I wish there was a better time to tell you this," I said when he came out. "It's about Astrid. Did anybody ever look at Lon Jessup?"

Gary frowned. "Lon Jessup. I know who he is, but I don't recall him ever being in trouble. And no, his name never came up in any of the case records I saw."

"I got a wild hair," I said. "Started putting things together and drove out to his place. I found that SUV, covered up with brush."

Gary's jaw tightened so hard it looked like he was going to break teeth. I assumed he was pissed because I'd overstepped my bounds by going out on my own.

But what he said was "Well now, that changes everything, don't it?"

At the same time, Madbird's eyes widened in sudden comprehension. Then they turned to slits.

"Guess we're looking at the wrong motherfucker," he said.

"I already figured Fraker's a dead end," Gary said. "He's babbling as fast as his mouth will move. The kicker is, we asked to search his truck and he shoved the keys at us. There was a clump of long black hair and a scrap of cloth caught on a door hinge—nylon and elastic, like it was torn from a woman's underwear. Right there in front of God and everybody."

I blinked in surprise. "That's the kicker that he's innocent? How do you figure?"

"He ain't that stupid. If he'd struggled with her, he'd know it would leave traces, and he'd have stalled us."

"Maybe he was just running too scared to notice it," I said.

Both men skewered me with impatient glares.

"What?" I said, bewildered.

"You brung us the mail, Hugh—now read it," Madbird growled. "Jessup gets spooked enough to hide his rig, Darcy goes missing right after. It's a smoke screen, that's how he operates."

I stood there, stunned, as his meaning filtered in. It was Lon Jessup who had abducted Darcy. He'd planted the hair and nylon in Fraker's truck, just like he had planted the photos we'd found in Professor Callister's study, and for the same reason—to frame another suspect and head the police away from himself.

He'd have known via Evvie's gossip mill that Fraker was seeing Darcy and had a rep for being rough with women. An adulterous public figure whose girlfriend disappeared was a scandal that would suck up law enforcement resources and sideline the Callister murder case indefinitely, giving Lon time to make his next move.

But the really chilling implication was that he couldn't afford to let Darcy return and tell the truth.

We were dealing with a man capable of committing murder purely as a ruse.

Gary was already issuing orders to Faith, the desk sergeant. "Call Jessup Real Estate and get Evvie Jessup. Tell her not to move from where she is or touch a phone, I'm coming over to talk to her. Start running a background check on her husband, Lon. Then get ready to mobilize all available personnel, on duty and off—surrounding counties, state troopers,

Fish and Wildlife, including air support. Jessup's a big bearded guy about fifty. He may have a young Indian female with him. I'll give you the go-ahead or abort as soon as I know more."

He swung back around to us. "If we go with it, it's a risk, Madbird. I hope you're okay with that."

It was a risk for Gary, too. As soon as Lon became aware of search planes and helicopters, he would know. Crafty and dangerous as he was, he might succeed in escaping.

"There ain't any choice from my end," Madbird said.

"Mine, either," Gary said.

CHAPTER 54

I'D NEVER ACTUALLY BEEN INSIDE Evvie Jessup's office, but it was just like thousands of others—nondescript carpet and furnishings that were neither expensive nor cheap, a few paintings like you'd find in better motels, and fluorescent lighting that gave everything a polyester sheen. The temperature was warm enough to dampen my armpits and the air was close, pervaded by the sickly-sweet smell of a freshener.

Evvie was sitting behind her desk, looking extremely piqued. As soon as Gary stepped in the door, she challenged him.

"What's this about?"

"I want to know where your husband is, Evvie."

"I have no objections to talking to you, Sheriff," she said crisply. "But I'd like to know why. And in private," she added, with a haughty glance at Madbird and me.

Gary stalked to her desk, planted a fist down on it hard enough to make her cringe, and leaned his face forward to within a foot of hers.

"We're talking *murder*, and you're implicated," he said harshly. "There's another young woman's life on the line right now. You play games with me one more second, I'll do my god-damnedest to see to it you get old in prison."

I never saw a human being's face change like Evvie Jessup's did.

It took her several tries to start talking. The words came out in a shaky voice hardly above a whisper.

"I don't know where he is. Maybe fishing. Maybe off on business."

"Business! He's got business, all right—he kidnapped that girl and he aims to come back without her."

Evvie's mouth quivered and tears streaked her careful makeup. It was not a pretty sight.

"I don't know anything about this, I swear. He was gone when I woke up, I didn't hear him leave. I—I take pills."

"Where *would* he go? Where does he fish?"

"All over," she said helplessly.

Gary exhaled explosively and stepped back from the desk, shaking his head. There were thousands of square miles of stream-filled woodlands around here.

"Do you at least know the vehicle he's driving, for Christ's sake?"

"He must have taken his pickup truck, it was gone this morning. But I think he has others he keeps different places."

"You *think*?"

"He has secrets. He goes away and says it's business, but he takes my money and runs around, gambling and having affairs. I don't dare argue with him, I stopped a long time ago. He can be very frightening." She covered her face with her hands and started sobbing, with mascara-darkened tears dripping through her fingers. "Oh, God, I always knew there was something wrong. What is going *on*? Please tell me."

I actually started feeling sorry for her.

Gary ignored her and took out his belt phone. "That's an affirmative, Faith—get the show moving," he said into it. "Aircraft crisscrossing low, I want him to know we're looking. Search area's everywhere within four hours' drive. Check out all vehicles registered to him, but he might be on foot in the woods, and none of that's for sure." He paused to glare at Evvie. "And send a unit over here to take Mrs. Jessup in for further questioning. Anything yet on that BG check?"

He listened for a few seconds, then grimaced and said, "Okay, thanks. I'll be back in a few minutes for a war council."

Now Gary's expression was sour, the look of a man realizing that he'd been taken in by a long ugly con game played out right under his nose, and he was seriously pissed at himself for not seeing it.

"They don't know who he really is, but they know who he ain't," he told us. "The only Lonnie Jessup they can find that matches his date and place of birth died in 1956, at the ripe old age of nineteen months. How about that, Evvie? Did you know *that* was one of his secrets?"

She buried her face deeper in her hands and rocked in her seat, her sobs rising to a thin wail.

CHAPTER 55

MADBIRD AND I SPENT MOST of the next few hours outside the courthouse to stay out of the way, taking short walks around the neighborhood, then coming back to check in and glean whatever information trickled out. We heard the drone of the low-flying search planes and helicopters and we occasionally glimpsed one, but they had a vast area to cover; it had started out being as far as a vehicle could drive in any direction, which meant a rough circle about five hundred miles in diameter, and it grew exponentially as time passed.

So did our anxiety. Our grim hope was that he would keep her alive in order to make her walk to the destination—if he was in the woods, he wouldn't be able to drive far on the backcountry roads, still mired in snow and mud this time of year—and Gary had rushed the aircraft into service to let him know that he was made, so he would realize that killing her was futile.

But they might have been too late. And he might do it anyway.

There'd been no sightings of anyone matching the description of either Lon or Darcy, or of the pickup truck registered to him, and the police didn't know for sure that he was driving that vehicle, anyway.

It was turning out that nobody knew much about Lon, and there was a lot to know. The information that they were piecing together—some from Evvie, some from a search of the Jessup house, some from sources those led to—was painting a picture of a man who, behind his bluff good ol' boy exterior, led a very complex life.

For openers, his true identity was still a mystery. He had used a time-honored method of establishing a false past— obtaining the records of a child born around the same time as himself who had died in infancy, and with that documentation acquiring a Social Security number and driver's license, establishing credit, and so on.

Then there was the question of exactly what he *did*. The tacit assumption had been that he was sort of a sportsman and gentleman rancher, and a businessman who helped Evvie with her realty transactions and had investments of his own. But the ranch was devoid of livestock, his business trips were in fact gambling and partying junkets, and he paid no attention to the real estate operation—except that he had pushed his wife to wangle the job of selling the Callister house, no doubt so that he could keep tabs on Renee and the photo cache he'd planted.

He didn't have or make any money of his own—it all came from Evvie's inherited wealth—but he'd set up at least two corporate entities. They were clearly fronts which didn't conduct any tangible commerce; it appeared that he used them mainly as conduits to sock away large chunks that he drained from her, no doubt into bank accounts that would be difficult or impossible to trace. Through them, he also leased vehicles, with frequent turnover—enumerating them and getting their descriptions was another paper trail the cops would have a hell of a time unraveling—and a network of storage units, where he maybe kept some of them and Lord knew what else.

By all indications so far, Evvie was being honest about

what she knew, although it was possible that this was an act she'd long been rehearsing.

According to her, Lon Jessup had first come to Montana about fifteen years ago to visit Astrid and Professor Callister. Astrid introduced him to her longtime friend Evvie—in her thirties, unmarried with no suitors, but rich—and romance bloomed.

The romance part didn't last long, but it wasn't one of those sordid situations that descended into abuse and despair. Lon simply wasn't interested in her. She and her money were a convenience, and he made it clear that he intended to use them as he pleased and do what he wanted. It took her a while to accept that, as it would anyone, but he was very effective at getting it across. He didn't use violence or outright menace. He was the kind of man who didn't have to.

Once that was settled, they got along quite well. He was outwardly solid and decent, and above all he was a husband, rescuing her from spinsterhood and giving her that societal credential. If there was a hole in Evvie Jessup's heart, she had plenty of things to fill it up with that most other people didn't.

But it had never occurred to her that he might be an entirely different person than he claimed.

He had never been a suspect in Astrid's murder. Besides his being a good friend of the Callisters and a respectable citizen, with no hint of a motive, Evvie remembered distinctly that he had been out of town when it occurred and had hurried home to offer his support to the family. But that was an alibi almost certain to fall apart under new police scrutiny.

What the motive might have been was still unknown. But an intriguing connection had surfaced. Lon had occasionally let something drop to Evvie that indicated military training— as a Navy SEAL, she thought. However, he had insisted that she never mention anything about it.

The fact that he didn't want that known inclined me

perversely to believe there was something to it. I'd never met a man who denied that kind of credential, and I'd run into several who claimed it when it wasn't true. It was a measure of how seriously Lon Jessup wanted his background erased.

Further, before coming to Montana, he'd been living in Colorado—the home of the phantom ex–Special Forces ranger who supposedly had led Astrid on a raid to shoot up a gyppo logging camp.

And who Astrid had counted on to blow up the Dead Silver Mine.

I remembered Buddy Pertwee's story about her sudden emotional upset and change of attitude not long before her death, as if something had gone very wrong.

Was Lon Jessup the commando? Did he and Astrid have a falling-out, maybe involving the demolition plan? Something that angered or threatened him enough to drive him to murder her?

Such as fear that the past he'd worked so hard to conceal might be exposed?

Then, just after three o'clock that afternoon, one of Gary's deputies stuck his head out the courthouse door and yelled at Madbird and me to get our ass inside.

A helicopter had spotted a woman with long dark hair in the mountains around the old mining town of Basin. She had run from the cover of trees out into a clearing, frantically waving her arms to flag them down.

CHAPTER 56

THE WOMAN WAS DARCY, AND the copter was able to land and get her on board. The immediate report was that she was cold, shaken, and scratched up, but otherwise unharmed.

The cops at the courthouse whooped and cheered and everybody exchanged high fives. Madbird got a big hug from Faith, and even Gary Varna and I gripped each other around the shoulders for a quick, awkward embrace.

They estimated that it would take another forty minutes or so to fly Darcy to the Helena airport and drive her here to the courthouse. Madbird called Hannah to tell her the news, then walked outside again. I went with him, assuming we were going to wait out front for Darcy to arrive, but he strode on to his parked van.

He went into the gear he carried in the back and got out a favorite Puma hunting knife and a whetstone. Then he sat inside the open rear doors and honed the knife, drawing the blade carefully across the stone in even, precisely angled strokes. He kept its edge like a straight razor anyway. After this attention, it would literally split hairs.

He paid no attention to me and didn't speak a word. I decided to leave him alone.

Madbird finished the task to his satisfaction, set the knife aside, and dug out a pair of insulated hunting boots. He laced those on and was rummaging around through his other stuff when the sheriff's cruiser carrying Darcy pulled into the parking lot.

She jumped out of the car, rushed to Madbird, and clung to him, sobbing, face buried in his chest.

"Okay, baby girl, okay," he muttered, patting her back gruffly. "Hannah's on her way here. She's bringing some burgers, you must be starving."

The deputies gently pried her loose from him, to take her inside and continue debriefing her. This time Madbird went with them. I stayed out of the way again and pieced together information as it was filtered to me.

The upshot was that while Lon Jessup had covered his bases with extraordinary cunning, he hadn't counted on the savvy and courage of a Blackfeet girl who'd grown up on the wild northern rez.

Early this morning, before dawn—Darcy remembered glimpsing her bedside clock reading 5:47—she had awakened to find a man beside her bed, holding a gun to her face.

When the police showed her a photo of Lon Jessup, she identified him positively, although he had shaved his beard and abandoned his tinted spectacles.

He had spoken to her soothingly, assuring her that he didn't intend harm, only wanted to have some fun. But he also warned her not to resist or cry out, and Darcy knew enough about weapons to realize that his pistol was small-caliber, probably a .22, with a sound suppressor on the muzzle; a shot would make less noise than the snap of a mousetrap. That, along with his chilling sense of authority, convinced her that he wouldn't hesitate to use it.

He ordered her to get dressed—and to go into her laundry hamper and give him the panties she had worn yesterday. Then they walked quietly out to his vehicle, where he had her crouch down on the floor of the passenger seat. She obeyed, assuming through her haze of fear and confusion that this would turn into a kinky sexual assault.

They went to a storage unit with a different vehicle parked inside it. He tied her up with an efficiency that made it clear he knew what he was doing, then zipped her into a mummy sleeping bag. Before he closed it over her face, he gripped several strands of her hair and yanked them from her head. He warned her again to stay quiet, and they took off on a longer drive.

This time, they paused along the way for several minutes—probably while Jessup broke into Seth Fraker's pickup truck to plant her hair and the nylon scrap from her panties.

After that they drove for most of an hour. She couldn't see anything, but the first and longest stretch was fast and relatively smooth—the highway to Basin. Then they turned off onto a slower, rougher road up into the mountains.

When they stopped for good, he pulled her out of the vehicle and freed her from the sleeping bag. They were deep in forest, far from any sign of humans. He untied her legs and they started walking.

By then, Darcy's mind had reached a state of frightening clarity. This man was not marching her out into the cold wet wilderness for sex. He made no more attempts to reassure her—didn't speak except for terse commands. And it had registered on her that he'd made no attempt to hide his face.

No doubt he was taking her to a remote hiding place, maybe one that he'd spotted on his fishing and hunting trips. The terrain was on the fringes of the Continental Divide—rugged, rarely traveled off-trail—and besides offering plenty of natural cover it was dotted with old mining excavations.

The odds that she ever would have been found were slim to nil.

She got her chance when they got to a deadfall-choked coulee and Jessup ordered her to stop; he climbed to the top of a small knoll, apparently trying to get his bearings. The distance between them still wasn't more than ten or fifteen yards, but as he scanned the surroundings, he half turned away from her. She sprinted the few steps to the ravine edge and threw herself over it, tumbling down the steep slope and digging her way frantically into its brush. He shouted at her to stop, and she thought she heard the popping sound of gunshots, but the cover was good and she wormed her way through it until she was shielded inside a jumble of rotting fallen timber.

Then began a desperate hide-and-seek, with her waiting, straining to listen for sounds of his pursuit—SEAL or not, he was a bulky fifty-year-old man, no match for lithe young Darcy in that kind of thick ground cover—and crawling farther each time she dared. He fired more shots that crashed through the brush around her, but she widened the distance between them steadily.

She guessed that the pursuit went on for an eternity of twenty or thirty minutes. Then, abruptly, the noise he made started to recede, and she wondered if he had given up and was heading back the way he'd come—or if that was what he wanted her to think.

She dug in, quietly covering herself with duff, and lay still for another hour, fearing that he'd found a vantage point and would see her if she moved. Eventually, she became aware of the drone of aircraft—and then, that the sound was more constant than just an occasional passing plane.

It finally dawned on her that that was probably what had scared Jessup into retreating. She dared to start moving again, at first still crawling and pausing to listen every few yards, then moving into thick forest and running. At least another hour passed before she heard a helicopter approaching close enough for her to flag down. By then she was on the edge of exhaustion.

Now all law enforcement resources were closing in on the area, looking for Lon Jessup. The immediate question was whether his vehicle was still where he'd left it when they started walking—whether he had gone back to it and gotten out, or was still on foot.

Darcy had only gotten a glimpse of the place, just enough to see that it was under the shelter of some decaying timbers. Now she couldn't describe the location with any accuracy; she'd never been in that country before, and she only had a rough idea of the distance and direction she'd traveled while running away. But authorities had identified a couple of possible sites and searchers were already on their way in to check them; the aircraft had narrowed their flyover zone and other personnel were ringing the overall area, hoping to spot and intercept Jessup.

It didn't take long for the experienced local men to get to those areas and relay back digital photos. Darcy quickly recognized the sagging, timbered overhang of an abandoned mine shaft in a cliffside; the tunnel was long since caved in, but the entrance formed a pocket big enough to shield a vehicle from casual view. Fresh tire tracks confirmed the find.

But the vehicle and Lon Jessup were gone.

Darcy hadn't gotten a good take on what he'd been driving, either; wrapped up in the sleeping bag, she'd barely seen it. She thought it was something like a Suburban or Expedition, off-white or gray, another of the generically common rides that Jessup seemed to favor, for reasons that were coming clear. It probably wouldn't have helped much, anyway. Interstate 15 was only a half hour's drive south, with highways branching off in all directions and places where he could rent or steal another car.

Madbird received the news with his usual stony face.

"Goddamn shame he ain't still in them woods," he said quietly.

Jessup had made a lucky decision to get the hell out of there. If he'd kept chasing Darcy long enough to get cut off from his vehicle, Madbird would have gone in after him, alone, and come back with his ears.

CHAPTER 57

As the excitement settled down notch by notch, I started realizing that I was worn out and deflated, drained by the long nerve-racking day. There was nothing that I could do here. I said my good-byes, let Gary Varna know I'd be at my place if anything came along, and headed home.

Of course, I was hoping there'd be a phone message from Renee.

During the hours of waiting, I'd had plenty of time to think about how this might affect the situation between us.

Her father was finally absolved of Astrid's murder. It was virtually certain that the killer was the man who called himself Lon Jessup. Renee had triumphed. The years of ugly suspicion were ended, and the hidden menace that had hovered over her was exposed and on the run.

The question remained as to whether Jessup posed a long-term threat to her. At this point, it didn't seem that he had anything to gain by harming her. But a mind like that was unfathomable.

Even with an APB out for him and national law enforcement agencies joining the hunt, I wasn't at all confident that he'd ever be caught. His escape plan hadn't worked like he wanted; he'd been forced to jump the gun. If he'd succeeded at diverting attention to Fraker, he'd have had time to quietly fade away while the police were occupied with Fraker, going on vacation or a "business trip" and never coming back. There'd have been no reason to connect Jessup to Darcy. If anyone eventually did get suspicious, he'd be long gone, and it was unlikely that they'd even try to pursue him.

Still, it was clear that he had the groundwork well laid. He'd gotten a head start of a couple of hours, and no doubt he had plenty of money stashed and another identity to slip into. Soon he'd be just another bland-faced, middle-aged, outwardly solid citizen with vague business interests. As long as he paid his way and didn't cause trouble, he'd be welcome most places in the world, no questions asked.

With any luck—and, I thought, in all likelihood—he wouldn't want to jeopardize his safety again, and he'd stay far away for the rest of his life.

That still left a lot of baggage for Renee and me to deal with, along with the other concerns of our very different lives—and the good man, Ian, who wanted to marry her.

The only thing that would resolve all that was time.

Driving out of town, I remembered that the larder in my cabin was bare, so I stopped at the usual market and bought deli fried chicken, potato salad, bacon and eggs for breakfast tomorrow, and a six-pack of Tecate beer. As I walked back across the parking lot to my truck, I realized that I was feeling and breathing the delicious spring air in a way I'd been oblivious to for the past weeks. I couldn't say that I'd achieved closure, but in spite of weariness, the worries that lingered, and problems that still lay ahead, a deep sense of of relief was penetrating into my being.

Then I heard a rumbling sound behind me. It was quiet—somehow stealthy—and approaching fast.

I turned to face it as its source came abreast of me—Ward Ackerman's big green rust bucket of a sedan. It was traveling ten or fifteen miles per hour, not aimed at me like he was going to run me down, but close enough to brush me. My instant thought was that he was going to slam on the brakes and jump out, and we'd go through another bullshit confrontation.

Instead, the son of a bitch threw open his door without slowing down. I just had time to cover my gut and chest with my right arm, like I was blocking a body punch. The door caught me hard enough to knock me clear off my feet and send me skidding, with the groceries flying in every direction.

Ward screamed something at me and stomped on the gas, screeching away and waving his raised middle finger out the open window.

But my bile was swept aside by a flood of illumination. My mind, all on its own, suddenly created—or maybe discovered—a realm called Pissant Purgatory, where all the nasty, sneaky little shitweasels like Ward would do time when they died. There were no burning flames, no demons with pitchforks. The punishment was that they were forced to hang around with others just like themselves, with no nonpissants to suck blood from.

I got up carefully, wary of my still-healing ribs. They let me know they'd been hit, but my elbow and upper arm had absorbed most of the shock. The only other part of me that felt impaired was my dignity. A couple of the eggs were broken, but otherwise the groceries were okay, too.

I gathered everything up, popped open a frothing can of beer, and drank it on the way home.

CHAPTER 58

THE LAST TREE-LINED STRETCH OF Stumpleg Gulch
Road opened into a football field–sized meadow at the front
of my property. My father had set the precedent of leaving a
few big firs around the cabin for shade, but otherwise clearing
a swath as a fire break, and I kept it that way.

So as I drove up to the gate, I had a clear view of a surprising and unsettling sight. My black tomcat was crouched
under the fence, not moving.

Like a lot of pets, he recognized the sound of familiar vehicles like mine and Madbird's, and he'd usually meet us, stalking around and yelling at us to say hello, or just complaining.

But he stayed right where he was, hunkered down tight.
He acted that way when he had a mouse or other varmint between his paws, but his tail would flip back and forth like a
windshield wiper, and within a few seconds he'd jump, bat
the critter around, and pin it down again, especially if he was
showing off for an audience.

Now he didn't so much as twitch.

I stopped the truck, got out, and knelt down beside him.
His eyes looked glazed, his chin was wet with drool, and he
was purring loudly.

"What's going on?" I said. I passed my hands over him

lightly, starting behind his ears—and immediately felt wet sticky fur at his left front shoulder. My fingers came away red with blood.

The bobcat. I'd damn near forgotten about him.

I stood and did a quick 360-degree scan of the surrounding tree line. The nearest cover was fifty yards away, and it was relatively thin for another ten or twenty yards beyond that; there were no suggestive shapes in there. Most likely the assault had happened someplace else and the tom had escaped, or maybe the bobcat had been spooked by the approach of my truck. But daylight was fading, and he could be hidden where I couldn't see.

I strode back to the pickup for the .41-Magnum pistol that Madbird had lent me, loaded it, and shoved it in my belt. Then I grabbed a hooded sweatshirt and went back to wrap up the tom. I'd never had to use an animal emergency room before, but I knew there was a veterinary hospital in town with an after-hours service.

"Come on, buddy," I said, picking him up gently. "You're going to hate this, but you've got to trust me."

He made a hoarse growl deep in his throat like he was ready to fight, but he stayed docile—a sign that he was badly hurt. It was a tribute to his toughness and a near miracle that with the big cat biting him so close to his head and throat, he'd managed to get away.

I carried him around to the passenger side of the truck to settle him on the floor, still watching the woods for any movement.

If I hadn't been on the alert like that, I'd never have seen the figure near the cabin, stealthily slipping behind a tree.

But, just as I'd known instantly when I first saw the bobcat that it wasn't a deer, I knew this wasn't the bobcat. It was hunched, but standing on two legs—human. And even in that glimpse, there was something familiar about the bulky shape.

I dropped to a crouch and lunged toward the back of the truck. There came the pop of two quick gunshots, the first one smashing into the passenger window and the second spanging off the metal behind me. I kept on scrambling around to the driver's side, got behind the protection of the rear wheel, and clawed the pistol from my belt.

I waited there, shaking, trying to understand who the fuck wanted to kill me *this* time.

The answer came fast. The reason the shape seemed familiar was because it was Lon Jessup. He must have come to get revenge for the part I'd played in outing him.

But the truth of that came clear fast, too. He had assumed that Renee would be with me. She was the one he wanted to kill.

I'd been an idiot to think he'd let her go. He knew perfectly well that everyone assumed he'd left the area, and he'd decided that murdering her now was a safer course than coming back in the future. In this isolated place, no one would hear his silenced gunshots or even know it had happened for a day or two—just like with Astrid and her lover, an eerie, ugly parallel.

And it was a gunshot from Jessup, not the bobcat, that had wounded my tom. He greeted strangers with the same kind of noisy show he put on for friends, letting them know that this was his place and they didn't belong here. Maybe Jessup had feared that the yowling would give him away. Maybe he was superstitious, and the feisty black cat had unnerved him. Most likely it was sheer meanness.

But that was what had saved me from already being dead—or worse, first being forced by Jessup to tell him what I knew about Renee's whereabouts.

That was when I made up my mind to kill him.

I'd heard that after you'd done it once, it was easier to do again. The first time had been unintentional, a fluke of self-defense, and I'd have done anything to relive that moment so it hadn't happened, even though the son of a bitch had it coming.

Now I just hoped to Christ I'd succeed.

I took off in a crouching run for the tree line across the road, keeping the truck between me and Jessup. The gunshots sounded like they had come from the silenced .22 pistol that Darcy had seen. At that range, moving fast, I'd be hard to hit—although he might also have a bigger pistol or a shotgun or rifle.

And he undoubtedly had a vehicle hidden nearby. He might already be on his way to it, figuring he'd blown his chance and he'd better get out of here.

Then again, he might be stalking me.

I was no Madbird, and no match for a man with SEAL-type training even if he was aging and out of shape. But I'd hunted all my life, and these woods had been my childhood playground. I knew every stick and stone. The fading daylight was in my favor; my eyes for the terrain were in my feet. The .41 Magnum was an excellent weapon for this, with long-range power and accuracy.

I settled the cat under a pine and kept on running down-road. For sure, I could cover ground faster than Jessup could, then work my way back up—cut him off he if drove out, or if he was still on foot, try to find him before he found me.

CHAPTER 59

I GLIDED ALONG LIKE MY feet were barely touching the earth, straining to listen for the rustling and cracking sounds of a big animal on the move. But the evening forest was as peaceful as an enchanted land in a fairy tale, with only an occasional birdcall and the whisper of the breeze through the treetops.

I worked my way around to a tree-sheltered rise that gave me a good perspective of the road and surrounding country toward my cabin, and waited for a longer time. I didn't want to put too much distance between us. If Jessup had seen me take off, he might guess what I was thinking and do the unexpected, like head in another direction.

After three full minutes, there was still no sight or sound of him, or of his vehicle. If I waited too long, I risked losing him.

I started back, this time in diagonal crisscrosses, going slowly in a stealthy crouch and setting each step carefully on the duff-covered ground, like I was zeroing in on an elk or buck. By now twilight was deep enough in the trees that I wasn't much more than a shadow, and I knew the paths where I could pass through noiselessly and still keep cover.

But my tense adrenaline high was cut by the fear that I was moving and he might be laying for me.

Then my straining ears picked up a sound that didn't belong—a metallic clank, coming from the direction of my gate, a few hundred yards ahead. I froze in place, trying to identify it. It was too loud for a pistol being cocked or loaded.

But whatever it was, it had to have come from Jessup.

I'd just started moving again when a much louder noise split the stillness. There was no mistaking this one—the growl of a vehicle engine starting up. I listened in disbelief, stunned that he could have hidden his ride so close to my place without me seeing it.

Then I recognized the rumble of my own pickup truck, familiar as a mother's voice.

That was what he'd been doing. I'd taken the keys out of the ignition, but somebody who knew their shit could hot-wire an old rig like mine in a minute or two.

The sounds kept coming fast—the engine revved, the clutch caught, and the tires spun. He was on his way toward me, fast.

I broke into a sprint for the road. But within a few seconds I realized that he wasn't staying on it—he was cutting off to the west where he could swing a wide loop, weaving through the trees until he got past me. I dug in a bootheel and spun to change direction and intercept him, gauging his progress by the sound.

I caught sight of the pickup just as it was coming abreast of me, thirty yards away, going like hell and bucking like a rodeo bull over the rough ground. It was hard to see clearly through the gloom and fir branches, and I couldn't make out his shape through the windows. I was hit by the abrupt terror that he wasn't even in there, that this was another of his diversions—that he'd wedged down the accelerator and he was really on foot, coming up behind me. But he had to be steering or he'd have piled into a tree by now. Probably he was sunk down in the seat peering over the dash.

I braced my right shoulder against a tree, spread my feet, inhaled deeply, and extended the big pistol with both hands, trying to sight just behind the steering wheel and two feet below the driver's windowsill. Following the bouncing speeding target was like trying to aim from a motorboat barreling through rough water.

It was the damnedest feeling, drawing down on the truck I'd loved and cared for all these years.

I released my breath and started squeezing off shots, letting the kickup of the barrel raise my aim a few inches each time. The .41 didn't make any little spang when it hit the metal. It sounded like John Henry rampaging through a junkyard with a pickax. The fifth round smashed a fist-sized hole in the window.

But the motherfucker kept right on going like he hadn't been hit by anything but a cloud of gnats.

Out of sheer frustration, I touched off the final round, now at a distance of fifty yards. I could just see a spiderweb of cracks streak the glass of my rear windshield before the old rig disappeared into the trees.

I screamed my rage to the darkening sky, then ran for my cabin. There I discovered that Jessup had cut a chunk out of my phone line.

By then, even the sound of my truck engine was long gone.

Renee's Subaru was still here and she'd left me the keys, but he'd done something to that, too—it was stone dead. My only other motorized transport was a '66 BSA Victor converted to a dirt bike, and I'd pulled the battery and drained the gas out of it last fall, tarped it up, and hadn't looked at it since. My nearest neighbor was a good fifteen-minute run away, and if they weren't home I'd have to break in to call the sheriffs. Splicing my own phone cable would be quickest; I had a partial spool of four-pair wire somewhere in a shed.

Finding it and making the repair took me another ten minutes—probably enough time for Jessup to drive my truck to wherever he'd stashed his own vehicle and get to the highway.

When I finished, I punched Gary Varna's number and braced myself to tell him that I'd had Lon Jessup in my sights for five clear shots, and he'd breezed on out of here as free as a bird.

CHAPTER 60

THE FLASHING RED AND BLUE of police beacons was not a sight that I ordinarily would have welcomed, but tonight I waited impatiently for their first distant flicker coming up my road. But time kept on passing—more than I expected, close to an hour. Gary had told me to stay put and he'd be along, but I was starting to fear that I'd misunderstood him.

When I finally glimpsed a vehicle approaching, it showed only headlights and turned out to be a single sheriff's cruiser.

I walked down to the gate to meet it and got there just as Gary climbed out. He looked weary, a little stooped, without his usual crispness.

"You can quit feeling sorry for yourself about your shooting," he said. "He piled up your truck at the bottom of Stumpleg Gulch. Took at least two rounds, smashed him up pretty good inside. Must have held on as long as he could and finally lost it."

I stared at Gary in disbelief. Then my gaze faltered and I turned away. Instead of exultation or even relief, it was like a cold steely hand reached inside me and twisted my guts.

"He's dead?" I said.

"Not yet—we sent him to the ER at St. Pete's. But from what I've heard so far, his odds don't look good."

The radio inside his car was crackling with brief, static-laced messages. Gary leaned back inside and switched it off.

"I know it'll be tough to shake off, Hugh, but you did the right thing," he said. "I wish I could say the same about myself. Before he came here, he killed Evvie."

My stare swung back to him.

"After we finished talking to her this afternoon, she wanted to go home and I let her," Gary said. "I figured Jessup was far away by then, and I never dreamed he'd do something like that, anyway. And I admit, I thought he might get in touch with her—I made her swear to call us if he did. Then when you told us he was still around, we called her and she didn't answer. Deputies went out there and found her shot point-blank."

Gary shook his head with a bleakness that gave me another of those inner clenches.

"It was my decision to let her go," he said again.

We stood there in heavy silence for a moment longer. The night wind was picking up, and not getting any warmer.

"Are you going back to town?" I said.

"Yeah, I better check in on Jessup. We'll need you to walk us through what happened up here, but it can wait till morning."

"Can I catch a ride with you? He shot my cat, too. I need to take him to a vet."

"Sure thing. Go get him, I'll radio ahead and tell them we're coming."

I'd built a fire in my woodstove and settled the tom on a blanket in front of it—the only help I could give him. He was still breathing, but he'd shut down further, eyes closed and no longer purring.

CHAPTER 61

THE PEOPLE AT THE VET hospital were pleasant and concerned, ready to whisk the tom away to surgery as soon as I brought him in. I watched him go with the helpless feeling of seeing a loved one disappear through those OR doors into a mysterious realm where ordinary people weren't allowed and everything was out of your control, and you knew they might not return alive.

I walked back outside to Gary, who'd stayed in the car to make calls.

"They're losing Jessup; he's passing in and out," he said. "I'm going over to St. Pete's. You want to come?"

"Seeing that evil prick is the last thing in the world I want."

"That ain't really a question, Hugh. You'll feel better in the long run, I guarantee."

The authority in his tone brought me around to something I'd never thought about—whether Gary had ever shot anyone. It was a good bet that in thirty years of Montana law enforcement, he'd been where I was now.

I exhaled tautly, and nodded.

He put the car in gear, flicked on the lightbar, and we started off. I'd never ridden in the front seat of a police cruiser, or for that matter, without cuffs on, before tonight. But there

was still no feel of being in a passenger car. Like the construction trucks I was used to, ambulances, and other such rigs, this
was a vehicle used for serious business, with the seriousness
underscored by the shotgun in its rack.

"This should make you feel better," Gary said. "I talked
to Renee. She said she tried calling your place and couldn't get
through; must have been while the line was cut. Anyway, she's
coming back tomorrow."

I let out my breath again, this time with relief.

"It does, a lot," I said. "Thanks."

Gary was an expert at getting where he wanted to go fast,
barreling past traffic that scrambled to get out of the way, and
barely slowing for red lights. St. Peter's was clear across town,
but we pulled up at the entrance within five minutes.

Personally, I hadn't been in all that much of a hurry.

The sights and smells inside the building were almost
alarmingly familiar. I realized that I'd had more dealings with
hospitals in the past few weeks than in the past twenty years
put together. I felt a lot the same about the medical profession
as the police—while I appreciated them hugely, I tried like hell
not to make contact.

A charge nurse led us to the ICU, where a pair of city
cops stood outside a room and personnel in scrubs hurried in
and out. The cops greeted Gary respectfully and gave me curt
nods. They didn't seem to know that I was the shooter, or if
they did, to care.

We stepped into the room. Jessup looked like a creature
being cloned in a sci-fi movie, lying on his back in a reclining
chair with a network of tubes attaching him to IVs, oxygen,
and blinking, bleeping monitors. He'd have been hard to recognize, anyway, with his beard shaved and his glasses gone.
His eyes were closed and his face was bloodless. It was hard
to imagine him as the big, hearty—and murderous—man that
he had been.

Maybe that helped me stay numb.

I stayed where I was while Gary talked to an ER doc. I could hear enough of what they said to glean that Jessup had extensive internal damage, and his belly was full of blood. Trying to operate would have been futile. He was in his last minutes and probably wouldn't regain consciousness.

But then I glanced at him and saw that his eyes were open. His gaze was fixed on me and focused, and I got the chilling certainty that he recognized me.

"Need—to tell you—something," he got out in a hoarse, painfully slow whisper.

I stepped forward like I was approaching a coiled cobra.

"Just did what I had to," he rasped. "Not personal."

He raised his right hand a few inches, extending it toward me as if imploring me to grasp it and render him absolution—a final con.

"It was personal to us," I said.

The hand dropped back to his lap and his eyes closed again. I turned away and walked out of the room.

Gary followed me and laid a fatherly hand on my shoulder.

"Pretty cold, Hugh," he said. "But right on the money."

I found out later that Jessup died within the next few minutes.

CHAPTER 62

THE NEXT DAY STARTED WITH good news—the tomcat was going to pull through. The veterinary surgeon had taken out a slug lodged between his heart and lung, and he'd stabilized during the night. The downside was that the shot had damaged his left foreleg so badly it had to be amputated below the shoulder. But the vet assured me that three-legged cats tended to get along fine, and pretty soon he'd never even miss it.

Then came a couple of hours around my place with a team of law enforcement personnel, giving them a statement and showing them what had happened where during my run-in with Jessup last night. I was given to understand that for a noncop to shoot a fleeing man was not regarded favorably, but the fact that he'd just murdered his wife and then took a couple of shots at me would smooth the path.

In the process, we checked Renee's Subaru and found that Jessup had done the same thing as with the phone line: cut a chunk out of the negative battery cable—covering bases with his usual thorough caution. It was an easy fix, another wire splice that would serve to get it to town.

When the cops were done with me, I drove the Subaru to a parts store and replaced the cable, then dropped it off at Renee's house for her to use when she got home. Madbird met

me there and loaned me a Datsun pickup that he used for haul-
ing brush and such. It was small and beat-up, but four-wheel
drive and king cab, so I had plenty of leg room—fine for running around for the time being.

My own truck was a question mark. It still ran fine—
the gunshots hadn't impaired anything mechanical and a
body shop could take care of the external damage. I could
get aftermarket interior door panels and seat cushions from
a GMC reconstruction outfit, and do that part myself. And it
was long overdue for a thorough cleaning, anyway.

The issue was whether I'd feel Lon Jessup's presence clinging to it. I decided that if I did and that was too disturbing, I'd
have to try to find another pre–planned obsolescence rig, but
saving the old one was worth a try.

By the time all that scurrying around was done, it was
two o'clock in the afternoon. I still hadn't had a chance to
talk to Renee, but I'd checked in with Gary Varna a couple
of times, and he'd told me her flight was due in around
three-thirty. He wanted to pick her up at the airport and
talk with her, so I wouldn't be seeing her until four-thirty
or five.

I suddenly found myself alone and with nothing to do. If it
weren't for Renee, I probably would have headed for a bar.

Instead, I drove back to her house, let myself in, and
started walking around—for the first time, taking a careful
look at the remodel work that was needed. The way things had
changed, maybe she'd decide to take the time for that before
she sold the place.

And I wanted to keep my mind off the man I'd killed,
although it was inescapable.

Jessup hadn't made any kind of confession before passing
on, but now the police had his fingerprints and some other information from tracking his business dealings. They had identified him with fair certainty as one Raymond Tice, wanted

in Florida for a fifteen-year-old string of crimes that included murdering two women there.

I'd only gotten a thumbnail account from Gary, but apparently Tice was a backwoods Southern boy who already possessed a large measure of natural cunning, who'd joined the military and acquired the kind of training he could readily turn to a criminal career—special operations and intelligence. After getting out, he'd quickly graduated from low-level drug dealing and scams to more sophisticated swindling, eventually setting himself up as a financial adviser who preyed on Miami's large population of wealthy, lonely widows.

His name became known to the police, but nothing stuck until one of his suspicious victims hired a private investigator and discovered that he was spending her money on a glossy lifestyle, complete with a stripper girlfriend.

It sounded bleakly familiar, and so did the follow-up. The woman pressed charges that would have sent Tice to prison. He got out on bail and vanished—but both the older woman and the stripper were found dead.

From there, the story was still largely speculation. It was known that he'd made his way to Colorado—he probably already had the Lon Jessup identity established—using the skills of his upbringing to get by as a woods hand. But that wasn't going to suit him for long. He was looking for his chance.

He found it when he spotted Professor Callister and Astrid, who were in Boulder to attend an ecological convention. Somehow he met them, no doubt picking up on the fact that Astrid was hot for more radical action than endless debate and counterproposals. He convinced her that his own sympathies lay in that direction, and if the story that Buddy Pertwee had heard was true, he led her to raid a gyppo logging camp where they shot and wounded one of the men. He then used his connection with her to come visit them in Montana, soon married Evvie, and returned to his former high-rolling lifestyle.

There things might have rested forever, except that Astrid decided she wanted more—his help in blowing up the Dead Silver Mine. But Tice knew perfectly well that he was dealing with amateurs who would certainly get caught—and that his past, including the Miami murders, was bound to come to light.

Had Astrid seduced him like she had the mine manager who'd died with her, for the same reason—to draw out information that she could use for her own purposes? Still playing her game, not realizing how dangerous Tice truly was? Had he let slip some damning story about his past, which she then threatened to reveal unless he gave in to her demands?

It seemed like a strong bet that that was what had gotten her killed. Just as with the other women, he hadn't considered it personal—simply a businesslike precaution.

That chilly emptiness was mirrored by the vacant lifeless rooms of the old house. As I wandered around, I became keenly aware by contrast of the warmth that once must have filled them. The intrinsic beauty of the inlaid hardwood floors, the high plaster ceilings, the carefully fitted trim was still there.

Sell it, hell.

I had just enough time to do some shopping before Renee arrived.

CHAPTER 63

I WAITED AT THE FRONT door for her, like the times she'd waited for me, and walked out to meet her when Gary pulled up to drop her off. He didn't get out, just waved to me, no doubt realizing that this was a situation where three would be a crowd.

My anticipation was cut by concern when I first glimpsed Renee's face. Her expression was one I'd seen before, suggesting that something had gone wrong. It changed to a welcoming smile as she stepped into my arms, but her embrace seemed like less than it could have been.

We walked on into the house. I'd gotten a good blaze going in the fireplace and turned on a cheerful array of lights. A pair of filet mignons and trimmings were in the refrigerator, and the aroma of baking potatoes was starting to fill the air. I had a dozen roses sitting on the table, flanked by bottles of chilled sauvignon blanc and Powers whiskey.

Her pleased surprise was obvious and she hugged me again. But I could still feel that undercurrent of trouble.

"Look, I got a notion," I said—speaking hastily, trying to push past it. "I could get this place in decent shape in a few months. So, you know, a couple of people would be comfortable living here again. It's the kind of job Madbird and I love. Wouldn't break the bank, just the cost of materials and his wages."

"Oh, Hugh, what a lovely thought," she murmured. She stepped back, holding both my hands and raising her gaze to mine.

"I feel like I owe you a debt I can never pay back," she said. "It's almost like one of those old myths—you saved me from the monster that was haunting my life."

"The only debt any of us owe is to our lucky stars, especially me. They lined up when I needed them."

"But I just coasted on through and never really got touched. You had to do the hard part, and you'll have to live with that forever. Are you okay with it? It must be such an enormous thing, I can't even imagine."

"It'll be there in my head," I said. "But I'm more than okay with it. Is that what's bothering you? Feeling like you've got to be nice to me because you're obligated? Lose that. You don't."

She lowered her gaze. "No. Look, I need a few minutes to get settled. Then can we talk about the house?"

"Sure," I said, relieved. "Whenever you feel like it. Take your time."

Then she started crying, breaking away from me and covering her face.

"I think Daddy knew," she got out. "That it was Lon who did it. He *had* to—had to at least suspect."

I stood there poleaxed, in a stillness underscored by the sounds of her weeping and the merrily crackling fire. Then I stepped to the table, opened the bottles, and poured us drinks, mostly for something to do. I took one of her hands and pressed the glass of wine into it. She sipped and gave me a tremulous smile of thanks, but it faded fast.

"That night I heard Daddy and Astrid arguing?" Renee said. "There was another part I'd blocked out. When she was mocking Daddy that he never did anything but talk—he snapped back at her, something like, '*I'm* the one who shot that man, not you. And for what? Just to prove to you I could.'"

"You heard your father say he shot a man?"

"I should have told you about it, I know. I didn't want to admit it, and it didn't seem to be part of this. But then when we found out about Lon, it made sense. I think he was talking about Lon taking Astrid to raid that illegal logging camp in Colorado. Daddy must have gone with them. Maybe Lon even maneuvered him into it—made him feel like an old man, competing for her." Renee shook her head, looking both wounded and angry. "That's how stupid I am. All along, I thought they were friends, but really Lon had that terrible hold on Daddy."

And Professor Callister had never summoned the courage to break it, because if he'd voiced his suspicions about Lon Jessup, Lon would have turned him in for the Colorado shooting, an unprovoked assault that would have carried a long prison sentence.

Talk about a devil's bargain.

So now, instead of experiencing the ecstatic relief of learning that her adored father was not a murderer, Renee was devastated by his cowardice.

"You haven't mentioned this to anybody else?" I said.

"Just you."

"Is that how you want it?"

"For now. Maybe forever, I don't know."

"That's how it'll stay, then," I said.

She nodded gratefully, but her eyes were starting to tear up again. "I'm sorry. I'm a mess, I've hardly slept."

"My fault; I should have realized that," I said. "Let's take a rain check on dinner, huh?"

"If that's okay. I wouldn't be much company tonight."

"You feel like talking?" I said. "Maybe unload a little?"

"I think I just need to crash."

I nodded. It was about as gentle as a dismissal could be, but it was still a dismissal.

Renee picked up the Powers bottle and pressed it into my hands. "Here, at least take this."

We walked together to the door. One warm, tear-salted kiss later, my whiskey and I were on our way home.

CHAPTER 64

ON A THURSDAY TOWARD THE end of May, with spring ripening into summer, Madbird and I finished remodeling the final cabin at the Split Rock Lodge. By the time we picked up our tools and gave the place a once-over with a Shop-Vac, it was three in the afternoon—perfect for starting a long weekend. We headed for the bar.

Pam Bryce brought us drinks on the house and set them in front of us, with her mouth turning down in a playfully sad little pout.

"I can't believe you guys aren't going to be around anymore," she said. "I've gotten so used to you, like . . ." she gestured in the air, bracelets tinkling, trying to find the right comparison.

"The junker cars?" I said. She laughed and swatted at my hand.

"Don't worry, we'll be dropping by," Madbird said. "We ain't that easy to get rid of."

There were a few regulars in the barroom, including our tool thief, Artie Thewlis. He gave us a cautious wave but kept his distance. Artie had made a big step up in the world—he and Elly May had become an item, maybe bonding over the trauma we'd caused them. He'd gained weight, put new tires on his truck, and now carried himself with an enhanced sense of authority, like a country squire who had come into his inheritance. I preferred him the way he'd been before, but he still wasn't too hard to take and he'd probably end up back there, anyway.

In general, things were pretty quiet around Split Rock these days. Darcy was gone, staying with her immediate family for a while in the reservation town of Browning. Madbird figured it wouldn't be long before she was in trouble again, but with any luck, it wouldn't be life-threatening.

When the Callister story had hit the news, including Seth Fraker's affair with Darcy, the congressman's political career took a predictable nosedive. He'd resigned his legislative seat, citing as a reason—I do not lie—that he wanted to spend more time with his family.

Whether or not he was actually guilty of foul play in the drowning of the St. Martin woman would probably never be known. I'd mentioned it to Gary Varna, and he answered sourly, "I hate like hell to say this, but it ain't my problem." I suspected that after a couple of years, when things settled down and memories dimmed, Fraker would make a quiet return.

Things were calm around my cabin, too. The black tomcat and I settled into life as usual. The vet was right about him getting used to his missing limb; at first he lurched around like a drunk, but pretty soon he was climbing trees and running fence rails, maybe just to prove he could.

And I finally had a name for him—Stumpleg, just like the gulch.

I hadn't seen any more signs of the bobcat. Probably with the warming weather he'd taken off into the mountains. But I didn't look too hard for him; my taste for wandering around my place had fallen off. As little time as Renee had spent there, it seemed I'd always see something that brought back one of those moments.

She was still in Seattle, living in her apartment and back at her job. At first we'd talked on the phone fairly often; she had asked if I'd come visit her and I'd said sure. But she never extended any actual invitation, and the intervals between calls had gotten longer. It had been a couple of weeks now.

She never mentioned her fiancé, Ian, which made me guess that she was seeing him. Probably that sensible life she'd been skittish about looked a lot better now, after what she'd been through.

And I couldn't help wondering if there was another element, along the lines of Darcy with Madbird when he'd sparked her breakup with Seth Fraker—if Renee had to blame somebody, however irrationally, for the emotional shock of what she'd learned about her father. Although I had nothing to do with it, it wouldn't have happened except for me.

As near as I could tell, nothing had changed at her house— no work being done, no FOR SALE sign. But I'd stopped driving by there.

There was one more footnote to the whole business, the kind of irony that inclined me to believe there really were forces of fate at work behind the scenes, and that sometimes they had a sense of humor that was hard to appreciate.

The Dead Silver Mine appeared to be coming back. I'd started noticing news articles to the effect that the market in precious metals was strong enough to spark renewed interest, and industry lobbyists were garnering support for allowing the Dodd Company to proceed on the good-faith promise of safe operation and cleanup, rather than a cash bond. There was opposition, but no firebrand like Astrid to spearhead it.

To be perfectly truthful, I didn't give a pack rat's ass.

ACKNOWLEDGMENTS

AS ALWAYS, THIS NOVEL OWES a great debt to many people, but I'll keep this brief. Heartfelt appreciation to all, including those not named.

My wife (and, too often, writing widow), Kim Anderson McMahon, and our families.

Carl Lennertz, my sine qua non editor, friend, partner in this entrerprise.

Jonathan Burnham, Kathy Schneider, Katherine Beitner, Deb Evans, David Koral, Pete Soper, John Zeck, and many others at HarperCollins.

My stellar agent, Jennifer Rudolph Walsh, and her colleagues at the William Morris Agency.

Otto Penzler, who gave us a terrific boost.

The great army of people in bookselling and related areas who do the all-important work of getting books from writers to readers. They're not in it for the money.

Susan Sakaye, Judy Loring, Jim and Martha Crumley, Frank and LaRue Bender, Mike Koepf, others who gave critical advice and support early on, and many friends who were close to Kuskay—what I've come to think of as the Madbird Clan, the ultimate foundation of these stories.